SLEEPWALKER

SLEEPWALKER
John Toomey

Dalkey Archive Press
Champaign & London

Library of Congress Cataloging-in-Publication Data

Toomey, John, 1975-
Sleepwalker / John Toomey. -- 1st ed.
    p. cm.
ISBN 978-1-56478-601-2 (pbk. : alk. paper)
    1. Executives--Fiction. 2. Self-realization--Fiction. 3. Dublin (Ireland)--Fiction. 4. Psychological fiction. I. Title.
PR6120.O56S54 2010
823'.92--dc22
                    2010019352

Partially funded by the University of Illinois at Urbana-Champaign and by a grant from the
Illinois Arts Council, a state agency

www.dalkeyarchive.com

Cover: design and composition by Danielle Dutton, illustration by Nicholas Motte
Printed on permanent/durable acid-free paper and bound in the United States of America

for Máire and September's baby

CONTENTS

Prologue 9

Sunday Morning—Early 11

Four Years Earlier—London 32

Sunday Morning—Late 55

Sunday Evening 72

Monday Morning 92

Monday Evening 118

Tuesday Morning 148

Tuesday Afternoon 176

Tuesday Evening 183

Wednesday Morning 213

Wednesday Afternoon 234

Thursday Morning 242

Thursday Evening—Dublin Airport 251

PROLOGUE

We had been school friends, of a kind. We had not seen each other for many years, until recently, when by nothing more formidable than chance, I spotted him across a busy room. I recognised him easily, even in all his disheveled ignominy, and spent an afternoon squatting in the dregs of his epic excess, mentally jotting him down as he spoke.

He held nothing back and I am grateful for that. For as long as I can remember, I've entertained vain dreams of writing properly (as opposed to the tripe I type up for my teen magazine employer) without actually doing anything about it. In the end, all I had to do was walk up, reintroduce myself to a young man that I'd known distantly as a boy, and write down what he said. Later, I wove it together and made sense of the chronologically sound but chaotic events. I entered into Stuart's story already in possession of some basic knowledge regarding several of the main players—the result of our shared education. I'm there too, of course, the ubiquitous narrator, godlike in my all-knowingness, but utterly toothless. I'm a true narrator, in that sense. And I've tried to be fair. I've endeavoured to preserve the integrity of what he recounted. But I didn't ask for it. All I said was, 'Hello.'

So, neutered narrator, Tom. That's me. Unwitting protagonist, Stuart. That's him. And in a bedroom, with an irrelevant girl, is where he said it began.

SUNDAY MORNING—EARLY

He awoke lying on his side, in a linenless bed, in a characterless room, staring into the face (the face rather than the eyes) of a rather plump girl. She smiled back with an uncertainty he interpreted as confusion, masquerading as mild amusement. She smiled as if she wanted to understand the joke. He smiled as if he knew he had made one, and she had got it, but he looked in his eyes as if he'd woke up, a red-blooded alpha male, wearing knickers and a bra.

He awoke. Well, he emerged suddenly. He sprung through and burst out. He surged meteorically from a black-out, or, at the very least, a patch-out, in mid sentence, and completely unaware of the subject he had been plodding inanely through a mere second beforehand. It was as if some internal earplugs had been popped from his ears, and an impervious film had been peeled from his eyes, so that he was suddenly, just at that precise moment, able to hear his spoken words for the first time, and see this Polaroid moment; like a deaf and blind man whose hearing and sight had returned in an instant, following a swift and divinely fortunate blow to the temple.

His ears and eyes were opened to the fractured reality of an urban Sunday morning. He heard himself finish his sentence but knew nothing of what he had said. In an effort to bridge this uncertain moment to a hopefully more stable future state of being, he rolled her closer and kissed her forehead. He hoped that his situation would reveal its full self during this stage-managed moment of intimacy. It did not, and he held her close too long for the moment to be passed off as genuine.

The room around him came into focus as she asked for her mobile phone. 'Where is it?' he asked.

'Side of the bed. In my bag.'

The room was vaguely recognisable. That is to say, it pretty much looked like any other spare room he had ever found himself in with a girl he barely knew. It was definitely a spare room. It was not her room. There was nothing to it but blandness. There were no personal artefacts, no evidence of anybody living here, other than a cocktail of clothes on the floor and their two bodies. This was a room for the discarded, a vacant space for the weary visitor, it was a last minute manger for the promiscuous, enough to be thankful for but not enough to welcome you to stay on another night.

Name please? he thought. Actually, no! Let's not prolong this. He reached for her handbag on the chair by the empty dresser. The room was familiar though, in specific ways, rather than in its sterile but dusty grimness; it wasn't just the emptiness synonymous with any spare room. It was the shape, the size, the lie of the sparse furnishing, the small stretch of carpet he could see through the gap in the door left ajar. It was the glimpse of red brick he caught through the slightest divide in the curtains, and the skyline that dripped over it. As he sat up in the bed, shimmering reflections in the mid-distant windows teased and hinted through a wider opening towards the top of the curtains.

'This?'

'Yeah. That's it.' He handed over the tiny, fake-leather handbag and, realising he was naked, and that she was merely half-naked, he looked around for something he could wear. 'Thanks,' she said.

'You know where any of my clothes are?' he ventured, with a perchance manner.

'Shirt's here.' She held up her left hand. 'And boxers are somewhere down here,' as she reached down under the grubby duvet. Stuart sat on the side of the bed, slipped his boxers over his ankles, up his legs, whipped them up over his buttocks, and stood up to put on his shirt.

Something was pressing on his mind, it may even have been the weight of such a burden that woke him. There was something he felt totally sure he ought to be doing. There was a pervading sense of urgency, a sense that he should have prepared in some manner for whatever it was that he had forgotten to do, but this nameless girl lay before of him, buffering the needling sense of unspecified duty. He just could not force a memory from the flotsam of his drink-soaked mind with regard to what that single pressing engagement might be.

With that, he climbed back into the bed in his boxers, with his shirt on but unbuttoned, and his bemusement displayed in every awkward contortion and inept facial expression. The nameless girl looked unimpressed, and fingered the key pad of her phone furiously, sending out an SOS maybe, as Stuart wriggled in beside her on the single bed. Once finished with her text for help, she dialled a three digit number and put the phone to her ear. Stuart lay there like a spare telephone, as she listened.

He had set out from his parents' house, where he had stayed on the Friday night. They had been out to dinner, a family affair filled mainly by vapid conversation and bristling tension. His wayward older brother, Owen, had failed to show, and, even more rudely, had neglected to call and explain his, no doubt, unnecessary absence. They had dined at a softly lit and quiet Italian place, Antonio's, run by the most un-Mediterranean in appearance local family, born and raised in Dublin, and never been near Italy in their lives, with a penchant for overcooked pasta. Still though, the décor gave the place a certain tasteful charm and a bit of time with the family is never badly spent in the grand scheme of universal karma. Whether time spent with your family counted for anything in the karmic universe when your entire family was emotionally retarded, was a question Owen might pose, and Stuart might sidestep. Perhaps it was on just such a premise that Owen decided not to attend, but Stuart, caring little for life's subtleties, towed the family line with docile obedience.

They talked. More accurately, his parents probed and pried and he slalomed his way through this minefield with ambiguous smiles and swerving, humorously designed, non-committal answers, intended to redirect the given subject down an even deader end, or stop the conversation entirely. His were commonplace answers, stock responses to uncomfortable questions, replies of the, So-so, You never can tell, We'll have to see, I'll cross that bridge when . . . variety.

His father asked questions, as he invariably did, that revolved around Stuart's financial future, and his mother asked questions about his marital future; his father not being so interested in Stuart's financial health as show-boating his own, and his mother not being so interested in his emotional health as she was in her family's locus in the social food chain. Little of what they asked Stuart was ever about him. Stuart was used to their ways though, and he rode the evening out in relative comfort.

■

Stuart's father, Patrick Byrne, a solicitor by trade, was always eager to remind anybody patient enough to indulge him, how he had battled his way from slum and humdrum to Killiney and all its trappings. Foresighted parenting had ensured that Patrick finished all the schooling that nineteen forties and fifties Ireland could offer a youth. Pulling hard on every string they could unravel, Patrick's parents arranged for him to be taken in and trained up by Frank O'Reilly, solicitor. Frank was a family friend and a devoted mentor.

Patrick spent several post-school years around O'Reilly's office sealing envelopes, licking stamps, running errands, and making tea. For the tenacity with which he went about these menial tasks, he was rewarded with a plentiful supply of recommended legal reading, plucked systematically from O'Reilly's many towering bookshelves, first hand experience of meetings with clients, and one on one crash courses in random aspects of the law. Whatever legalities a given meeting might throw up, O'Reilly would sit down with Patrick and talk him through the theory and practice at the end of the day.

O'Reilly paid him a small wage and covered exam fees. He encouraged Patrick to take an interest in the wider world. He set aside half an hour every morning, before the office opened, for Patrick to flick through all the local and national papers, as well as the international, when available. They selected articles of interest to be read supplementary to study, for when Patrick returned home in the evenings. It was an apprenticeship of true worth. Patrick grew to rage against mediocrity and complacency, determined not to fail those who struggled selflessly for him.

In reading the papers he became politicised, and onto Seán Lemass, Taoiseach and innovator, he projected the traits he most admired in O'Reilly and hoped for in himself: a strong work ethic and staunch professional optimism. Though he loved his parents, it was O'Reilly and Lemass he revered. In high-spirited debate, O'Reilly and Lemass were interchangeable characters and influences, shaping the dovetailed success of Patrick and the country. Here were men present and correct at the birth of the nation, who were not satisfied with mere past glory, men who saw the folly of isolationism, men who embraced rather than feared the future. These were visionaries, who always had one foot in the creditable past and one eye on a hopeful future.

Patrick worked hard at becoming the best solicitor he could be, and learned from the wealthy and successful clients whom he served so well. He learned the value of property and he provided well for his family.

Patrick's ventures had not been an immediate success—'The market wasn't the thriving beast it is today'—but he stuck to his guns, the twin-shooters of hard work and optimism, and those early days were the building blocks for the comfort in which Stuart, his sister, his brother, and their mother had become accustomed to living in. It wasn't easy, he would tell them—'It was fucking hard, kids, but you get nowhere without graft and a streak of mean!' The father had done it all for his family and insisted they know it.

Stuart's mother, Elizabeth Sheridan-Byrne, had always been concerned about Stuart's underdeveloped sense of social opportunism. She always felt that he could do better if he were only more discriminating with the ladies. She felt he should aspire to girls who knew about dinner parties, functions, balls (never acknowledging the double entendre), girls with a mischievous, double-dealing business sense to match their rich fathers' ever expanding empires—that kind of idea; girls who knew when to stand behind their men and when to bend over in front of them. So girls with accents neither South County Dublin bland nor outrageously posh, were a strict no-no. Girls who drank beer were frowned upon, and those who tippled on pints of the stuff were finished before they started. Girls with short hair—'Not very lady-like, you see'—or overly big breasts—'Discretion is a successful wife's finest asset, and sticking your tits in a man's face just isn't discreet'—found it difficult to deal with his mother's hissing and spitting remarks. The skinnier the classier, was the way the mother saw it—'Never eat more than he or drink bigger drinks than he, never!' It wasn't that she wanted women to be passive and pander to the whims of men, it was that she demanded something more Machiavellian.

Her ideas, like her language, were anachronistic. She never even seemed of her own generation. She was a generational hybrid freak, an unhappy mix of old world family values, sixties feminism and modern self-assurance. Unlike her husband, who felt his history was sewn into the fabric of the country, Elizabeth Sheridan-Byrne seemed without history: a woman conceived as a person on the matrimonial altar. Just before Stuart's birth, she assumed the double-barrel surname, rescuing Sheridan from her mysterious past and relegating Byrne to second billing. Other than this unexplained crisis of identity, and a misty memory of Granddad Sheridan, Stuart knew nothing about his mother, other than how she had always been: a complete, immovable personality, devoid of any visible influence or mitigating experience.

■

She was dressed before him. She got out of the bed about sixty seconds after he climbed back in. She had spent the sixty seconds with the phone clasped to her ear and her elbow cordoning off her private space. Stuart lay quarantined on the other side of her elbow, as she listened to her messages. When she was finished she got up and threw on the rest of her clothes as he lay still and half-dressed on the bed.

His eyes were barely open, but he could see her as she lingered. She hung in the middle of the floor for an awkward moment, a few yards from the bed, while looking in her handbag for something either impossibly small or nonexistent. She never looked at him once. She wasn't needy, mind, it was more that she seemed uncertain of how she could tactfully take her leave. He pulled the duvet up over his chest, drowsily. She turned to face him, leaned down, pecked him on the lips, and with absolutely no eye-contact, said, 'Got to go. Seeya!' Stuart blinked, and grumbled something deliberately inaudible. She pulled her tiny handbag onto her rounded shoulder and walked out.

He was still not one hundred percent on exactly whose place he was in, despite the oppressive familiarity of the room. He heard voices on the other side of the door. The nameless girl left, and a call followed, 'Hey Stuey, you want breakfast, pal?' This clarified the matter for him immediately. He turned on his side, facing away from the window, and slept for half an hour.

When he woke again, he dressed himself in more of the previous night's smoke-soaked and beer-stained clothes, and made his way to the living area. Gary was an old school friend. Stuart had known him since they were seventeen and he had arrived at St Christopher's Christian Brothers' Secondary School. They had many good times locked away in their late teens that welded their histories together. Added to which, they had some epic disagreements, during and since their teens, with one in particular, that fastened that bond tight for better or worse. They had just brokered the latest of their peace deals a week earlier.

This was Gary's apartment, and Stuart had indeed stayed in that impassive spare room on a number of occasions in the past. But he had not been here in a few years. Gary had lived there for five years. His parents bought the apartment for him and he shared it with his girlfriend of a year and a half, Anna. It was a second floor apartment with the living room and the spare room facing out onto the quays, looking over the Liffey, as it cut the city in half, north and south. The apartment was well served by several big windows, apart from the spare room which was darkened by an ugly, heavy, black curtain. The windows were covered by drawn cream blinds that morning and the apartment was suspended in a twilight hue. The air was musty and stale with Saturday night's sweat and flatulence added to Sunday morning's kitten-breath and smoky clothes.

As Gary pottered about, speaking in a winding, unstructured monologue, Stuart looked around at the most impressive en-dorsement of accessory culture you could imagine: a NADIR wide-screen TV and matching DVD player (also VCR—held for posterity, presumably), and a state of the art, surround-sound stereo system by some exclusive Japanese crowd—all in match-ing chrome; the CHALLENGE flat-screen PC and, on the coffee table charging, a matching laptop; the latest and tiniest handheld, digital video camera rested on the chair by the PC; the shelves were full of CDs, DVDs, trashy lads' magazines, and empty bot-tles of obscure beers from around the globe; on top of the small but fully stocked drinks cabinet were the only two books in the apartment—*Rock N' Roll Doggy: A True Story* and *The Biggest Book of Freaks*; and in the hallway against the wall were two pairs of skis, and beside them were four scuffed and worn life jackets, and, spilling out from the utility room, a black and chrome motor-cycle helmet. Gary was exceptionally well taken care of.

On Saturday morning, after leaving his parents' house, Stuart had gone back to his apartment for a shower and change of clothes. He met Gary in the city. They had not seen each other for over a year, until a week beforehand, when Stuart bumped into Gary and Anna at the cinema. Stuart was with Rachel. They introduced the girls to each other and went their separate ways. Gary and Anna headed off to *Varsity Virgin*, the latest in a long line of Hollywood teenage slapstick, while Rachel had convinced Stuart to go to a more thoughtful drama, *Kaleidoscope Heart*. The next day Stuart got a text from Gary saying that he was on his own the following weekend, and they should meet up and have a few drinks, like old times.

■

Rachel is beautiful. Upon meeting her for the first time, that is the single most towering factor that comes from any appraisal—she is beautiful. She happens to be a lot more besides, but it is for her beauty that she is most commonly lauded. She is also discerning and charming. She appears to have it in spades, but all narratives have twists and turns and trap doors, and all characters, real or fictional, have fatal flaws and chronic injuries. Rachel is no different. Our narrative's resident goddess has an Achilles' heel, albeit a fittingly endearing imperfection: she glides through life with her heart wide open, and she loves at the drop of a hat.

She is pursued by the arrogant and pompous for her trophy beauty, and they are allowed success because of her unshakable belief in love's wisdom. This paradoxical combination of intelligence and blind faith in love has meant she has not been protected from a long, steep, dirt track of relationships, with a succession of aesthetically pleasing snakes in the grass for boyfriends.

Her men have in the main been lofty, good-looking, well dressed, flashy, sneaky bastards. They have, without fail, cheated on her, lied to her, broken her trusting heart, and made her feel like a right asshole for not seeing through them in the first place. She continues to believe though. Her love is true and truly felt, and, even after she has been belittled by infidelity and dispirited by neglect, she finds hope in the next man. Rachel's intellect is too often overridden by an emotional naïvety—dare I say, stupidity—when it comes to tall, reptilian-natured men; but, my lord, how beautiful!

Through all the mistakes, and there have been quite a few, Stuart has been there for her: a shoulder to soak the despair (despair—never tears); a gentle hand to stroke soothingly through her perfect brown hair; a reassuringly simple man of simple desires, without the complication of ever having shared carnal knowledge of her. Stuart does it by instinct (an instinct that is sadly absent in all other respects), he does the comforting so well because Rachel is the only person he has ever felt so unguarded with, and he loves her purely, and defends the purity of his affection ferociously should anybody imply an ulterior motive.

For the benefit of anyone interested, Stuart is willing to explain the sanctity of his friendship with Rachel, detailing the facts as he feels them: he could never risk the friendship (not that he has any feelings for her like that anyway, you understand); Rachel doesn't look at him that way either; he just likes spending time with her; he has known her longer than anybody and better than anybody; they have been there for each other through some tough times, and all the other kind of hackneyed, run-of-the-mill responses that usually precede the best or most embarrassing sex of our lives.

Perhaps none of us believe Stuart's protest for reasons more deeply personal than the throwaway, quasi-Shakespearian reasoning—The boy protests too loudly! Maybe we don't believe Stuart because we've all made such claims about the unrequited lusts of our lives. We feel he must be lying, he must be suffering the same desperate aching for somebody unattainable that we felt when we couldn't pursue the person of our private fantasies, for reasons of friendship, commitment, or just because that person was out of our league. And because we lusted so surreptitiously, so must Stuart. We cannot believe that he might be a bona fide platonicist, because none of us truly believe in platonic love.

But Stuart is a gentleman when it comes to Rachel. He claims, with beseeching sincerity, not to entertain lascivious desires, and his inaction, to date, supports his claim. There is something different about Rachel, he might say; the emotional landscape of their relationship is stunning in its uniqueness to him. The complexity of Rachel is a revelation to Stuart, it's awe inspiring; the wonder is all in the details—the things that make her laugh, the things that make her smile, knowing what gets her goat and what tickles her pink. He dares not move emotionally for fear of frightening her away, sitting quietly like a cat in the long grass, watching her thoughtfully. Perhaps it is out of fear that he keeps his cock in check. But that does not matter, the reason is irrelevant, because for now, at least, Stuart is as good as his word; he has not dipped so much as a sexual finger into his platonic pie.

As for Rachel, her feelings for Stuart are not so clear-cut. Not recently. Her latest empty vessel of a boyfriend, all year-round tan and dot-com money, has been messing her around, and she feels sure he is sleeping with somebody else. She is not entirely sure whether this is a paranoid product of her own insecurities, given her aforementioned record with the boys, or whether this meathead is actually cheating on her. What she is sure of is that his mobile phone seems to run out of battery an awful lot, and he works late too often to be believed.

Rachel has been around at Stuart's a lot lately. They watch American sitcoms, Sunday omnibuses of trite soaps, films, and they order pizza together. Sometimes she stays over on Saturday nights and they fall asleep together on the sofa. They wake up in the early hours of the morning and say, 'I suppose we should get into the bed.' And then they do. They climb into a big double bed, get under the duvet—Rachel in her knickers and a T-shirt, and Stuart in his boxers and a T-shirt—and Rachel lays her head on Stuart's chest, and he lobs his arm around her, and they fall asleep. Stuart sometimes wakes erect, but they laugh it off, because what else is going to happen? even if they are only friends. Then they get up and go out to the shops for Sunday papers and something nice for breakfast. Stuart does the bacon and sausages and Rachel does the eggs, and then they sit with the papers, Stuart with the Sport, Rachel with the News, Review and Magazine sections. When Stuart flicks on the TV around midday, they both sink into the sofa and take the piss out of the soaps for the afternoon.

Rachel calls over when she's bored or upset. Lately, she has just been calling over. Stuart is tall and handsome. His complete ignorance of all affairs, cultural and current, has always been something of a quirky cuteness in Rachel's eyes. She would say, 'Who's Julian Barnes? Only one of the best writers around, that's all,' and like clockwork, he would retort, 'And what can you tell me about the Argentina team of '86?' and they would laugh—same old point made the same old way. Lately, she has begun to notice his broad shoulders more than his quirky ignorance, and when they lie in bed late on Saturday nights/Sunday mornings, she often feels her mouth go dry, her heart beating with a little more thump than usual, and she has to stop herself from wanting to tilt her head and move her lips to his.

Like Stuart, she's afraid, and so she keeps herself in check. But unlike Stuart, she has the capacity for reflection. Reflection has been making it harder for her to deny her fast-developing, sensual aching for Stuart's touch, her best friend, the one person who knows all her ugly details, and she wonders does their friendship or her past count against her?

∎

Stuart knew he would be heading in Gary's direction on Saturday morning, after staying with his parents on the Friday, and the drink sounded like a good idea. Stuart was renting in the city, not too far from Gary's place. If it doesn't work out, Stuart thought to himself, I won't be too far from home and can make up an excuse and head off at anytime. So they met up and Stuart was looking forward to it. It was about half past one on Saturday afternoon, and they sat down and had a pint.

'You dirty dog, Stuey!'

'Well, you've got to take it where you can get it,' he said, still suffering from impaired recollection. 'What happened out there last night, Garr?'

Gary tilted his blond head slightly, winked his eye, and flashed a dentist's smile Stuart's way. 'It's like that, is it?' he said. 'Come off it, you filth bag, how much do you really remember?'

'How's about a few pints in Boland's.'

'Get out of it, you've got to have more than that, pal. I just met your girl leaving there. Not your best work, but given the state of you last night . . .' he said, raising an incredulous eyebrow. 'Come on,' he said, turning to the kitchen area, 'and we'll see what an extra-black coffee and a greasy fry can do for your memory.' Stuart followed him into the kitchen, dragging his heavy and clumsy-feeling body across the carpet. He sat on a high-stool at the counter, put his elbows down, dropped his head into his hands, and stared silently and red-eyed into the glass of sickeningly fresh orange juice that Gary had swept across the pristine counter-top, and under his nose.

The blinds were open now. Gary lit up a cigarette, put on some music, and began darting round the kitchen, readying breakfast, detailing his own memories and salvaging a few of Stuart's from the realms of the unrecalled. Stuart began to drift back to that pressing engagement or obligation that he felt sure needed to be honoured. He looked at the clock on the microwave and the flashing green digits claimed 9:33 A.M. Not too bad. He would never have made any promise to anyone that involved anything before noon. If time was not completely on his side, it was at least playing a neutral role.

As he sat at the kitchen counter unable to drink the juice, and taking in Gary's crass attempts to appear cultured—two appallingly cheap and nasty Picasso images, carelessly forced into two expensive, wooden frames—he let Gary's soliloquy wash over him, responding with nods and short, snorting laughs. Stuart was trying to understand how Gary could have put these almost photocopy-like Picassos (Stuart knew Picasso to be a famous artist, and he was fairly sure he was dead; of course, he was also fairly sure he was French) into such expensive frames without cringing, when he noticed that one of them was so hastily forced into its frame, that there was actually a ripple in the paper at the lower right corner—Picasso's final self-portrait was without its hairy left shoulder. The gaunt face with huge, ghoulish features was unsettling; the long, ever broadening nose, and the hard, dark lines of the eye-sockets and eyeballs, dominated the image, while the rest of the face seemed to be dying around them, as if they were part of his immortal character, part of his soul, intrinsic elements of his restless genius, still boring outward while the mortal body perished with age.

Had Stuart cared anything for art, the careless ripple and the photocopy paper might have troubled him, but he did not, and it was the intensity of the portrait that unsettled him. However, knowing enough to say that even a good copy of a Picasso wasn't likely to be on A4 photocopy paper, mounted in a kitchen, hung over the breadbin, and labelled, PICASSO, with a felt-tip marker, he took some smug pleasure in the moment.

The other Picasso hung on a bare wall just above the small kitchen table. It was *Guernica*, and Stuart found it equally unsettling;

the violence, pain, derangement, and fury of the image were too much, it was too busy for the quivering hangover (had fascism buckled so easily at the knees, Pablo would have been thrilled to bits). While he was unable to dwell on Gary's Picasso's, their careless pretension did serve to make him fat with unspoken superiority. Gary may have had money, but he didn't have a clue. Theirs was a fractious friendship at the best of times, a skin allergy likely to flare up red and sore at any time, and with a history of doing so.

Stuart refocused on the clock—9:57 A.M.—as Gary placed a yellow plate of assorted fried food on a tablemat beside his untouched juice. Stuart was set to bring an end to Gary's marauding monologue. Gary mentioned something, maybe it was even just a word, that ripped Stuart with all the brutality of an icy shower from his slumberous, hangover haze. His head shot up, his eyes rolled manically into alert focus, and he halted his half-boasting, internal slating of Gary's crassness with a sharp, wide-eyed—blind panic rather than innocence—'What? Who? I don't remember this. When did this happen?' What was it Gary said that tipped Stuart off? Was it, 'some girl,' or, 'from college,' or was it the, 'private number' bit that got him?

'Yesterday. Late afternoon, I'd guesstimate. You got a call, private number. You answered and took it outside. When you got back you said you remembered why you don't answer to private numbers. Said it was some girl you were at college with. Jackie, Julie, or something.'

Maybe it was just the 'phonecall' part, but then Gary didn't even say that. But the word 'phonecall' was definitely the word that resounded in Stuart's mind. It was the trigger word, the word that set off this chain reaction of panic and tip-of-the-tongue desperation. Maybe it was just the way Gary set the scene. Maybe it was just a fleeting moment of storytelling genius that fell luckily into his lap, like a fortune into a pauper's hand.

'Yeah, Jenny! That's it. Fuck! I forgot all about it,' Stuart said, absolutely sure that this was the pressing engagement he had forgotten about. Must ring Jenny, he thought to himself. But then, no, he mustn't ring Jenny until he knew what he would be ringing about, and why this ostensibly innocuous call from a college acquaintance was causing him to feel like his heart had swelled so big in his chest that he couldn't breathe, and his brain was running faster than his body could ever take him. Fight or flight? His instinct, ever prescient, chose flight, but his half-wit body, shackled by impaired reaction, stood still and waited. It waited for what his instinct already knew had to be bad news. His mind was racing.

'You rode her, didn't you? I knew it,' Gary said, shaking his head with a you-should-have-known-better grin. 'Denied it yesterday when I said it, but I knew it. Read you like a fucking Disney plot!'

'No! No, I didn't. Not really. It was nothing,' Stuart said, spiking his runny egg with the fork. As the yellow stream of piping egg yolk haemorrhaged over the sausage and into the blood-orange beans, he put the fork down on the plate, got off the stool, and told Gary he had to leave, immediately.

'You haven't even eaten my magnificent . . .' he yelled after Stuart.

But he was already to the door with his mobile phone in his hand, the key-lock off, and preempting Gary's protestation with an apology. 'I got to run. Sorry, again. Thanks for the bed. I'll talk to you.'

'Breakfast,' Stuart heard Gary finish.

The front door closed behind him.

He stood on the path outside Gary's apartment breathing heavily. His unlocked phone was in his hand. His hands were sweaty and trembling. There must have been tequila, he thought. The streets were empty, and littered from the night before, with fast-food wrappers and boxes, fallen chips, and some plastic glasses rocking in the breeze. Shutters were down on all the shop fronts along the quays, except for the mini-market on the corner, where a grizzly, wire-haired, brown dog was lying on the path outside, with his sad, long-nosed face resting on his lazy, Sunday morning paws. Stuart was breathing deep and looking stunned; a holiday post-card of perplexity and self-reproach, sent from the MTV generation. He stared at his mobile phone screen, wondering who to call, then looked up the road and down the road. Three cars passed. Then a van. Then an Alsa Shipping Line truck rattled past leaving a cloud of fumes in his face. Then another car.

He thought: Jenny . . . phonecall . . . plump nameless girl . . . taxi . . . dinner with the folks . . . Jenny (again) . . . phonecall (again) . . . Rachel . . . meet Jenny . . . ring Jenny . . . Gary's Picasso's . . . where did I meet that girl? . . . Sunday morning, I think . . . taxi (again) . . . must get home . . . text Jenny—no, don't do anything yet . . . why did the plump girl seem embarrassed? . . . what have I done?

. . . calm down, calm down . . . ring Rachel, must ring Rachel—always Rachel . . . definitely Jenny . . . get home, shower, then ring Jenny—or text her . . . taxi (again)—where will I get a taxi? . . . ring or wait for a taxi? . . . got to get home . . . ring somebody for a lift—stupid idea . . . home, shower, calm down . . . where did I meet the plump girl?

'Taxi!'

Screeching halt. Window rolled down. Tired, cheerful face, leaning across the handbrake onto the passenger seat, and peering up and out the window. 'Where you going?' Smiling, rings under the eyes, been up all night, definitely the last run of the shift, probably going to rip you off, not even supposed to be taking any fares.

'Home. I got to get home.'

'In you hop then, sir.'

'Thanks.'

'No probs, sir.'

'Yeah, thanks. Harcourt, please. Thanks a lot.' He dropped onto the back seat of the taxi, laid his head back on the headrest, and closed his eyes with the taxi heading east down the quays.

FOUR YEARS EARLIER—LONDON

The syrupy globules of ink had hardly encrusted at the tip of his cheap biros, bought to see him through his final exams, before he had bounded aboard a budget flight to London, the self-confident Irish Sea bloating below him, soaring into the interim months between youth and adulthood proper. He planned on a summer of wonderful decadence, centred on the twin pursuits of girls and intoxication. Working the bars of a major foreign city—as clichéd a rite of passage as it may be—was simply the most appealing way for him to pursue his post-education kicks.

He landed in Luton Airport at ten A.M. on a swelteringly sticky Monday in early June. By twelve o'clock he was standing outside Kings Cross Tube station, not quite sure how he got there or how to continue his journey. His over-packed rucksack was wearing through his T-shirt and into his shoulders, and his back was ringing with sweat in London's breezeless, muggy air. A friend's brother, Dave, who he knew only vaguely upon his arrival in London, was putting him up for a week in his rental-house in Camberwell and had the option of job in his bar lined up, if needed.

From the moment he arrived on the platform at Kings Cross train station, the sheer size and human concentration of London, with its sprawling urban tentacles, cloyed at him like an oppressive, mental attack of hyperventilation. London dragged traffic, human and motor, in towards its greedily congested centre. A young man hailing from the breezy coast of Dublin wasn't ideally suited to the clammy populousness and claustrophobic summer heat. The air of expectancy that had characterised the months leading up to London was temporarily usurped, by a non-specific anxiety, as waves of faceless commuters pulsated past him.

Camberwell? It sounded very London, undoubtedly, and Stuart had envisioned leafy avenues flanked by fine Victorian houses, local pubs, the buzz of the markets, black cabs and red buses whizzing happily up and down, and a plethora of nationalities, all coalesced into one happy carnival of life. In Stuart's mind, London, and Camberwell in particular, was one massive continuation of a sixties love-in, just waiting open-legged for him to arrive and be adored by the locals, for his uniqueness, for his marvellous accent, for his voracious Irish appetite for a good auld laugh. Upon deciding London was his summer destination, a profusion of random images, procured from a twenty-one year lifetime of television and films, congealed in Stuart's mind and produced his idea of London—a London of possibility and bohemian promise. This was to be a place halfway between popular myth and parody: *Alfie* meets *Austin Powers*. The summer ahead was eagerly anticipated.

But what met Stuart there, at Kings Cross, the heart chamber of the city, where the Tube lines—the Victoria, Northern, Piccadilly, Circle, District, Metropolitan—and National Lines, from all around London's unbounded boroughs and suburbs, pumped people into the city and pumped them back out through its arteries and veins to other illustrious places, like Leicester Square, Charing Cross, Oxford Circus, and to places less well known to fresh-faced Irish youths, like Cockfosters, Amersham, or Morden, was a feeling that would stalk him discreetly, at first, and finally envelop him over the course of the next four years: a feeling of awful, unexplained anxiety, tinged with apathy.

He had gone on one last night out with college friends the night before, the final meeting of classmates, where they all reminisced and spoke hopefully of the future, before going their separate ways for the summer or a lifetime. The ambitions of some were so defined that they were almost tangible, while others hoped, rather than aspired, towards vague notions of career and lifestyle. Stuart sat silent, not knowing what future he wished for, and wondered what kind of work could ever inspire something as grand as passion in him. The conversation made him feel empty, and filled with booze, that emptiness draped over him like a pall.

In the morning he was occupied by the rush for the airport, but the shroud of gloom still poured over him in folds and creases. He was in London by the time he had a moment to pause. Having navigated what seemed like a maze of Underground tunnels in the still heat, sweating and disorientated, watching constant streams of commuters rush past him, sometimes knocking him onto his heels with an overhasty shoulder, he felt anxious and deflated at the same time. That this feeling was fast in passing, and didn't visit him again for some time, should not detract from its portentous intent.

Dave's house was a mess. It looked like Dave spent little time there and when he did he spent it throwing his clothes and dirty dishes around. The ceiling and walls were stained dirty, as feasibly the result of Dave's chain-smoking alone as decades of feckless tenants. The furnishing was minimal, and what furniture there was, was either in disrepair or too offensively stained to feel comfortable sitting on while any of your skin was exposed. There was a TV. However, the screen of the TV was shattered, and a now dust- and glass-covered souvenir baseball sat inside the set. 'There was never anything on worth watching,' was as close as Dave, shrugging his shoulders, ever came to a meaningful explanation.

Dave apologised for his hovel, but explained that he felt it hard to care about a place he spent so little time in. He was almost always at work at his bar, The Green Lion, in Brixton, and most days, upon finishing, he would stay behind for a few drinks that would turn into a few more, and end up too tired or too drunk to go home.

At thirty-five, Dave was fourteen years older than Stuart. And he was a tired thirty-five. He looked anaemic and weathered. He was sullen and reticent when stone-cold sober, though never rude. A warm, gentle, self-assuredness occasionally lifted his demeanour when he talked of home, or The Rolling Stones, or when he was reasonably drunk. It was hard to tell, at a glance, whether he was happy or miserable.

It was the autumn after his finals when Stuart began working for Ramsey & Stanley Foods. He had returned from his summer working in London three weeks early, following an unexpected and successful phone interview with the company's director and co-owner, Alan S. Stanley. By the time Mr Alan S. Stanley contacted Stuart about the job in his marketing department at Ramsey & Stanley Foods, at the beginning of September, Stuart was ready to leave London. He was living in a cramped, three-bed flat off Holloway Road and bartending at a large franchise pub at Bank.

Stuart had been checking his e-mail in a grotty Internet café, one afternoon in late August, before heading off to work, when he opened up what looked like some junk mail, advertising marketing posts in a food company based in Dublin. The ad claimed R&S Foods was looking for 'bright young professionals' and said the company offered excellent salaries and opportunities for advancement. He responded, e-mailing them some of his details and his qualifications. There was nothing to lose and he didn't think about it again until a personalised e-mail arrived in his inbox two days later, from an R&S Foods secretary, saying that the company would be interested in seeing a more comprehensive CV, with a view to a possible interview. He had his CV typed and printed and posted it back to Dublin.

At the beginning of the following week, while at work, he was called from the bar to take a phonecall.

'Hello,' he said. 'Stuart Byrne speaking.'

A reassuringly careful but formal voice responded. 'Hello, Mr Byrne. This is Tamara Beckondale, from Ramsey & Stanley Foods.

I am ringing in response to the enquiry you made regarding a position in our marketing department.'

'Oh, yes,' said Stuart, a little rattled.

'In your accompanying letter you mentioned that you were working in London at the moment and that you would need some advance notice should we wish to interview you.'

'That's correct,' he said, trying to sound a little more business-like, standing in the back corridor, by a payphone, wearing a greasy apron.

'Well, Mr Byrne,' said Ms Beckondale in her soothing voice. 'We feel dragging you back from London is unnecessary. I have our company director, Mr Stanley, on the line, and he is propos-ing a phone interview.' She paused, putting the onus on Stuart to take the initiative or make his own excuses. Stuart floundered in a bottomless silence, until she took pity and threw him a clue. 'If that arrangement would suit you,' she said, as if imparting infor-mation to a simpleton, but without ever losing the tidy rhythm of her sweet tones.

'Right now?' he asked, compounding his hesitancy by failing to take his prompt.

'I appreciate that we have called you at the work number you provided, Mr Byrne, and if right now doesn't suit, I'm sure an al-ternative time could be arranged. Though, as I'm sure you appre-ciate, that time would need to be soon, as we are eager to fill the position, and Mr Stanley is a very busy man.'

'No. No problem. Now is fine. I just wasn't sure if you meant . . .' Stuart said, trailing off as Ms Beckondale thanked him and handed him over to the humbly waiting Mr Stanley.

'Stuart. Hi there. Al Stanley, here. This will only take a couple of minutes.'

'No problem,' said Stuart, trying to be as calm under unexpected fire as possible.

'Listen, we were very impressed with your CV,' he said. 'And we want fresh, innovative people in here working for us. We want to take you in on a competitive basic salary, with good opportunities for bonuses, and with the right temperament you'll have all the prospects for advancement you could want. We're a forward-looking company, Stuart, who want the freshest ideas from the best young people to drive our marketing campaigns, and capitalise on our strong foothold in the market. We want you to be the right guy for us, Stuart. We'll take you in and train you up for six months, fully paid, with bonuses all backdated to you if you're still with us in a year's time. In six months, once your training is done, we'll throw you in the deep end and see if you float. And if you start swimming lengths for us, you could treble your basic. Now, that's our bit. That's what we're offering you. But I need to ask you a few questions before the job is yours, you understand. I'm pretty sure this one's for you, Stuart, but I need to go through the procedure to keep the girls in HR happy. Okay?'

'Yeah. Sure. Of course,' said Stuart. 'I'm on it,' he shot out, attempting to reflect some of the parlance he'd just been bewildered by. 'I'm good to go!'

Five days after arriving in Camberwell, having done a couple of eight-hour shifts for Dave at the Green Lion, to pay for his board and food, Stuart was set for his third big night out since arriving.

Dave had taken a night off to show Stuart the real nooks and crannies of the big city, as he experienced it. Dave said they were going to do a proper tour of South London, and maybe a bit of East London, before he would leave Stuart to his own devices and the tourist cesspool of London's city centre. Dave said that he couldn't allow him to come to London and not see real London. He spoke of the working-summer dead-end that most students hurtle down, only to emerge at the end of the summer having encountered nothing new or valuable. He said it was the fate of the unguided working student in London to head to the hub of the place, be dazzled by its lights, seduced by its flawless neon and glittering reflection, and be trapped there for the remainder of the summer, never knowing that there were far more rewarding experiences to be met if only they were willing to journey out in search of the many satellite bars and social villages that are scattered so liberally through the boroughs of the great city. There were, he swore, just as many girls and even better chances to be taken, if the spell cast by the lights, famous place-names, and novelty factor of a new city could be broken. Dave said if Stuart continued to be drawn to the obvious and the path of least adventure, he would be committing as great a sin as the many Irish who for decades poured into the city, found their nearest Irish pub, and swallowed down their potential in colossal gulps for the remainder of their lives.

Dave's tour took Stuart from heaving bars in Brixton mainstreet, with the smell of the market still wafting in through the open windows and doors, to trendier Clapham bars with pretty girls and flowing drink. They sat and talked and flirted with girls whose accents seduced and whose names seemed irresistibly exotic. They travelled on the Tube and those red buses. They got out at Clapham North and stopped in for a couple of drinks in the busy Southern Star before boarding a red bus, on Dave's insistence, and heading up the street towards Clapham Common, and settling in at another busy pub. By the time ten o'clock came and Dave proposed his next spot, something a little more conventional but still colourful, a Brazilian night in Brick Lane, moving on held no appeal, and they settled into the squatting tub-chairs around a low, rectangular table on a close evening in Clapham.

Dave had spruced himself up for the night. He had pulled on a short-sleeved, white cotton shirt. It was loose around his wiry body. He wore some brown cords and a pair of sandals. He looked casually smart. Despite his neat attire, he looked awfully close to the latter stages of a terrible illness. His mid-length, black hair was thin and drooped greasily over his ears and across his forehead. His skin appeared grey in contrast with his white shirt. His teeth were a see-through, light yellow. With every drink his eyes became dimmer, yet more bloodshot. Yet there was something convivial in his manner. Dave spoke slowly and thoughtfully. He listened attentively too, and engaged meaningfully with careful questions and clever quips. He looked like a corpse though, and it was only in his rumbustious laugh that his latent depth and intelligence found animation against all the odds.

'So you're telling me, in all honesty, that you'd prefer to have the Lion rather than some bar in central London? If you had the choice.'

'Absolutely, Stu. No doubt in my mind. You know why? I've been here for twelve years, just over twelve now. I started off working the bars like you. And when I first arrived I made straight for Covent Garden. All that shite; spending every penny in my pocket every time I went out, chasing women, eating shite, and drinking every night. And it was great. For as long as I thought I was only here for the summer. It's just now I feel different about the place. It's not that it's my city now, London's not anybody's; certainly not blow-ins like me. But there's much more to it than the theme bars and clubs and West End shows. Like the London you imagine when you read Dickens or something. You look out from anywhere along the river at night, and there's Big Ben and the Houses of Parliament, and all that—it's like somewhere you've always known. But it's an urban mirage. When you get down off the bridge it's gone. So you try Camden and Covent Garden, but there's nothing there either.'

'You've lost me, Dave?'

'Okay.' He set himself. 'That old London—the history, the culture, the good old London—that's out there, beyond the lights. When I was a kid and I heard about London, or read about it, I imagined it a certain way. It was the best place. It had atmosphere, it was *Oliver Twist* and Shakespeare and Sherlock Holmes. Places like Camden or Covent Garden were supposed to have that character, they were supposed to have retained something of its spirit, of its human soul. But they've been bastardised by theme bars and half-ass markets. Now, I haven't known places like that in any other way. When I came here first those markets and places were already swarming with tourists, and I was one of them, but I wasn't looking for a postcard of London. I just know I was disappointed when I first saw those places. They weren't what I'd hoped for. But when I finally got out of there, and started moving further out the Tube lines, I found local markets the way I imagined them. I found little towns with proper pubs that were more personable, and people who stopped and took time, people with real lives and stories. I shacked up with a sweet little Indian bird for a while, a year maybe. She worked in her uncle's pharmacy on the mainstreet; well, she said he was her uncle, but trust me, the way Indians throw around terms like uncle and auntie, it can be hard to tell. But when we got together she would take me all over. She was great. I got to know places, and this city stopped being a postcard for me. And, fair enough, those places I ended up don't look like the London I imagined either, but there's something in their character that is closer to my imagined London than all the Covent Gardens or Camden Towns will ever be.' Dave finished and sat silently, reflecting on his own words, as if it was the first time those thoughts had been spoken aloud. He drew deeply on an ever-present cigarette, his features obfuscated by a steady train of smoke.

'Yeah, I get it, I think,' said Stuart, a little too quickly. 'But I want the rush of London, a thumping city centre bar on a Friday at five P.M. I want to mix in with that. I don't feel like spending my summer slumming in dirty Camberwell—no offence. I want to be able to go out where there are lots of people and be part of it. I mean this is good, I like it here, Clapham is nice. But I came here to do the big city thing.'

Camberwell had not turned out as expected. The hardness of a city was palpable there. The littered streets screamed of neglect and indifference. When he first stepped out of a taxi onto the pavement at Camberwell Green, the abiding image in Stuart's mind was of a grey-bearded Jamaican man, limping from the low-budget supermarket, in a chalky, seasonally inept overcoat. He struggled, with two heavy carrier bags, towards the back of the long queue for a bus to some place on the Brixton route—Denmark Hill or Cold Harbour Lane. He looked lonely and beaten, not violently, but like a cliff-face over time. The queue he joined was composed mainly of middle-aged and elderly black women, and a few men, with a scattering of pasty, young mothers leaning on buggies, smoking, while their plastic carrier bags swung from the handles of their buggies; infants, and older children, were strapped in and sat passively, without stimulation and disengaged.

Young men—mainly tall, skinny, and white, with bad skin, and mostly dressed in tracksuits and baseball caps—rushed in and out of pub doors, across to discount shops, or to have a mock-furtive word in the ear of another youth. Some gnarly old guys could be seen through the pub window, sitting at the bar and reading the form for the horses or the dogs and tossing tattered dockets into ashtrays. Several new-looking restaurants and pubs with clean fronts looked out of place, they looked desperate as they tried to force a niche in a dead market and regenerate the systematically neglected.

All society's phobias—poverty, unemployment, drugs, crime—could be tasted in the air. Its bleakness kept rent as reasonable as could be expected in London, attracting out-of-city university kids and burgeoning professionals at the start of their working lives, while managing to remain a comfortable step or two from the harsher lives of Peckham and Brixton. Stuart was not scared of

Camberwell's brash decay, he was saddened slightly, and relieved also. In a rare moment of reflection, he could not avoid what glared at him from the streets of Camberwell, comparing it to the life he knew, though he is not one for dwelling too long on the uncomfortable.

'Yeah,' said Dave. 'I hear you, Stu. You want the posh and the privileged, you want the aspiring women, the sharp suits, and the big tips. And maybe you're right. You want the High Street, the airbrushed lifestyle. You've got the look of somebody who's somebody, you could survive there. You're a lone wolf, and that's the best way to be if you're going on a summer slutting round the city. You need to be free to leave or move on when you've had enough.'

Within a few days, Dave found Stuart a job in a café-bar in Camden called Afroditie's. Stuart did everything from waiting tables, to helping the chefs, to cleaning and serving drinks. Stuart's preference was waiting the tables. He liked being out front and feeling the swell and deflation of the crowds as busy periods came and went. He liked observing the busy pathway outside and making small-talk with the customers. However, after a few weeks of erratic hours, Stuart decided he needed a second, more reliable job.

Afroditie's proprietor was a fifty-two year old Greek bachelor. He had lived in Camden Town for twenty-seven years. Whether it was living in Camden or his Mediterranean roots that made him so entirely eccentric, Stuart couldn't say. Stuart didn't know what his real name was, but his sometime boss called himself Eddie. Eddie, without explanation or apology.

The uncertainty of working for Eddie the Greek did not diminish the pleasure of the experience in any way. Eddie's employees never knew when they were working. There was no roster and no set opening hours. There were general guidelines for closing, along the lines of, 'We closes when our customers' bellies are full!' Unfortunately, that same customer-centred ethic wasn't so prevalent when it came to opening times. Eddie the Greek called his employees an hour before he wanted them at work. When they arrived he would have a cooked breakfast and cup of coffee waiting for them. As the employee walked in the door, he would point them to their breakfast table, drop over some tabloid dross to read, usually a week or so old, and say, 'My friend, you have thirty minutes. Eat, relax, wipe shit out of the eyes, and find smile for my customers.' The call could happen at six A.M. or as late as ten.

Sometimes, the café-bar wasn't open for three or four hours in the morning, sometimes they had two people working when they needed six, and other times they had six when the place was deserted. Some days there were no chefs in the kitchen, some days Stuart was hunched over the Belfast sink in the basement, scrubbing seldom used pots and pans while there was nobody upstairs to wait the tables, only Eddie. Eddie could open extra hours for a couple of strangers chatting over the cold dregs of an hour-old coffee, or kick out ten regulars because he wanted to close up early—conveniently disregarding his bellies-full mantra. There were no rules and no certainties, but the business ticked along and people continued to come back no matter how discourteous or unreliable the service. Those who did complain were mainly American, people less used to the customer only sometimes being right. Maybe it was because it was in keeping with the fabled spirit of Camden, or because people were unnerved by Eddie's eccentricities, but complaints were rare and Afroditie's boasted as regular a custom as any conventionally run business might hope for. Whatever the reason, Eddie the Greek's Camden café-bar remained open for business, and Stuart loved the work.

It was Eddie who got Stuart his job at the Bank Inn. Eddie knew one of the old barmen there, and he put in a good word for Stuart. 'Stuart, you crazy Irish, I cannot see you leave this city because of no work. As my good friend, Dave, help you come to my business, I show you to other man's. I have you the job by tonight.' That night Stuart began working at the Bank Inn.

For the rest of the summer, Stuart chugged along without much to complain about. He worked mainly at the Bank Inn. Having overcome his initial wariness of the Underground, he found his job was ideally situated. Working at the Bank Inn left him at a convenient Tube junction of Central, Northern, Circle and District lines. Upon finishing work he was no more than six or seven stops from any of the areas he might want to find himself: Camden, where Dave had found him his first job and where he continued to work on and off throughout the summer; central London, when he wanted something less parochial; Holloway, when all he wanted was a shower and a bed.

The job was exactly what he wanted, vocationally and geographically. It asked virtually nothing of him—no meaningful responsibility, no brain power—and provided him with an abundance of social opportunity in return. He spent the summer between the two jobs, working and drinking late at the Bank Inn, and socialising with Eddie the Greek and his ever changing group of employees. Stuart had a wide social circle. He accumulated friends of little importance and had adventures with girls accented, coloured, and morally conditioned from one end of the spectrum to the other.

He shared a flat in North London with an Italian student who smoked dope all day by herself in front of the TV and a London mechanic (who fancied himself as an MC in the evenings) who was hardly ever home. Stuart was hardly there either. He met up with Dave regularly enough, dropping into the Green Lion on his days off. They spent many nights at the bar, long after closing, playing music on the jukebox, shooting pool, or throwing darts, well into the morning. Stuart always thanked Dave for getting him the job at Afroditie's, and Dave always made light of the favour.

Following his successful phone interview with Mr Alan Stanley, Stuart announced to his friends and his employers that he would be returning home slightly earlier than planned. He told everybody on a Thursday that he would be leaving on the Monday afternoon; it was the cheapest flight available, and since he had saved no money, and was eager to avoid any unnecessary debt, as he would be looking to get his own place at home as soon as possible, the end to his summer in London was necessarily abrupt.

He worked his final shift at the Bank Inn on the Friday. He stayed late for good-bye drinks and farewells. On Saturday morning, early, Eddie the Greek gave him an impromptu wake-up call and invited him to work a final, courtesy shift, waiting tables for no pay whatsoever. In convulsions of laughter, Stuart agreed. Upon arriving at

Afroditie's, at ten-thirty, Stuart was met with a surprise breakfast in the company of all Afroditie's peripatetic and misfit staff. The café-bar remained closed until a quarter to twelve, as his workmates and eccentric, sometime boss saw Stuart off in style with a fine Mediterranean breakfast, complemented by champagne. At a quarter to twelve, Eddie opened up and Stuart was expected to work his shift. He worked till five o'clock before saying his good-byes to all, including a comically rude Eddie—'Now leave, you Irish dog! The boozing is all dried up.'

As he moseyed through the Camden crowds towards the Tube station, he felt a flush of wistfulness. He looked back at the rectangular, wooden sign that jutted out at a right angle over the path from Afroditie's. It had a long, curly-haired mermaid figure, with the name in ornate script arcing from one shoulder to her other. It was hand-painted and as odd in its mismatch of mythological references as Afroditie's unusual proprietor. Stuart wondered why he had never really noticed the sign before. He wondered what Eddie the Greek's true name was, and whether Eddie the Greek was Greek at all.

He turned his attention once more towards the station and Holloway. The crowd was busy and hurried. He ambled through, soaking up the smells of frying onions and jumbo sausages from the street vendors, the cacophony of accents and diluted accents going about the end of their day. He understood what Dave had said about Camden's pandering to tourists, but there was still something different in its shabby streets and colourful stalls: Regent's Canal, the bridge over the Lock, the irregular twangs in blended accents hinting faintly at multiple histories, the motley personalities it attracted in search of an urban myth. It was as if the commercial had tried to enclose the essence of the place in its greasy fist, only for it to sift free, like something ethereal, through its bony fingers. The Hippies, the Goths, the Freaks, the Loons, and all those who came just wanting something different from urban life, made the place ungraspable. It survived and innovated despite its self-contrived aura of otherness; as if it wished itself into mythical existence. For Stuart, it was not devoid of charm. It held the warmth of personal experience in its cobblestones, slabs, memories, and faces. He felt he would miss it.

On the Monday morning when he was leaving the flat in Holloway, his Italian flatmate was on the dope trail, already dumbing herself down for the day with a dose of morning TV. She was sitting on the small, two-seater sofa in her blue, silken pyjamas, huddled, with a cushion pulled onto her belly, and with her feet tucked in under her arse, staring at the TV and rolling in autopilot. He attempted to engage her, but she hardly lifted her eyes from the hypnotic screen as he left the key on top of the fridge and told her he was going. She nodded her head, 'Ciao,' and licked the Rizla paper before sealing it.

Stuart walked out of Arrivals and into the main airport building. He had his rucksack on his back, and it was now half as full as when he left three months before. He had dumped the clothes he would not need again, clothes that were over-cautiously packed in anticipation of all strains of weather.

Dublin Airport was cool and busy. He looked around for his father. His father had taken a half-day and was picking him up. He would be eager to know what kind of a career the new job offered Stuart and would have questions about salary, bonuses, and perks, lined up for him to answer one at a time. The inquisition would be structured and prepared. In a brief phone conversation when Stuart announced his news, and asked could he be met at the airport, his father had failed to elicit a satisfactory amount of information. Now he would be ready and have Stuart penned in for an hour, at least, on the way home.

Patrick Byrne stood grey, tall, and brooding by an airline information desk, one elbow propped up on the counter. He was in a smart, grey suit and an immaculate white shirt. His top two buttons were undone, and his tie was folded and draped over the side of his jacket pocket. He held a folded broadsheet in his hand, resting by his side. He looked deep in thought. Stuart caught his eye and watched as his father straightened himself up, smoothed out his suit jacket, and loosened his shirt with a roll of his shoulders. Patrick's mind returned from wherever it had absently been wandering.

'Hi, Dad. Thanks for coming.'

'You're welcome. It will give me a chance to catch up on your news. I fancied a half-day anyway. It's been hectic at the office lately. Bring on retirement,' he said, making a play for light-heartedness, a mood he scarcely had the temperament for unless he was in the early, social phase of drunkenness.

'You'd have to actually spend time with Mum then.'

'No need for that, son,' his father said, sharply.

'How're Owen and Sara?' Stuart asked, showing dutiful interest in the welfare of his siblings.

'I'm sure you know better than I do. They never tell me anything. If they have something to tell me, they know I'm here. Although, Kevin and myself are investing together in a new development.' Kevin was the brother-in-law; a shameless capitalist and right down Patrick's street.

'Oh, I didn't know that. And how is Damien?' Damien was Sara and Kevin's child, the cosseted only grandchild.

'He's still a handful, but he's good. No major incidents lately.'

'No news from Owen though, no?' Stuart asked, fairly disinterested in either his brother-in-law or his nephew.

'Nobody ever knows what that boy is doing,' he replied irritably. They walked the rest of the way to the car in silence.

The questions began as Patrick's brand new, black *Pretenzia* pulled out of the airport. He struggled a little with the steering on his new car as they hit the first of Dublin Airport's roundabouts.

'When did you get the car?' asked Stuart, hoping to head off the questions before they began, while noting that it was more of a younger man's car.

'A couple of weeks ago. Still trying to feel my way around it. I should have stuck with the old *Pinacel*.'

'It was hardly old, Dad. Two, three years, was it?'

'I needed something with a little more room, for when I retire. I plan to do a bit of travelling around the country.' Stuart allowed the issue of the *Pretenzia*'s unsuitability for a national tour—too flash, too city, too impractical—to slide by unchallenged. 'Anyway, what's the news on this job? R&S Foods. I've read about them. What basic are they offering? I hope you negotiated. Companies like that have lots to spare, and they won't respect you if you just accept their first offer, no matter how generous it sounds.'

'It's done already, Dad. Contract signed.' Stuart lied to end the enquiry. 'And it's a good one with good prospects. Better that anybody else I've heard about from college.' It did not work.

'Listen, you can't go judging what's good enough for yourself by what other people get. You decide your own value. I've never sold myself short, and if you've any sense . . . Did I ever tell you about the first contract O'Reilly offered me?'

'Dad! It's a good job, I've taken it, and at least let me work a day before you start saying I could do better.'

'Okay. Okay, Stuart,' he said, nodding his head compliantly. 'Is it performance related, though? Target based? I'm telling you, bar working for yourself, that's the only way to make serious money.'

'Dad!'

'Okay. Sorry. We'll talk again. I'm sure it's for the best.' Stuart braced himself for a further onslaught, but it never came. The rest of the car journey was spent complaining about the traffic on the motorway these days, toll-bridges, the weather, ads on the radio, and anything impersonal. There was not another mention of Stuart's job. The ease with which Patrick gave up was surprising, and Stuart thought he must be preoccupied.

Patrick drove home through the city, as much a force of old habit as bad choice, and then they crawled along the sea road to Blackrock. Stuart felt contented. The southside suburbs were where he felt at home. He was glad to be back. The sun peeped out from behind an overcast sky every so often and the beauty of the coastline soothed. The breezy, low-rise vista of Dublin's east coast road was in total contrast to the soaring municipalism of what he had just left behind.

Turning into the driveway, Stuart's thoughts turned to what was to come. He wondered first about Rachel: where would she be? She had remained home for the summer to help in her mother's book shop. She would have been paid well enough, and saved herself rent and food expenses before starting her first teaching job, which she already had lined up for September. He had in mind, too, a few drinks with his brother, if he could manage to contact him.

The one thing he did not want was an awkward evening in with his parents. He wondered were they fighting today or just ignoring each other politely. He wondered which member of the community his mother was doing a hatchet job on this month. The car came to a halt on the driveway. His mother was standing in the wide porch, beneath the hanging baskets, with a watering can. She was as smartly dressed as ever and had her sunglasses on. She turned to greet the arrivals with a stiff smile, as if posing for publicity shots with the local council. It was her attempt at warmth.

'Darling,' she said, putting down the watering can and descending the four steps from the porch with her arms in half-bloom. She laid her hands lightly at his elbows and leaned in to kiss his cheek. 'Welcome home. So good to see you.'

'Hi, Mum. Nice to be back. How've you been?' he said, routinely.

'Fine. Are you hungry? We're having a homemade soup starter, and sirloin steaks with a pepper sauce.'

'I'm actually supposed to be golfing this evening, Liz,' said Patrick, as he kicked a loose hubcap into place. 'So . . .'

'For Christ's sake, Patrick,' she said. 'He's only in the damn door. Can you not reschedule this ridiculous game? You knew he was coming home.'

'Well, I could, but I'm letting you know now that I've got a game on Wednesday, and Friday too. No matter who's coming to see us, the Pope or the fucking Taoiseach, I'll be playing those. You've got . . .'

'No, don't change your plans, Dad. I was going to see if I could get hold of Owen, anyway,' Stuart said.

'So the two of you are going out. That's great! You can both microwave baked beans then! Sure you'd probably be happier with that. Ungrateful . . .' Father and son looked at each other as mother stormed into the house. They would all be dining together. But there was a parting shot, before they would come together again over dinner. Elizabeth Sheridan-Byrne stopped and turned, halfway down the hall, still just audible, and said, 'Oh, that tramp from the bookshop was sniffing around here. She probably thinks you love her by the looks of things. You should call her. Put her straight.'

Stuart looked at his dad. 'Bitter auld wagon,' his dad said, shaking his sour head. 'I'd better take the clubs back out of the boot.'

SUNDAY MORNING—LATE

Rachel was sitting on the floor outside his apartment. She was wearing stonewashed blue jeans, a tightly fit pink T-shirt, and a short, desert-brown jacket to keep her bare arms from the cool drafts of a sun-sheltered corridor. She sat back to the wall, arse to the skirting-board, and knees pushed to her chest by arched feet and tensed toes. The rubber sole of her tan flip-flops gripped the laminate floor, and held her legs steady and her knees locked. Her handbag lay slumped beside her, and on her other side stood an almost empty bottle of mineral water; a bottle of water already flushing the system and the day had barely started.

Rachel always looked healthy and whole, slim but never skinny. She was an advert for clean living, or for regular fruit and vegetables, at least. She was well-fed, well-bred, well-dressed, well-proportioned, and well-balanced. If you lunched or dined, or were lucky enough to breakfast with Rachel, she always ate. She never politely declined or checked the calorie content with regret. She never looked between you and your slobbering kebab at the end of a boozy evening, caught between ravenous envy and bitter rage, in a manner that said she was compelled to either swallow your kebab, fellatio style, or decapitate you on the spot. You looked at a girl like Rachel and you just couldn't imagine her red-eyed, late on a Tuesday night, blubbering into a box of extra-soft tissues, cradling a tub of chocolate chip ice-cream, watching some whimsical New York sitcom, in the throes of self-pity because her arse looked too big in her new pants.

From time to time, Stuart would find himself pondering the sincerity of their friendship. Less so now, these days, but during his mid to late teens, when his heart clenched in jealousy at the sight of a new boyfriend, the question nagged him on almost every drunkenly melancholic occasion. He questioned the friendship's platonic conformation and whether he could truly swear to not entertaining a salacious fantasy or two. There were those even less convinced than Stuart. Among friends, Rachel was a source of jocular mistrust—'Go on, I bet you have! Would you do it if you got the chance?' His mother spoke of Rachel with alarming distaste, even by Elizabeth Sheridan-Byrne's own caustic standards, her comments always loaded with venom and intent on undermining the 'so-called' friendship.

Stuart loved Rachel no less for this. In fact, he loved her more because of the scepticism, because he had to. She was the only person who could testify to the truth of their friendship, the only person who believed and could confirm that nothing had ever happened between them, and furthermore, she was the only one who believed he didn't have a 'what if' scenario floating around in his devious, philandering, playing with a safety-net, want to have your cake and eat it, mind. They enjoyed the same things. That was the simplest and most appropriately sterile response to any inquisition he had ever been able to devise. It seemed to cover all the bases without ever really saying anything at all: a timely platitude while the emotions weren't mature enough to formulate and grind out an adequate response. Never say never, Time will tell, We enjoy the same things; they mean something else, and he meant something else. He meant that the whole thing was too complicated, too loaded with history, too cumulative a bond to be dissected so easily, and yet it was also too embryonic to be exposed to the harsh glare of sex and lust.

Stuart was not accustomed to such complications. He drifted from one girl to the next, without pause for thought or consideration. Those other feelings just never developed. There was too little of him to share with objective emotion, with selfless regard for another. He was never sure what he wanted from Rachel, other than her omnipresence.

She heard him coming through the security door, but she never lifted her stare from the floorboards until he was standing side on, with his key in the lock, and he paused to look down and said, 'Hey. What's up, Rache?'

'Just thought I'd come and see you. Haven't seen you in a while, that's all.'

'Well, a week, eight days, maybe,' he said. 'He must be some prick if you want to spend time with me on a hangover.'

'I didn't know you'd have a hangover. And he is.'

'It's Sunday morning, Rache. You should've known. You look very fresh, by the way.' Rachel held out on display the almost empty bottle of water as he reached down for her limply outstretched other hand.

'I've been re-hydrating since early A.M.' He hauled her to her feet, leaned down and picked up her handbag. He put his other arm around her waist as she rose, and she rested her temple, briefly, on his shoulder, as he guided her through the open door. 'And what's wrong with your mobile?'

There was nothing wrong with his phone. But sitting in his inbox were seven messages from the previous night and very early that morning. All of them asked about his whereabouts, each one got successively more desperate and ratty, and despite the fact that they had all been opened, Stuart remembered nothing of any of them. She had texted him seven times between 23:16 and 03:07 when, Stuart assumed, she passed out, either drunk or exhausted. Rachel's latest man was a prick. There was no other way Stuart could see it. He recognised all Seb's lies, excuses, body language, and 'keep 'em keen' tactics. What Stuart didn't understand was why Seb would treat Rachel this way. It didn't make sense to Stuart, and he disliked Seb wholly and at once.

■

Seb: the big, D-KhD sports car; the deck shoes and designer pants; the dumb-fuck, collars-up, jock-bastard, rugby shirts; the overly sized, real-leather wallet that insisted on having two fifties at all times, and being complemented and supported by an array of credit cards, and he always, without exception, used the plastic, so confirming the tangible currency to be as pretentious and redundant as it appeared. Seb: the smarmy, nasal, South County Dublin accent, and his condescending looks; his slap-on-the-ass-go-get-me-a-drink manner of addressing Rachel when he was around his friends; his high-standing University of West Brit, or wherever, education. Seb—what a prick!

I want Stuart to be a bit more balanced here, but this is how he feels, and to be honest, I don't care much for Seb myself. I mean, Seb? Sebastian? What kind of a name is that? Sounds like a name for a dyed in the wool, Tory colonist. Why not just call him Cromwell and be done with it!

■

Stuart had asked to be dropped off at the local mini-market by the taxi and walked the rest of the way to his apartment. His heart was palpitating, by no means the worst palpitations he had ever known, but enough to signal the likely onset of paranoid anxiety. He knew the drill well. He shopped for breakfast, having skipped Gary's fry-up.

In recent times, most noticeably after heavy drinking, anxiety attacks had set upon him. They ranged from mild to almighty. People joked about it, 'Ah, that's just the beginnings of getting old. You can't escape the hangovers forever.' But they were more than hangovers. Owen (and who would know better?) suggested that there must be something wrong, a source of anxiety in his everyday life that found itself exaggerated and heightened in the midst of a hangover. He said the combination of alcohol, not eating properly, lack of sleep, or some worthless, drink-induced sleep, could conspire to play tricks on the mind. Stuart dismissed the idea of a general anxiety in his life; everything was fine. He had a good job and his own place, he was young and free and wanted for nothing.

But then came the sober anxiety attack; he was lying in bed unable to sleep and there was nothing on the TV. He had nothing to do. It started with a pang of guilt. Laura worked as a receptionist at R&S Foods. She was plain and pleasant. They had found themselves seated next to each other at dinner, following an overnight, company team-building exercise in a country hotel. Laura was vivacious in conversation, and as the evening tumbled on this was more than ample reason for Stuart to fall into bed with her, and Stuart's obvious attributes proved equally sufficient cause for Laura; they toppled onto the bed in suite twenty-nine, sometime after two A.M.

In the morning, there were no expectations or repercussions. But some weeks later, Stuart ill-advisedly disclosed the chronicles of suite twenty-nine to a young, R&S Sales Rep., after they came across each other in a late-licensed pub, including some unnecessarily lurid details. When Laura Buckley became Laura Suckley, she was terminally embarrassed. The betrayal stung her, and Stuart had just heard that she had handed in her notice. He did not know why, for sure, but even Stuart is capable of that measure of informed speculation.

Sleepless and unoccupied, he began to have thoughts. There came a jolt of conscience which turned to a guilty ache, maybe even shame. He felt lonely, and he was filling up with potent regret. Then, out of a place he never knew existed, in the idleness and silence, came fears he never knew he had; he was afraid of what he could not undo. He was afraid of his future. He sensed the ominous presence of a fearsome deity preparing to balance the books. His heart was pounding. The back of his neck was sweating, so were his palms. His throat was sapless. All he could see was his badness coming back to haunt him. He felt he was in the wrathful grip of fate and destiny. He thought he could see his heart throbbing under his vest. He wanted to fix things, but even if he dealt with the fears one at a time, it would not be enough; none of these were the problem in itself, they were symptoms, parts of a spiritual whole, or a spiritual hole, perhaps. This was about life, and he had no idea about life. In that instant, he just knew that his was dreadfully misaligned. It was about basic decency, love, guilt, and fear. He lay awake and alone for hours, in the dark, before the anxiety was finally subdued by exhaustion. He passed out.

When he awoke, the anxiety was untraceable. The only evidence of what he'd endured was the sweat-dampened sheets. The thoughts that had badgered him to distraction seemed trivial in the morning. He had been unable to get any perspective the night before. He had been unable to get his mind to function logically. It was gone now, though. But as time went by, and hangover, anxiety attacks continued, Stuart began to acknowledge the similarities between that sober night of terror and the delirium tremens.

So he knew the drill well; the body needed food, hydration, and sleep; the mind, if the anxiety and paranoia were to be kept at bay, needed to be occupied, preferably by human company. Alternatively, another drink or two would settle body and mind. If combined with food, pure water, and distraction from himself, the drinks could facilitate a comfortable recovery. For this reason, Stuart was happier than usual to find Rachel waiting for him. She offered salvation—delectable, sugar-coated, inch-perfect salvation.

By midday they were slouched on the sofa, cup of tea in Rachel's hand and mug of coffee in Stuart's, watching the Sunday omnibus of *Sunrise Road*, the usual soap-opera tripe. It was an amazing stretch of the world, filled mainly by devastatingly gorgeous young people with ever eventful lives. The characters all seemed like caricatures, familiar yet completely unreal—caricatures of themselves somehow; where did the characters end and the actors begin?

They never seemed to work or study, although much of the dialogue was spent complaining about the amount of both they had to do. Not too dissimilar to real students, Rachel commented. Stuart enjoyed Rachel's attempts at engaging him in something marginally more meaningful than the fanciful plotlines. 'We were all like that. I remember you and me talking about how broke we were, as we sat in the pub sipping on drinks and eating a lunch. Why do people do it? How come we can't see the stupidity of what we're saying at the time? Look at this lot. They just sit around talking about how little money they have, but at the same time getting pissed in the pub, and drinking bottled water, and buying gourmet foods,' she said, noting the lethargy of a generation so crudely reflected in the Sunday afternoon filler. 'But we did it too. How come we have to wait for time to give us perspective? Is it some cruel trick of nature, that our ability to express ourselves develops faster than our self-awareness, so that we are condemned, through hindsight, to embarrass ourselves horribly with our youthful twaddle? It's not fair, Stu, but we didn't do it for the cameras, at least.'

'It's only TV, Rache.'

'Okay. But I get the feeling these aren't great actors, and yet their performances seem so convincing. I'm not sure these people aren't supposing themselves to be in some kind of parallel reality. Maybe this is reality TV, so cleverly edited that we believe it's a soap. It could be a docudrama, or a mockusoap,' she said. As she looked at the TV screen to see the show's token fat and hairy man about to make a fool of himself with an impossibly sleek and unblemished young woman, she continued and ran, without a breath, into, 'But I know enough to say—what a big, fat effing idiot!' She pointed at the screen, 'Don't do that!,' as the big, fat fucking idiot produced an engagement ring; they laughed a loud, cosy laugh and rolled their bodies until they were closer on the sofa. Stuart slid his arm around Rachel, as he normally would, and she nuzzled her shoulder under his arm and poured her contented head into the hollow of his chest, beneath the collarbone. Meanwhile, the big, fat fucking idiot got what all big, fat fucking idiots get on TV—he got ridiculed, broken, and pitied; while Rachel and Stuart settled back into their own improbable tale.

With the omnibus over, mid-afternoon was spent down in The Auld Harte, a typical city pub: wood and cushions, not a lot of natural light, but a lot of flattering light. On a Sunday it was comfortably populated. You could get a seat without any hassle while always having sufficient customers to maintain an atmosphere.

They did a tasty, combo lunch with goujons, potato wedges, cocktail sausages, chips, fried mushrooms, and a few spicy sauces. They also did a fine pint. Stuart had a nice European beer and Rachel had a red wine. Usually they would sit at the bar. This sitting at the bar, casual and chummy, helped maintain the appearance of pure platonicism. On this afternoon, they broke with habit and sat in a discrete corner of the pub instead. They sat down and ordered food and drinks.

'So, how was dinner with your folks on Friday?'

'Ah, the usual. Owen never showed and was unreachable for an explanation. Sara arrived with Damien and bitched about married life at every opportunity.'

'Where was Kevin?'

'Work. Sara probably didn't tell him there was a dinner. Save herself the bother. And sure it would be harder to slate the fella when he's right there at the table.'

'There's no wonder Damien is an evil shit, with her bitching Kevin out in front of him.'

'Yeah, I know, but that kid was fucking evil from the start.'

'Bitter egg met bitter sperm to make bitter little child—Damien,' Rachel offered.

'Yeah, exactly,' he said. 'And wait till you hear this. He had a birthday recently. Party at the house for all his school buddies, and all that. So the invites go out and there's all the usual suspects—Johnny, Billy, Daisy—and whoever.'

'Right.'

'But there's this one name that Sara's never heard before. New friend she figures. Everything's fine. So party day arrives and all's going well; there's fizzy drinks, sweets, chocolate, popcorn, and presents galore. There's even a bouncy castle, and it's a beautiful day. The lads deliver the castle, inflate it, and everyone piles into the back garden, Mum and Dad and all. The kids are all knackering themselves out, burning off the sugar rush, and nearly wetting themselves with excitement. As things start to wind down, Sara hears these awful wails coming from inside. She thinks, Shit, one of them is after falling, I'm going to have some parent on my case for the next year. She dashes inside. But there's no obvious sign of anyone. So she follows the noise until she comes to the cloakroom. She goes to open it, but it's locked. And when she opens it up, inside, white as ghost and inconsolable, is the new kid. Somebody's gone and locked him in the cloakroom for the whole afternoon.'

'Oh, no. It wasn't?'

'Too right it was. Turns out Damien's been pulled up a few times for bullying the kid. He obviously thought, I'll get him on my own turf and we'll see what happens. There was uproar.'

'What a child to have! I'm telling you, a dark angel if ever there was one,' Rachel confirmed.

'Un-fucking-believable! The Omen.'

'And he looks such a lovely little boy.'

Just then, their food arrived over. 'Trying out some new seats, eh? How're you two doing?' The barman laid the large plates down on the table and straightened up. He smiled and rubbed his eye with his index finger, as if to wipe some sleep away.

'Not too bad. How're you?' Rachel asked.

'Okay. Were you out last . . . ?' and there was a call from the bar. 'Sorry. Busy, got to go. Talk to you later.'

'Who's that?' Stuart asked.

'Don't know. He's here a bit on Sundays though.'

'I'd say he's here for you.'

'No he's not.'

'Well, looks to me as if . . .'

'Seriously, Stu, leave it alone.' There was a quiet moment before Rachel opened up the next can of worms. 'How's work?'

'Don't know. Pulled a sicky on Friday,' Stuart threw out flippantly, biting down on a cocktail sausage.

'Why?'

More than flippancy was required to answer that. 'I just couldn't face it. I sat on the edge of my bed for twenty minutes just wishing I didn't have to go. I couldn't stand up. I felt knackered. I felt like puking. Finally, I just picked up the phone and told them I couldn't come in.'

'What's wrong with you?'

'Nothing. It's just work. I'm . . . I'm bored. I just dread it sometimes.'

'That's your second sick day in the last few weeks, Stu. They're . . .'

'Third. I took the Friday the week before, too.'

'You don't think that looks bad?'

'It does. I just . . . I'll get my head together and I'll be fine.'

'What about the promotion? I thought you were excited about that.' Rachel began cutting into her panini.

'I was. They flashed the pay rise at me, and I left feeling great. New title too—Regional Marketing Manager. More money and more perks—a whole new me. But then I get into work and I'm still spending my day talking about chocolate bars, crisps, and fizzy drinks. I feel like I've been doing it for forty years. I could do it my sleep.'

'But you're busy and you're working hard.'

'Yeah, but anybody could do it.'

'Sounds to me like R&S could have saved themselves a big improved pay deal if Al Stanley had just given you a bit of a hug.'

'It's not that. It's like . . . the other day we were doing some endorsement work. This guy gets collected from his pre-season training camp and driven into the studios to do thirty minutes' work. He's going to get a small fortune for his face and his time. All he has to do is hold up the can of Bucks Lemon, take a drink, smile, and say, 'Put the fizz back with a Bucks!' That's all he has to do. He doesn't even have to swallow.'

'You'll edit cleverly to save him the indignity of actually consuming the product he's being paid to promote,' Rachel laughed. 'You can't ask fairer than that.'

'But he says it tastes like piss, it's screwing up his diet, and going on to give us a full rundown of his daily meals. He's on the phone to people while the director is trying to talk to him. And I just don't know why I'm there. It just annoyed me, so I took a day off.' Stuart was slouched in his chair now, looking fairly glum.

'You've got to be careful, Stu. You could lose your job,' she said. She changed the subject. 'Have you heard anything from Owen since Friday?'

He had not heard from Owen. This too was on his mind. It was not unlike Owen to forget a planned family occasion, or to turn up piss-drunk or loaded up and be missing from the next few family bashes out of shame, or by request of his parents. But at the last get-together, their uncle's funeral, Owen had attended and behaved himself well. He had arrived sober and sombre (the way their parents preferred him) and he had refrained from drinking until he was a safe distance away from family affairs, sparing their mother's superficial sensibilities in front of the in-laws and their father's sense of his own incredible success. He had earned a reprieve. And yet he hadn't turned up and he hadn't returned Stuart's call on the Friday evening, or picked up the following morning. The snub brought out the worst of Patrick's vitriolic dismay, 'What else could you expect of an out and out lazy, fucking drug fiend? Too lazy to stop. Is this what our great statesmen struggled for? So that you lot could take the whole show for granted, all the things previous generations were willing to work, fight and die for. Lemass would be sick to the bottom of his gut.' Stuart, instinctively feeling that his brother needed defending, was on the verge of suggesting that Lemass could go fuck his own arse, but he bit his untaught lip and allowed the major moment of tension in the evening to drain away.

Stuart and Rachel sat at the table, closed off from those around them, for over two hours. They ate and talked and they had a few drinks. Stuart told Rachel about Owen's non-appearance and Rachel told Stuart about Seb and his conveniently faulty phone. They spoke confidingly across the small table. They enjoyed the familiar timbre of voices closest to the heart. They soaked up the inspiriting smells of afternoon beers, cigarette smoke, cooking food from the kitchen, and they lounged in the familiar sounds of clinking pint glasses and the gentle bustle of Sunday afternoon business. They sat closer than the small table intended, leaning into each other's words. Only the occasional, unconscious gesture of hand stirred them from their wordy intimacy as the touch of fingers on fingers, or tender hand to arm, would momentarily haul into the contrast the gulf between their closeness on the one hand and their distance on the other. These ungainly junctures in their dance of denial would cause them to instantly recoil into self-conscious laughter or meaningless toasts—'Well, here's to alcohol!' or 'Bugger 'em anyway!' On this afternoon, the two were saved from their usual subterfuge, following one of these devilish moments, by a phonecall. Stuart's phone rang, almost jumping off the table with urgent vibration. Flashing on the screen in uppercase, and in full sight of Rachel, was—JENNY! JENNY! JENNY!

'Go on, you better answer it. You're going to have to find out what she wants sooner or later.'

'I don't want to. Not right now,' he said. 'I'll deal with it later. I'm enjoying this.'

'Last meal of a condemned man kind of thing?'

'Yeah. I suppose.'

'She probably just wants to meet up with you. You did sleep with her.'

'No. Not now. I'll text her later, or something.'

A little while and a little residual tension later, they finished their drinks and walked out of the pub together. It was half-four. Stuart still felt unready to be alone, and he was much relieved when Rachel made no moves towards departing. They strolled back to Stuart's apartment, locked together, arm in arm, with any unease from the Jenny call forgotten. It was a nice afternoon with a gentle sun darting in and out, piercing the blanket shadows cast by large city buildings. The city streets were tiring earlier than they would on a weekday, and the pleasant industry of a Sunday was entering its early evening lull. They teased and joked, each putting the other at their ease and distracting one another from their respective problems. Their heads were delightfully light with booze and bubbles.

They reached the steps of Stuart's apartment almost unawares. Their arrival seemed to catch them by surprise, so that they had to stop abruptly, before bouncing up the steps. Stuart keyed in the entry code on the security door of the building. Rachel peered through the glass, for nothing in particular. The shine on the glass prevented her from seeing clearly down the hall, but she could make out that there were some people approaching.

As Stuart opened the door and stopped to gesture her in, she saw a young couple. The woman was a few steps in front of the man. She was dressed in black pants and dressy shoes, and a long summer-coat was buttoned up to her made-up face. The clothes and make-up couldn't conceal her disconcertion. The man, dressed in a suit and a casual light blue shirt, was following quickly behind her, shaking his head, sighing, and shoving his wallet into his breast pocket. Through the angry space left between the young couple, Rachel caught sight of another person, another woman. She was pacing a couple of steps backwards and forwards with folded arms, and she appeared to be sighing heavily. Rachel had taken a step through the door, in front of Stuart, when she realised the woman was outside Stuart's apartment.

The woman swung her attention to the incoming friends. She looked past Rachel, lingering uncertainly on something other than

Rachel, before firing a look back at her that took everything in all at once; it weighed Rachel up, took her measurements, assessed her importance, compared her accordingly, and, finally, summed her up. The summation would be concise, unambiguous, the one word type—Tramp! Bitch! Whore! even. They had never met, but Rachel knew, and as she turned to look at Stuart, he was looking at the young woman outside his door, with an expression that had been hiding behind a relaxed demeanour all afternoon. He'd had his stay of execution, now it was time to face what he had known he must face. The burning sense of urgency, of an imminently serious situation, that he had felt when he first woke up in Gary's that morning, had risen from the shallow grave at the back of his mind, where it had only half-successfully been buried for the better part of the day.

'Jenny,' he said. He looked at Rachel.

'I'll go. It's alright,' she said.

Rachel stepped back out the door, down the steps, and out of sight and earshot of the rest of Stuart's afternoon. Stuart closed the security door, and waited for what came next.

SUNDAY EVENING

Jenny was irate. She was incensed. Stuart still didn't know why. There was no eye-contact. There are not many conflicts Stuart would be willing to look in the eye. He is afraid of people looking right into him, fearing they might see through the shallow waters of his green eyes into his soul. If Jenny wanted a fight, she was going to have to force the spineless to stand up. She stood face to face with him. He was having none of it. He looked down or over her shoulder.

'Hi. How're things?' he said, glancing to the wall clock. She was going to have to smoke him out, he could hide away in his den of detachment all day long.

'Shit. Shit actually. I'm fucking well properly shitty, as it happens! Where the fuck have you been?' There was an intemperate use of 'shitting' and 'fucking' in her opening exchange, and even the slender-vowelled, south Dublin 'fucking'—more 'focking' than 'fucking'—didn't succeed in softening the threat of her rancorous anger.

'Just out. With Rachel. We . . .'

'Rachel! Fucking Rachel! That girl-next-door slut that you use as a crutch. Are you, like, actually fucking her?'

'Sorry?' Stuart snapped, rushing impulsively from the cover of his foxhole, smoke stinging his eyes, into God knows what. 'She's a friend, not that it's any of your business.' He was a bit irritable himself now, and emboldened by the afternoon pints. 'You turn up at my door, like . . .'

'I'm pregnant!' There was a pause. It wasn't a Pinter pause, so full of suggestion and ambiguity, so much as it was a stopped dead on your arse pause, a gaping pause that was far more than the sum of its temporal parts; it was a pause filled with more than a couple of seconds seemed capable of holding. It was the type of pause where pennies drop and gravity dawns. 'You remember that don't you? You remember me telling you that while I cried down the phone yesterday, and you remember arranging to meet me, and I'm sure you remember me stand-ing outside your door—two fucking minutes ago!' she let fly, 'while I waited here for you, like an asshole. Waited! Like some stupid . . . dog!'

Jenny was sitting down now, cupping a mug of coffee tightly be-tween her two hands and still trying to establish some kind of eye-contact with Stuart. He kept himself busy with small, menial tasks: washing a glass, putting away the few drip-dried dishes that lay on the draining board, refilling the electric kettle, herding some stray bread-crumbs and sugar granules on the counter-top into a single pile, and then into his hand with a cloth. Jenny spoke,

73

quieter now, but still simmering, still capable of eruption and precariously poised on the brink of major activity.

'Does this mean anything to you, Stuart?'

It had all come rolling and crashing back to him. He remembered the previous day's drunken phonecall. He remembered her tears, hearing the waterlogged words spill heavily and succinctly out.

He recalled being uneasy with the manner and tone of Jenny's breaking news. There was an element of precision in her words that he couldn't reconcile with the tears and the drama. Their problem seemed to be something other than a problem to Jenny, or more than a problem. Although she cried, there seemed a preparedness in the manner in which Jenny broke the news. Stuart heard her words—'Stuart, I'm pregnant. We need to talk.' There was something measured behind those two sentences. There were things supposed and presumed in the seamless transition from 'I'm' to 'We.' And beyond that there was a suggestion that there were options, a range of choices when it came to dealing with this problem. Within the proposal to talk there was an inference that this didn't have to be all bad. The 'we' and 'talk' appeared to offer a possibility of a sweet and contented ending that a different phrase could never have implied. She could have said, 'I'm pregnant. I need to get this sorted,' or, 'I'm pregnant. I need your help,' or if she was to insist on 'we,' she could have said, 'I'm pregnant. We need to sort this out.' But she didn't. She said that they needed to talk.

Would she have gotten pregnant deliberately? No, Stuart didn't believe that. But she wasn't completely distraught at having become

74

pregnant as a result of a one-night stand with a college friend who had shown little interest in her before or since the night in question—a college friend with whom the only common ground shared was the Business Marketing degree they both independently chose to pursue, around six years previous to the night in question. They were brought together by a choice made when they were eighteen and didn't know each other, a choice made about a degree course he could imagine that neither of them weighed up too carefully before choosing. While they may have known each other better at the end of their three college years, they never became any closer. For Stuart's part, despite the sex, he would say that there was no more intimacy between them now than there was on the first day they shared a drink together, them and all their college classmates. Nothing had ever developed further than niceties. They slept together. That was all. Why? Jenny was fairly attractive. They were both drunk. Sex happens. But there was nothing more to it.

'What do you mean?'

'I mean, does the fact that I'm pregnant mean anything to you? What are we going to do?'

'I don't know. It's not like I've been in this position before.' He was now lamenting the same pints that had seemed to embolden him only minutes earlier. He was afraid of saying something slurred or ill thought-out. He was trying desperately to establish some kind of rational high ground, some place he could reside while steadying his tipsy ship.

'And you think I have?'

'No, I'm not saying that.'

'Do you, like, think I've done this on purpose? You bastard! You do.'

'No,' Stuart said, gesturing open-palmed for some calmness. 'No, I don't. I don't think that at all. I just don't know how people go about doing whatever they do when this happens.'

'You mean abortion. Just say it, Stu! That's what you mean, isn't it? Termination,' Jenny said, accusingly. She was fired up by Stuart's ducking of the subject. She sensed uncertainty in him and was watering at the mouth with predatorial opportunism. She felt compelled to force the situation to melodramatic heights. She appeared to want tears and joy all at once.

'Well, yeah. I suppose that's what has to be done. Isn't it?'

But at the final moment, she drew back from her emotional instinct and said, 'I haven't decided what to do yet. But you have, like, absolutely no interest in this child? And before you answer, because I understand that this is so big, it's scary, but my parents have said they'll help, if that's what we decide to do. I know you're not so close to your parents, but mine said they will be there.'

'You told . . . what do you mean you know I'm not close to my parents?'

'That's just the impression I always got.'

'What . . . ah, forget it,' he said, and then remembering what had really angered him, he lashed out. 'You told your parents already? Christ, give a man a chance to think! Why didn't you . . . ?'

'Why didn't I talk it over with you first, Stu? Is that it? Why didn't I wait till you had come back off whatever piss-up with your mates that was more important than this? Why didn't I wait while you went out chasing your slutty friends? Because this is difficult for me, I needed to talk to somebody.'

'You spoke to them first. You don't even know how I feel about it and they're already talking about helping us. I hardly know you. We're only slightly more than,' and it came to him, 'acquaintances! And you have us shacked up and saddled with child. And taking donations.'

'Oh, screw you. It wouldn't be charity. My father could, like, help with your career. And . . .'

'I have a job, thank you very much! I don't even know these people. I hardly know you, Jenny.'

'Well, I suppose that settles that then,' she roared, and stood up. They looked at each other for the first time. There was runny mascara, red, blotchy cheeks, and tears. 'You don't care at all about me. Does the baby mean anything? Or is it that you just can't see anything except yourself?'

'Stuart, I'm pregnant. We need to talk.' He was in the pub with Gary and had taken the call outside. The words sobered him. The world slowed. He felt physically punctured. His shoulders and chest sank. His chin dropped, with the phone still held to his ear. He gulped a mouthful of beer, placed the glass on the ground, and with his elbows on his knees and his head fallen on his free hand, he sat hunched over on the edge of a metallic seat in the beer garden. He had been fairly drunk already when she broke the news.

After she hung up, he did all the things that shocked people do: he stared into nothing; he shook his head; he sighed some more; he went to move and then stopped; he had another mouthful of beer; and finally, he made a decision—for you have to start again in some small way, eventually. His decision was to drink some more. He returned inside and rejoined Gary at the bar. He drank a lot more. As he drank, he became more distant and contributed only what was strictly necessary to the conversation. Gary didn't notice. Stuart forgot for moments at a time what lay ahead, only to recall those words and become drained again. He felt hollow. Slowly, he drifted free of any kind of sober responsibility, and put off till tomorrow that which just wouldn't go away.

Jenny erupted into heavier tears, and before Stuart could speak, she whipped the coffee mug up over her shoulder, behind her ear, and hurled it violently past Stuart's head, shattering it against the tiled splashback and raining ceramic shards into the sink below. She screamed a wild scream, just a scream, a roar, no word in particular—'Ahhh!' Stuart drew back suddenly. The force of her fury startled him. He looked back at her, and she scooped her handbag up from the counter-top, tucked it in under her elbow, and made for the door with her wavy, blonde hair flowing behind her—full dramatic effect achieved. It was nearly six o'clock.

Stuart found himself slumped in front of the TV with the evening descending upon his apartment. He had sobered well enough now, after finding out for the second time in under twenty-four hours that he was half-responsible for an unwanted pregnancy, or half responsible for a half-wanted pregnancy. Perhaps they were two different experiences. The subtle differences had an enormous effect on his fragile sense of decency. However petrified and shell-shocked he felt the day before, he felt far worse right then having had Jenny's scorn and disappointment added to the equation. The day before, after overcoming the initial shock, and with the adrenaline flowing freely, he had only felt inclined towards self-preservation—trying to flee, escaping downstream on a river of booze. Now his conscience was a contributory factor, and his instinct had been blunted. He felt sluggish and rueful. Fear and panic, the elements that might have saved him, had dissolved and evaporated into the moment.

He sat in front of the TV for an hour before becoming conscious of anything he had watched. Pieces of information from the TV seeped into his consciousness: '. . . the death of religion has left an enormous hole in society; the consumer culture, the accessory culture, has left young people with pressures to achieve material success, but it is a pressure without any spiritual or emotional reward, even if achieved; people are unfulfilled; the fast-food models of entertainment are leaving children with difficulties concentrating, and inhibiting their development; the pace of modern life is wearing people down; the breakdown of the nuclear family is the cause of many social problems; single parent families are on the increase year after year; there is a high rate of depression among young people, particularly young males; the binge-drinking culture is the most glaring symptom of a troubled Irish society . . .'

It was a political forum. There was a bishop, a teacher, a government minister, a businessman, a publican, and a student representative from Trinity College. Stuart recognised none of them. They all spoke. They all had complaints, and between them they pretty much seemed to blame everything people enjoyed for the awful statistics that were flashing across the bottom of the screen. Sometimes, one of the panellists would say their piece, blaming alcohol, promiscuity, loss of values, and their argument would appear to make sense to Stuart. Then somebody else would retort and punch a few holes in that argument, and Stuart would swing round to the other opinion. Then, all of a sudden, a third party would offer an opinion between the two, in an act that seemed to appease, almost always receiving applause, only to sneak in the most nebulous link to their preferred agenda, and spin the whole debate back out of focus. Stuart couldn't follow as speakers leapt from agenda to different agenda, blurring the issues with news-speak and spin, leaving arguments unresolved and positions unclear. Stuart couldn't distinguish any clear lines of thought. He couldn't tell what any of the panellists were championing. He was unable to untangle his own opinions from the cerebral knots that the panel tied, as they pranced from one topic to the next.

The student rep from Trinity referred to the mass disillusion inherent in a generation entering the society as tax payers for the first time. Stuart wondered what that meant; how were tax and disillusion and youth bound up together, in what could only be a conspiracy of the highest and most furtive nature? He wondered how this young guy, he had to be at least three or four years younger than Stuart, knew about such things. Where did he learn that? What degree was he doing that taught him about the 'disillusion of a generation'? And why wasn't he in some student bar drinking his face off? How had his finger come to rest so intuitively on the pulse of his generation? Stuart was fairly positive this student wasn't out getting drunk girls pregnant at the weekends;

he took an oddly proud pleasure in that thought, before refocusing. He found himself crying out for the other panellists to shut up, and let the lad finish. He seemed to have something to say, and Stuart found himself physically yearning to hear it. But every time the young man got up a head of steam, somebody jumped in and cut him off, either patronizing him or shouting him down. Fair play to him though, Stuart thought, He keeps going, keeps trying to say his piece. But it was too chaotic and broad a debate to wrestle any answers from.

In the heat of this rare engagement, Stuart had briefly escaped the enclosing gloom of his Jenny problem. His mobile rang on the counter. He jumped up, as if suddenly woken from an exciting dream, and grabbed it.

'Owen? Where've you been? I've been trying you since Friday afternoon.'

'Sorry, Stu. I was away for the weekend. What you up to tonight?'

'You missed the dinner. They were expecting you.'

'I know. Listen, I'm down at The Lantern, if you fancy a drink. Come on down. It would be good to catch up.'

'Sure. About half an hour, forty minutes, yeah?'

A blast of deodorant, a splash of aftershave, a casual shirt, and he was out the door. Seeing Owen was exactly what was needed. They would have some drinks and a laugh, and the next morning, Stuart would get up and do what needed to be done. The perfect solution to getting through the night. Stuart was more upbeat, and his mind left Jenny, feeling content that the situation was in hand for the moment and could not be improved upon by dwelling on it.

His thoughts drifted back to the Trinity student. The credits of the appropriately entitled programme, *The Forum*, rolled. The presenter—a tanned, suavely suited, forty-something year old—thanked his panellists. As the camera fell on the wispy student, the presenter thanked and named him: Eamon Quigley. Stuart stopped, looking for a pen. No pen. But he spotted a pencil, absentmindedly removed from the local bookies and laid prostrate in the empty fruit bowl. Now for a piece of paper. Again, nothing. He picked up an unopened electricity bill and wrote the name, Eamon Quigley, on the back of it, folded it, and stuffed it in his trouser pocket.

Stuart passed down the corridor of his apartment and through the doors where just hours earlier he had first caught sight of Jenny. It could have been days ago. It was of another time. Maybe it was the effect of sobering up, of being more sober now than he was during their exchange. Maybe it was just the disorientation you get when you sober up in full consciousness, rather than in a drunken coma.

He wandered out into the beautiful, calm summer's evening, surprisingly at ease. It was approaching half-eight with the twilight braced and ready. The sun had begun to lightly smear the clear blue of evening with a warm orange. Traffic on the roads had calmed so that it was the mottled sounds of individual engines you noticed, rather than the hum of one car after another. There was a light breeze through the leaves and it felt cool but not cold. That this might be the calm in the heart of a life-changing storm occurred to him, but he chose to ignore it.

The quiet streets were thinly populated, mainly happy couples and dog walkers. The couples and the dog walkers slinked their way along the paths and across the roads with an identical aloofness. They were, each couple of same or mixed species, their own island. In each other's company they needed no other, and were immune to loneliness and inadequacy. Then there were the single men, hurriedly pulling on jackets or buttoning shirts as they left doorways or descended steps. There was a girl in a short, floral skirt and yellow stilettos, clicking briskly across the slabs of grey pavement, trying to hail a passing taxi. Stuart caught her eye and she smiled, pleased with herself; two passing strangers silently affirming each other. The tanned legs made him think of Rachel.

As he approached The Lantern, a message beeped in on his mobile. He read it as he walked. It wasn't what he feared, it wasn't what his heart dreaded when it jumped and sprinted during the three or four seconds it took to unlock his key pad and find who the message was from; GARY: HOW U DOING NOW? SOBER YET—HA! HA! Stuart didn't reply. He had no sooner replaced the phone in his pocket when it began to ring. RACHEL! RACHEL! RACHEL!

'Hi,' he said.

'Hey, how are you? What happened with the bird?'

'Oh, don't start. Very long story.'

'She want your body still, then? I told you that.'

'Yeah. Anyway, I'm meeting Owen for a pint in The Lantern, if you're interested? I'm just here now,' he said, swinging open the door to the pub.

'Maybe later. I'm meeting Seb for a chat. Let me know where you are if you're moving on.'

Owen was sitting alone at the bar. He had a pint of Guinness in front of him and a cigarette was tilting into an ashtray on the counter. He had his back to Stuart. The Lantern was a regular meeting point for the brothers. Stuart approached the bar and lay a hand on Owen's shoulder. Owen turned and offered his hand in greeting. His eyes narrowed a little as he looked Stuart from face to chest and back to face again. He spoke warmly as he took hold of Stuart's hand. 'You look like shite, Stu.'

This was quite something coming from Owen. For Owen, whose own appearance could best be described as generally unkempt, to notice his brother's fall from polished grace was something of a moment.

.

Stuart had no memory of Owen ever seeming older than him. Owen refused to accept any assumption of responsibility based on the timing of his birth. Although age and conventional wisdom would never concede it, Owen believed he was under no obligation whatsoever to be either a role model or a credible influence on his younger brother's life. Owen was who he was by whatever fluke of circumstance determined such things, and in a world of chance and random acts, he believed everyone else, including his brother, to be in the same boat and at the mercy of the same random elements.

Owen was restless, life-smart, and spasmodically engaged with ideas of selfhood, identity, and society, while Stuart was an uncurious slave to contented indifference. Owen had enjoyed a number of long-term girlfriends, predominantly of the crusty, tree-hugging variety. Stuart didn't do girlfriends. He had had a couple but he got bored, or they did, or there was nothing left after the sex became monotonous. Stuart never had need of a girlfriend. Owen often protested that within Stuart's assertion that he did not need a girlfriend was the converse implication that Owen did. 'But it isn't a matter of need,' Owen says. It's that Owen likes the familiarity of a body he's intimate with in the bed beside him when he wakes in the mornings; he likes the proximity, the overlapping of two seemingly incongruous lives, differing over grand issues that affect neither of them directly but somehow unveil the intricate mechanics of each other's emotional engines, the slurping soup, the folding of towels in a particular way, the slightest stutter, or the tears of sentimentality. And to this, Stuart would say, 'All the difficult, irritating things, you mean?'

■

'Do I?' Stuart looked over the bar and into the mirror behind the spirits bottles. He did appear a little bedraggled. His thick hair was ruffled, he was unshaven, his shirt was creased, and his eyes were tired. As he wondered why the girl with the legs had been smiling at him, he said, 'I do, I suppose.' Reaching for the back of a barstool, so he could manoeuvre himself onto it, he noticed that the stool was already occupied by a light woollen cardigan, and on the bar there rested a small, rustic-brown, ladies' wallet.

'Oh sorry, Stu. That's Christina's. Sit in here,' he said, pulling a vacant stool around and placing it at the apex of what was now a seating triangle. 'She's just in the toilet. She'll be out in a minute.'

'Christina?' Stuart posed, with a punch-pleased grin beginning to ripple and tug at the sides of his mouth. 'Is she new then?'

'Not that new. She's been around for a while. I love her.' The declaration did not cause Stuart any surprise. He had heard his brother tell of past loves enough times before. It wasn't that Owen was insincere, he never was. But he had loved a handful of women, and love was the obvious after-effect of time spent with a woman. Owen developed feelings and a sense of closeness where Stuart would find himself struggling to breathe.

'How come I haven't heard about her before?'

'I was about to tell you, when I had the great idea to bring her along to the dinner the other night. Let her meet the parents and that. Get it over with. But then that didn't work out. I had a few rocky days.'

'What kind of rocky?' Stuart asked.

'Potentially very rocky. But I worked through it my way. I took a step back. I'll never fit into their ideas, I know that. So when I meet them it has to be clear in my head what I'm doing it for. I mean, if I'm going to spend an evening with two people I can't stand, who can't see any worth in me whatsoever, I should have a good reason for that, shouldn't I? It wasn't clear to me why I was going. And I'm not sure I want to subject Christina to that either.'

An unfussy woman in her early thirties, dressed in pale-blue jeans and a loose but not baggy white T-shirt, walked lightly and confidently from the ladies' toilet. It had to be Christina, because she was so unlike anything Owen would ever hanker after, and this breed of surprise was in perfect keeping with Stuart's weekend so far. As she sat down, Stuart observed her shoulder-length hair, a nose slightly too big for her face that managed to come across as striking, her lightly freckled skin, and her make-up; she wore none. She was average and conventional. She reached out her hand and sat down, smiling constantly. Stuart reviewed his initial impression. She was remarkable, somehow. Was it physical, or just the self-possessed certainty of her entrance that made her? He wasn't sure.

'Hi, you must be Stuart then,' she said.

'Yeah. Nice to meet you. I've just been hearing about you,' he said, still taken aback.

'Likewise,' Christina replied. 'I see you're still empty-handed. What are you drinking?'

'Now that's what I call getting off on the right foot,' Owen interjected, before Stuart had had the chance to nod his head and say, 'A pint of whatever, please.'

'Yeah, we should get along just fine,' Stuart squeezed in, before Christina called out the order to the barman.

∎

As children, their differences were dramatically pronounced. Now, as men, a shared in-house sense of humour would incline an outsider to believe nurture had prevailed. An outsider could be forgiven for thinking that they were simply the product of some fine, consistent parenting, their sensibilities forged in the same scorching furnace. The truth was more complex; family truths are always more complex than the individuals they send out into the world.

Owen came first and was separated by the middle sibling, Sara, from Stuart. Necessarily, their parents came before them all, though not only in chronology.

Owen had been a cheerful child, full of wide-eyed excitement and adventure. His curiosity threw him from trees, into playground fights (from which he always emerged the worst, not being shrewd enough to defend or vindictive enough to prevail), detentions, teenage drinking and soft drugs, minor brushes with the law, expulsion from a couple of schools, squandering of student loans, heavier drinking and harder drugs, self-rehabilitation, and an assortment of jobs, never careers, with the odd alcoholic lapse at family occasions thrown in for good, black-sheep measure.

Sara complied with her parents' wishes, until she was fifteen, and then she lied and deceived, and continued doing so for several rebellious years, only to compromise in marriage by finding herself an acceptable husband whom she could never love.

Stuart was quiet, above-average at school at practical and numerical subjects, always neat, athletic, and free of all rebellious spirit until his mid-teens, when his sins paled in comparison to outcast number one and only—Owen. All the misplaced expectations put on Owen were transferred to Stuart. Stuart found that by being reasonably normal, he met his parents' expectations fairly easily.

Sitting at the bar in The Lantern on this night, the two brothers may have seemed a natural friendship; they may have seemed obvious brothers, but it was shared experience—good, bad, painful— that was the solder binding them so closely together. They split the impossible load that is dislike for one's parents between them and their sister; it is the Gordian knot of family politics, an irresolvable conflict that pursues a person through their life—what to do when you don't like those you try hardest to impress? In the friction and fall-out of hard times in the home, loyalties were earned, debts were accrued, and warmth was found in those closest to the wreckage.

■

Back at the bar, Stuart was drunk again, or still, but more drunk than when he arrived. So were Owen and Christina. It was approaching closing when the main door to The Lantern opened to reveal to the world outside an almost empty pub. A wide beam of bright light from a street lamp lit up the pub's carpeted floor, cutting a lambent catwalk from the door to the tipsy trinity by the bar. Onto this airy stage stepped an instantly recognisable figure. Making a grand entrance in a slimming, buttoned white blouse, knee-length red skirt, and heels was Rachel. She spotted the group immediately, and aware of the time, made straight for them, introduced herself to Christina, hugged Owen and kissed him on the cheek, put her arms around Stuart and hugged him tightly, before ordering a round and excusing herself to go to the ladies'. She changed into a pair of green khaki trousers and a yellow T-shirt, pulled from her bigger than usual handbag.

'Wow,' said Christina. 'Those are some legs to be going and covering up.'

'She's looking great, Stu. Where's she coming from?'

'From a talk with her boyfriend, ex-boyfriend, reunited boyfriend—whatever. He's a real shit.' Owen smirked at Stuart.

'Not to mention she's hot,' said Christina cheekily, suspecting that she may have pushed it a step too far with the brother she'd only just met. 'Sorry,' she said. 'It's between the two of you.'

'It's okay. I've had this stuff for years. Mostly from him,' he said, gesturing towards Owen.

In the minimum of time, Rachel was back at the bar, straightening her belt and flattening down her T-shirt over her trousers, just in time for drinks. Printed on her newly donned T-shirt were the words—WHO'S GONNA KNOW? She dove right in. 'Can I stay at yours tonight, Stu?' Stuart nodded and she continued, 'Cool. We'll have to taxi it though,' she said, kicking her left foot into the air to reveal her high-heeled shoes. 'So Owen, how've you been?'

'Pretty good, actually. The world's a little brighter these days. Maybe it's all about ageing gracefully. You?'

'Good. I'm good too. I am now.'

Now, Stuart thought. Now, as opposed to earlier. She was good now. What did that mean?

'Why the change of clothes?' Owen asked.

'Well,' she said, 'I liberated myself from a big mistake tonight.' They all braced themselves as she continued; Stuart and Christina were holding metaphorical hands in anticipation. 'And I wanted that mistake to have a good look at what he would be missing, as a parting shot. A touch catty, maybe, but I had my reasons. Now I just feel like kicking back, and this feels more comfortable.'

From there the room assumed an entirely new dynamic. From two brothers and one girlfriend, to two brothers, a girlfriend, and a girl friend with an asshole for a boyfriend, to the final composition of two brothers and their two girls. A balance was achieved with the removal of the fifth party, the silent partner, the casting vote. The four were cosy, a little boozy before home, and for the time being, all problems had been glossed over without discussion or consideration. They ordered one, very last, last round and went their separate ways. They went home to comfort and intimacy, caught up in a near perfect moment that stretched for hours.

MONDAY MORNING

Rachel's eyelids began to flutter slightly, threatening to open. Her eyes were breaking their seal—eyelash by eyelash. She rolled heavily to the side, lifting her cheek from Stuart's bare chest. She became aware of the cool air as her skin pulled free of Stuart's warm body. She untucked her hand from Stuart's hip and unwrapped her arm from around his stomach and waist. Simultaneously, she unhooked her foot and leg from between Stuart's half-spread legs. She breathed in deep through her nose and opened her eyes while exhaling steadily. She was lying on her back now and became aware of being clothed only in her T-shirt. Suddenly, she started, and looked around in a panic for something with a time display. Stuart's digital alarm clock read 7:52 A.M.

'Monday morning! The shop!' she said, internally. 'Shit,' she said, out loud. Her exclamation stirred Stuart and he began his battle towards consciousness. 'Stuart. Stu,' she said, jabbing him bluntly with the flat of her fingers. 'Five to eight, Stu. I've got to open the shop for Mum today. We got to get up. Can you give me a lift?' Stuart was unable to get it together. He couldn't decipher the statements or the question, he couldn't manage to connect the urgency of her words with their meaning. He understood what she said in a literal sense, but he was unable to respond appropriately. There was no adrenaline, only mental torpidity. He was too sleepy, still too filled with booze, too dehydrated to understand and respond. 'Stu, come on. I've got to go. I promised my mum.'

'Stay in bed,' he growled, through a throat-worn voice.

'I can't, Stu. I gotta go. I feel awful, but I have to be there today.'

'I don't think I can, Rache,' he said, eyes still closed, rolling onto his side, with his bare back to Rachel as she sat upright on the edge of the bed. He pulled the duvet up around his shoulders. Rachel looked a little rough by her own demigoddess standards. 'Take my car. I can't go in.' The dry-mouthed, aching-body, throbbing-head hangover was becoming more pronounced as Stuart came closer to being awake.

'You sure?'

'Yeah, definitely.' Rachel crawled over to his side of the bed on all fours, leaned over him, and with her hand on his shoulder she rocked him towards her, kissing him on his lips as his head turned, to say thanks. She lingered there, bent over him, feeling a coolness on her bare arse-cheeks as the T-shirt rode up her back, until he opened his eyes and looked up at her. They talked and joked as she threw on her clothes. She was ready within minutes and made hastily for the bedroom door. The morning light rushed by her, as she opened it, into the blind-darkened room, illuminating all around her once again. Stuart was still watching her as she turned back and said, 'I'll see you later. When I drop the car back, yeah?' She looked buoyed.

'No problem,' he said, and she left, closing the door and taking the brightness with her. There was comfort in that final silhouette, in Rachel's familiar contours, in the flow of her hair as the light of morning shimmered through individual strands, rippling free on the slightest of drafts. In her voice was the residue of simpler times, and although these visceral comforts could never protect him fully from the complexity of his immediate future, they attested to a possibility, a chance of something better than what awaited just around the corner. Rachel provided respite, but darker thoughts were not far off. Other issues, other people—other girls—didn't inspire such sincerity in Stuart.

Rachel was gone about half an hour. Stuart had turned from one side to the other several times. He had buried his head under the pillow. He had searched for the cool of the bed-sheets. He had lifted his head and dropped it back down to the firm pillow; he looked at the ceiling; he dangled his arm off the side of the mattress at such an angle that his fingers began to tingle for lack of blood; he forced himself to sit up, quarter-erect, and sip some water from the pint glass on the dresser; he rolled, kicked, tossed and contorted. But nothing helped, and finally he had to get out of bed and face the day that was in it.

Phase 1: find his phone, make the call; the landline wouldn't do, he hadn't been able to remember a number since the advent of the mobile phone pandemic. Phase 2: sort his head out, do something about the Jenny situation, get through the day. Phase 1: to find his phone? On the face of it, a straightforward job. However, Stuart's rate of productivity was heavily impeded by holistic malaise: the morning-after syndrome, where the mere tying of a shoelace is an ordeal, the challenge of dexterity being too much. So the locating of a misplaced phone, without the benefit of sober patience, was inevitably infuriating.

After shaking out the duvet cover, turning the pillows, opening and closing the fridge three times, shoving fingers down the back of the sofa, checking all pockets, inside shoes, sweeping the bathroom military-style, Stuart, now sweating and close to cracking up, collapsed sodden onto the living room rug. He lay flat out on his back with MTV droning in the background—the odd soporific song squeezed between a gratuitous show paying homage to some soulless ego, and a series of self-promoting ads—and cursed his lot. He retreated into something less than consciousness for a few minutes.

His left temple was the first to note a slight bulge beneath the inside corner of the rug. As he rolled onto his shoulder, his cheek took some therapeutic pleasure from the firm pressure applied by the weight of his head on a solid corner of a soft rug. The incompatibility of these two sensations didn't strike him at first. The conflicting facts survived separately for nearly a minute, until, in his first show of urgency this day, he shot his hand up under the rug, towards the hard corner at his temple. From there he lifted his phone. Phase 1, underway.

Now, all that remained of Phase 1 was to carefully develop the intricacies of his feigned illness and construct a thirty second conversation that relayed his pain and discomfort in a laconic but convincing manner. Although, Monday's lie would need to be informed by Friday's, consistency being the mother of plausibility. His lie required an inconclusive line, so as not to paint himself into a corner of deceit. At the same time, it required an idiosyncratic detail or two, for the sake of authenticity. In order for him to take any pleasure from his sicky, he had to convince himself he'd put in a good performance; he had to hear in his own voice a genuine pain, and in the voice of whoever he relayed his illness to, he needed to hear sympathy, in fact, he needed to hear empathy, so that he could be comfortable in his deception.

Stuart began to feel ill. He felt tired and nauseous. This was what he had hoped for. He had to turn green and feel rough in order to act out his part. The hangover would aid his performance. Once the phone went down, after the call, he knew the symptoms would be alleviated, just like when as a kid he had lain strewn on his bed, apparently kowtow to anonymous illness, only to be wrested from death's door and into vigorous life upon hearing school was out for the day. Here too, an overwhelming and liberating relief would surge through him once the seeds of fraudulence were successfully sewn, and his well-being would be only slightly tinged by professional chagrin. He would be left with a mere hangover.

He worked himself up into a psychosomatic queasiness. He was set to vomit. The thought of vomit temporarily distracted him, as it dominoed from vomit to morning sickness to Jenny. Stuart did not even know if Jenny would have morning sickness yet, or whether morning sickness actually involved puking, or whether it was just a case of glorified nausea; some vaguely received but hardly noted knowledge informed him that morning sickness was in the early stages of pregnancy, but how early? He sat himself up on the edge of the sofa and dialled the number. His heart pounded and his head went light.

'Good morning. Ramsey and Stanley. How can I help you?'

By ten o'clock he was showered and dressed. No clean clothes, but he managed to find a not too dirty T-shirt and yesterday's relatively clean trousers. There was no possibility he could remain in the apartment. Between professional chagrin, the hangover, and personal angst, the possibility of spending a slovenly day in front of the TV was a non-runner. Any one of the factors alone would ordinarily have been enough to bring on the panics. The three of them together were a lethal mix. He was not prepared to lie at home just waiting for uncontrollable palpitations of the heart, clammy hands, irrational fears, and an exhaustion that wouldn't let him sleep.

Stuart had to get out of the apartment. He had to keep his mind occupied and he had to get some food into him, and some liquids, but no stimulants—no coffee, no tea, no alcohol. Given the early diagnosis, and provided the correct treatment was administered, he could expect to be well on the way to recovery by lunch time. He would keep himself busy and arrive home exhausted, in the early evening, and sleep like a baby. The next day he would rise early and fresh and go into work, and get back to reliable routine—and no more sick-days.

With his car gone, he decided to take a walk towards the city centre for a fried breakfast and a read of the Monday sports. He walked towards the canal, crossed the lock, and continued along the uneven footpath that ran the banks of the canal, taking in the passing traffic as it built ominously from the late Monday morning trough towards what would eventually be a crawling and intense peak, as the week got more serious.

It was warm but overcast. All the school kids were off for the summer. He noticed a few as they passed, some on foot and some cycling, probably making their way to various places of summer employment. A gang of younger kids were standing on the side of the canal, throwing stones at the ducks. The nervous ducks flapped and squawked each time a stone burst the surface of the water near by. They were petrified, and kicked off in random directions as the gang continued to torment them. A stone finally clocked one of the ducks on the breast and it let out a sustained screech. An old lady leaning out of a window on the far side of the canal shouted out at the children to stop. She was tearful in her plea, but she was met by a small, freckled, red-haired kid who stuck two fingers up at her and threw a stone in her direction. It fell well short, but his point was made.

Stuart walked on, away from the red hair and the freckles and the learned aggression, towards St Stephen's Green, in search of breakfast. The emissions-filled city air was preferable to the stagnancy and claustrophobia of his apartment, and he felt better. The streets around the city centre had a constant flow of people. An air of insouciance prevailed as the residue of a sunny weekend's rejuvenation was borne on people's faces; not everyone overdid it like Stuart.

He sat down at a small table in a café. Rush hour had come and gone, but the café was still busy enough, full with the corporate legions, armed to the teeth with filofaxes, briefcases, laptops and mobile phones, all chowing down before well thought-out late Monday morning appointments and loading up on caffeine, and there was a scattering of civilians too, thrown in the mix like a personalised afterthought of the city. There were three people waiting the tables and a woman behind the counter making various coffees—cappuccino, espresso, decaf, mocha, arabica—and teas, and barking orders into the kitchen behind. Stuart unfolded the tabloid he had picked up along the way and turned to the back pages. A girl who had just finished wiping the next table over came and placed a dried rose in a tall, glass vase in the middle of the table. She stood over him and took out her pad and pencil, ready for his order. She was foreign and earnest.

'What do you like, mister?' she enquired. He heard a thick Dublin accent behind the counter say, 'Sir! It's sir. That drives me mental.' The girl continued, unaware or unconcerned, 'Mister?'

'Hi,' said Stuart. 'Could I get the bacon, eggs, sausage, beans and toast, please?'

'Yes, mister. Would you like some tea too?'

'Coffee,' he said, without thinking. Before he had time to correct himself, she was handing in the order to the life-ravaged woman behind the counter. Stuart called out, 'Excuse me,' and the waitress turned and waited for what he had to say. 'Sorry. Could I get orange juice instead?'

'To the breakfast?' she asked, baffled.

'What?' Stuart replied.

'You want juice, no breakfast?'

'No. Sorry,' he said. 'I want the breakfast but with orange juice instead of the coffee. Sorry.'

'Oh,' she said, and clarity relaxed the skin on her face and smoothed the furrows of concentration.

With the mix-up unjumbled, the leathered lady leaned over the counter and said, 'Sorry about this love. She's new. What's it you want? The full breakfast, is it?'

'Yeah,' said Stuart. 'But with no coffee. Just juice.' The waitress placed her pad back in the pocket of her black apron and went off about her job again, the unkind, implied criticism shrugged off. Stuart called out towards the counter, 'I think she had it actually.'

The woman behind the counter turned and gave a customer service smile, the kind that thanks you for your interest and dismisses your input at the same time, and then went on about her work while talking to the man behind the counter. As he turned his attention back to the back pages of the tabloid, he heard the woman say, 'We'll have to put her back in the kitchen.'

Stuart enjoyed his breakfast and was beginning to feel better. He was ready to pay the bill and looked around for the waitress so that he might leave a tip. He could not see her. He went to the counter to pay, still looking around for the waitress. He had some change in his hand, waiting, when the lady behind the counter pushed a tips jar in front of him.

'We share it out all equally at the end of the day. If you want to leave something, love.'

Stuart had not intended for the tip to be part of a central fund, and he could not help but feel he was about to donate to the woman's greasy till, rather than subsidising the waitress's paltry wage. He dropped half the change in his hand into the jar. 'Thanks,' he said, and went out into the street.

He wandered towards Grafton Street, past the grand Georgian houses operating as centres for big banks and businesses and state departments. He paused outside an electrical shop, looking in the window for nothing in particular. On the other side of the road, parked along the Green, was an unoccupied one-horse carriage. The harnessed horse stood patiently, while the carriage driver talked animatedly into his mobile phone. Nailed on to the back of the carriage was an advertisement for a casino.

Stuart turned down Grafton Street, onto the red-brick underfoot, and into retail heaven. He wound down the street, its four and five storey buildings looming close on either side. The glass-domed roof of Stephen's Green Shopping Centre was just disappearing behind him as he passed Harry Street and the flower stalls. He stopped into a sports shop, but decided against buying anything he would have to carry for the rest of the day. In the record shop he refrained again from impulse purchasing, despite the overtures of a funky little shop assistant with a tongue-piercing. But he was growing bored, and quickly. After twenty fruitless minutes, he caved in and made a purchase, returning to the funky record shop girl with the piercing and buying a miniature radio and earphones.

By the time he had got to the end of Grafton Street, he had heard two ads for R&S Foods as he flicked through the stations, looking for anything but ads, especially his own. He stood, stressed a little by the inescapable adverts as they beat a crude path to consumers' wallets: *Chocnut—half the fat, all the satisfaction!* He immediately switched stations.

As he walked along the walls of Trinity College, he tried in vain to find a music station that played music. If it wasn't ads, it was awful disc jockeys filling the airwaves with useless irreverence and contrived humour. Some shouts became audible over the voices on the radio as he walked. He looked over the wall and through the bars of the black railings, down onto Trinity's grounds, to see a group of untroubled students playing a seven aside football match. Within a couple of minutes, he was pitchside. He sat down on the grass and in the shelter of a tree, with the radio still talking in his ear. After a few minutes, he began to feel sleepy. He drifted into a light snooze in the warm afternoon, as the disc jockey encouraged listeners to text in to his show: 'So accidents in the kitchen, folks. It's pretty much fifty-fifty, women to men, from what we've heard so far. Who's worse? What do you think? Text us and let us know. And coming up is two songs back to back. Right after the news and ads.'

The Dublin sky had had enough of summer and it began to drizzle. Snoozing Stuart did not notice, sheltered beneath a tree from the initial droplets. As the grounds gradually emptied and became quiet, and the drizzle cranked itself up a notch to a fully fledged shower, Stuart was woken by a bloated, cartoon blob of rain that dripped slowly from an overhanging leaf, and burst all over his forehead. He sat up suddenly. He looked around and saw the last survivors running with their heads sunk low into their shoulders, as if their heads were being hammered further down into their upper bodies with the weighty blow of each bull's-eye raindrop. Their sunken heads made their arms appear over-long, and they looked simian as they ran with their lanky, spindly arms jerking formlessly up and down.

He took his lead from a couple scurrying across the tarmac perimeter of the fields, dashing from beneath the tree, onto the tarmac, and up a paved wheelchair ramp. He kept going, down some steps, and onto some cobbles and past the Book of Kells. Then he turned sharply, barely avoiding impaling himself on a black, iron pylon, and raced for the shelter of Regent House. Bicycles were chained around the square. He got there a little wet, pushed through the small crowd into the centre of the high-roofed octagon. He stood by the internal mailbox, decorated by a no-smoking sign and surrounded on the walls by flyers and posters. There were some students around, but mostly it was tourists. Many of the tourists had their windsheeters on or were taking them out of their little pouches; ever prepared, the tourists were the only ones who never got caught out by the Irish weather. Stuart scanned the notice boards—Student Union notices, Arts, Swimming Club, Golf Captain's Prize, posters for upcoming debates and events—while the tourists scanned colour-coded maps and decided where to go next.

The shower continued to come down for twenty minutes. Stuart was getting restless and manoeuvred his way back through the crowd gathered under the arch, to check on the weather. He looked out, but the rain persisted.

A small waif of a young man came clapping over the cobbles, wrestling with an umbrella in the rising breeze. His thick-soled shoes seemed too heavy for his rickety legs, and his awkward steps on the cobbles made his knees contort so badly that Stuart feared they might snap with the next step. The young man stopped about ten yards in front of him and lowered his long umbrella before coming under the archway. He pushed past Stuart, excusing himself to those around him, and then somebody called out and caught his attention. Stuart looked to see who had called. Three students walked towards the skinny, pale man, now standing beneath the roof's single hanging light, shaking the rain from his umbrella. The group of three average-sized people, two young men and a young woman, engulfed the space around him, and were chatting excitedly. Stuart could hear parts of the conversation.

'Well, thanks very much. I appreciate that.'

'No, seriously, you were superb.'

'Really showed them. Brilliant.'

'Thank you. Thank you,' he heard the little man say.

The man had his back to Stuart. But as the group shuffled and gesticulated, he caught glimpses of an eye, or an ear, or a patch of hair. The group were surrounding him but not infringing. There was a reverential distance between the three groupies and the small man at the centre of the fuss. The group came to a consensus of some kind, and they moved to one side, waiting for the little man to lead them away. He looked over his shoulder, in Stuart's direction, as he prepared his large umbrella. Stuart reached into his back pocket. His eyes narrowed with concentration as he took out the unopened electricity bill. He looked down at the name scribbled in pencil on the back—Eamon Quigley. He looked from the name on the envelope to the man's face, and back again, as if trying to identify him from the letters that made up his name.

He stuffed the envelope back in his pocket, keeping a close eye on them as they passed through the tall, narrow archway of Trinity's enormous, wooden doors, and out of the strange twilight.

Stuart trotted quickly to the doors in time to see the ungainly Quigley nearly do himself serious injury on the slippery manhole in the midst of the treacherous cobbles by the front gates, falling into one of his companions, who, quite unnaturally, didn't even snigger, but merely caught Quigley by the elbow and lifted him upright again. What Dublin had now was a stubborn drizzle; there was a decidedly dreary greyness to the day. Stuart followed them into the rain.

Stuart was at the gates to see the group making their way back towards Grafton Street, with Quigley steadier now as he skated along the pavement, free of the perilous cobblestones. The green man at the pedestrian crossing flashed into action, allowing Stuart to cross the road without pause. He was twenty yards or so behind them. He checked his phone for the time. It was two o'clock. Abruptly, they came to a stop by Molly Malone, in all her hearty voluptuousness—Molly, falling out of her low-cut dress, with it slipping off her shoulder as she manoeuvred her empty cart, all her cries of cockles and mussels come to a successful end. Stuart's eager momentum continued to take him closer.

They turned right and Stuart had to lift his pace for a few steps to make sure he didn't lose them. He rounded the corner without hesitation, only to be met by Quigley's stare. Quigley had come to a standstill outside a pub. He had lowered the umbrella, shook it, and with his free hand held the door open for the rest of his party. As they trooped in the door, Quigley looked down the street and caught Stuart's eye, right on. Stuart was startled: the allegorical child with his hungry hand in the cookie jar, caught doing something he shouldn't. He ducked right back where he'd come from, and walked into a newsagent and stood by the papers and magazines. He felt like he had just been caught peeping, he had feelings of slight shame and awkwardness; he was pissed off too, he did not deserve to feel like a peeping pervert—this was a straightforward stalk. He picked up a copy of a glossy magazine and tried to look occupied—ridiculously playing to a nonexistent audience, like the guilty atheist trying to appease a judgemental deity he doesn't believe in with a gesture of goodwill.

How could Quigley have picked him out specifically? There must have been ten or twenty people around him. He could not have been looking at Stuart. At least, he could not have been looking at him with any knowledge of what Stuart was doing. It was just a glance, Stuart thought. He flicked absently to the last page of the magazine. There was a bright red crisp packet with crisps tumbling out the top and a caption that read, *New Chilli Flavour from Crunchers*, and underneath the bouncing text concluded, *They're Just Sensatious!* Stuart let a mental scream. He dumped the magazine back onto the pile and left the shop. He was going into the pub. He had an undeniable feeling of a man about to be rescued.

Stuart took a high stool by the window, looking out onto the street. He ordered his pint of cordial and sat down. He sat at an angle that allowed him to appear as though he was people-watching out the window. Quigley was at the bar, in casual conversation with his three groupies. Between the low music and the bustle of people, there was no way Stuart could listen in on their conversation. He was too far away for that, but he dared not go any closer, just in case Quigley was some sort of surveillance genius, and had actually spotted Stuart for the stalker he was.

Stuart was prepared to instigate a conversation, but he had no wish to play the irritating stranger to Quigley's Mr Popular. Quigley was already getting all the ego-plumping he could want from The Three Stooges. While he did not suppose there was anything too imposing in a passing introduction, and commenting that he had seen Quigley on the TV and thought he was interesting, it was hardly invitation to sit down material. And that was what Stuart wanted, he wanted a sit-down, he wanted an answer from Quigley, albeit an answer to an as of yet unarticulated question. What he needed was Quigley alone.

So he waited. Twenty minutes for the first pint. Twenty-four minutes for the second. It was nearly three o'clock by then, and two messages had beeped in on his mobile, and there had been one unanswered call. They ordered their third pint and Stuart was still sitting by the window with an empty glass. About halfway through the third pint he thought he'd finally got his break. The dam had burst. One of the young men and the woman took a toilet break. Surely, Stuart thought, Quigley can't be far behind.

They returned from their toilet break but there was still no sign of them leaving Quigley to his own devices, or of Quigley himself giving in to nature. Stuart was getting edgy. He was beginning to look shady, still sitting there with his empty pint glass. He did not want to order another one though, in case that would force him to the toilet. He could lose Quigley altogether. Eventually, Quigley broke, just as Stuart was beginning to suspect the little slip of a man had a bottomless bladder hidden in his little body. Stuart followed him down the stairs and into the toilet. He lined himself up two urinals down. Quigley stood, with his head thrown back, whistling a happy tune to the discoloured, sunken ceiling.

'I saw you on the TV last night,' Stuart said.

Quigley looked at him. 'Was I any good?'

'Yeah. I thought so. I found it very interesting, and it's not my kind of thing, to be honest.'

'Not your kind of thing? That's a curious statement. What's not your kind of thing? People? Standard of living? Society? Taking care of the young and the elderly? Misuse of tax?'

'I mean, I don't usually watch those sort of programmes. I'm not very . . . very political.'

'Not political,' Quigley said, bemusedly. 'Our whole lives are politics, my friend.' Stuart felt like he was talking to someone's father. Quigley was deliberate in his speech, he sounded like he had an abundance of informed opinion at his disposal. His face was lean and young. His body looked hunched and frail like an old man's. He was a compellingly clichéd mix of erudition and physical vulnerability; had these been schooldays, and had Stuart not been in the middle of a disempowering crisis, he might have pushed Quigley's face to the urine-splattered tiles and taken his lunch money.

'I've just never paid attention, I suppose. But I was watching the show last night and I thought to myself, This Trinity guy is on to something. But I couldn't hear you. Every time I thought you were about to really nail it, somebody interrupted, or you went another way with it.'

'That's just rhetoric, my friend. Political rhetoric can make a man seem wise and learned, when he's only taking potshots in the dark, and stalling for time. But let's suppose I was, what point exactly is it that interested you? Maybe I could clarify it for you now.'

They were both still standing at the urinals, but finished. Stuart did not want the conversation to end there with nothing resolved. Quigley, realising he was conducting a conversation while out of his trousers, zipped up and made for the sink. Stuart followed suit. They both finished washing their hands.

'There was just something. See if I can get this straight,' Stuart said.

'Take your time.' As they walked out of the toilet and back up the stairs, Quigley invited Stuart to come and sit with him and his friends. Stuart declined, suggesting he would be out of his depth. Quigley reassured him. He said, 'Your questions are as valid as my opinions.' Stuart bought the mawkish sound-bite, managed not to be offended by the condescension, intended or not, and joined Quigley and The Stooges. 'You have as much right to politics as the TDs and the Taoiseach himself!' Quigley exclaimed, as they reached the bar. The other three all laughed as if this was an old classic. Stuart laughed too; he was ninety percent sure he could name the Taoiseach, if push came to shove.

Quigley asked Stuart's name and introduced him to Larry, Moe, and Curly. The conversation from the toilet was shelved as the four tidied up on the details of what they had been discussing. In stark contrast to Quigley, the others looked and sounded very much their ages. They were as unremarkable as any other second or third year student. It was not too long before the three were off to put up posters, or give out flyers, but Quigley remained.

'So tell me, what was it about last night's debate that is on your mind?'

Stuart was impressed that Quigley had paid attention. 'Right,' Stuart began. 'Would you like a drink, by the way?'

'Sure. The black stuff please. Everything else just runs through me like water. I'd be in the jacks every ten minutes.' Stuart ordered the drink and got himself another pint of cordial.

'You said something about jobs, and religion being dead. And tax. And you were talking about . . . I'm not sure. I can't quite get my head around it. I only caught the last part.'

'Okay. Let me have a go.' He took a sip of his unsettled pint and wiped the cream moustache from his upper lip with a brush of his fingers. 'We're the same generation.'

Stuart was not so sure about that. 'What age are you?'

'Twenty-five,' Stuart replied.

'Right. I'm twenty. People of our generation don't believe in anything—there's no plausible religion, no creditable doctrine out there. There's no faith in gods, or society, or in people in general. We don't exactly accept corruption and deceit in our institutions and leaders, but we figure it's inevitable, and as time passes, one false hope after another will be revealed in a 'sensational' kiss and tell in the Sunday papers. That's our experience of politics and institutions, in general.'

'I must have missed this part. Sorry. This isn't what I was thinking of.'

'Hold on,' Quigley said, knowingly. 'I think I know what you're looking for here, but this is all part of it. I believe that people need to have faith, that they need to contribute to the world they live in, in order to flourish in it. But don't get me wrong here, I'm no bible basher. There were many before us who didn't believe in that either, and they got along just dandy. Rhetorical question: Why was that? Rhetorical answer: Because of vocations! Lack of faith didn't matter because people had vocations. Their jobs gave their lives meaning and importance. The village tailor made the clothes, the farmers provided the crops and dairy, the blacksmith the bits and pieces for whatever. Mother looked after the family, and everybody was happy. Everybody had a function, and although it wasn't all joy and whistling in the fields, there was a job that needed to be done and you did it. You were relevant and needed. Today, our generation has no god, no faith, and no vocations. That leaves a gaping hole. Societies crave meaning, and individual members of the society have to be valued if they are going to be asked to work for their community, rather than against it. In our world, people work jobs for no reason other than money. When you have enough money and you get more, what do you do with it? You spend it. You think, This will give me some pleasure. And it does. The first few times it does, and then the pleasure attained by the accumulation of luxury items lasts less time each time you do it. It's like the buildup of tolerance to a drug in the system. Every time it needs to be more and bigger, if you're to get the same satisfaction. This week it's a CD, next week a new stereo. Next month, it's a stereo for the car, and at Christmas it's a new bloody car altogether! There's no meaning in our lives, in our work. Where do we find the meaning then?'

'That's an impressive rant,' and it was to Stuart. 'But I still don't really get you. In fact, I don't get it at all,' Stuart said. 'And don't women want more than babies and housework?'

'Ah, very true. But that's a whole other aspect of it, the 'be careful what you wish for' line of thinking, as grey as any other area of life. However, let's keep the focus here, put the mother thing down as an erroneous example in point. We've got no value system, you see. We don't know what we value, not the way our parents did, or the way a stereotypical Buddhist or a Muslim does. We're in transition, we're the transitional generation. All the old cornerstones of society and morality are disintegrating before us; religion—Catholicism—is a sham to us, we're closer to libertines than Catholics. But there's still the residue of that moral framework, we've got an uneasy relationship with ourselves and the lives we've chosen. We lap up the money and luxuries, but we can't reconcile that with the hopes our parents had for us. We enjoy the excess—food, drink, drugs, sex—but can't help feeling that somehow it's all too easy, it can't be right. We're adamant about our freedom—freedom to choose, to vote, to protest, to fight, to fuck, to indulge, to fundamentalism, if we want it—but we're uneasy with the choices we've made, as a collective, with that freedom. At some point along the line, that discomfort with ourselves as a collective filters down to us as individuals—What have I done with my life? Am I happy? Are my priorities right? Do I really love my wife? Did I ever truly chase my dreams? Why did I waste so many years on money and conformity? And where do we go then, when half our lives, the most oomph-filled half, is already in the past, and we're nothing like we hoped we'd be?'

'We might be onto something here, but I'm still not quite with you. You see, it isn't about religion, or any of that rubbish, you know. I've never given it a second's thought, until last night. I just get up and go to work, enjoying myself whenever I can.'

'Except that you don't. You're not doing that right now.' Quigley paused and thought for a second. 'Change of tack,' he said. 'What do you do? What's your job?'

'I'm a regional manager for a food company.'

'What does that mean?'

'Well, in my case, it means I oversee ad campaigns and launch new products.'

'Marketing. God help you. You lot are worst off. What happens if you don't go to work tomorrow?'

'Nothing. In fact, I didn't go today. Or Friday. This is one of my problems.'

'You've barely begun your working, adult life, and already you're struggling with the shallowness of your proposed model. Great! You're rebelling against consumer culture, and that's from your position as one of its architects, however lowly an architect you may be.' Quigley seemed delighted.

'I'm not. Really, I'm not. I just couldn't get it together to go to work. And today was more the hangover than anything else. And then there's this girl. And now this other girl, which is really complicated. Seriously, I'm not anti- anything.'

'Okay. Why couldn't you go to work on Friday?'

'I just couldn't get off the side of my bed.'

'What do you mean? Physically? You couldn't?'

'Yeah, I suppose. I felt sick. I thought I might cry. I just didn't want to go, and not going seemed the only way to make it all better.'

'Beautiful!' Quigley yelled, loud enough to draw some attention to the two of them. 'I'm a fan of this already. Your body is rejecting consumer culture.' The drink had clearly hit his euphorituary gland. 'Or your part in it, anyway. Your body is a socialist entity, brainwashed by a mind unconsciously imprisoned and controlled by a prevalent capitalist philosophy. And it's just had enough.'

'I think I'm just unhappy,' Stuart said, feeling like those five words constituted about as profound a statement as had ever been made.

'If you get fired, what happens to the company?'

'They carry on. They get a new guy in, I suppose.'

'And if the company went belly-up? What then?'

'I don't know. I suppose a lot of people would lose their jobs, and there would be no Crunchers, Chocnut, or Bucks in the world.'

'How would that affect the world at large?'

'When you put it like that, it wouldn't make any difference. Other than to the people who just lost their jobs.'

'You're right, of course. Those people, who are now without jobs, are the flaw in my argument. People have to work. But vocations are no longer, not in a western world of plenty, and there is no faith to speak of. So what am I recommending? I recommend people contribute to their society. I recommend that if you have the soulless job, you hold on to it, and give it its due importance—it pays the bills. But take some of your spare time to ensure that while you have plenty, others aren't left short. Get involved in the local council, do some voluntary work, work for charity instead of just throwing them your pennies every so often. Get involved in politics, make sure you vote. Always look for the injustices and do what little you can about them. This to me is why politics is so important. Our communities, our societies, are full of people who feel worthless, who feel they aren't valued by others because they don't make any difference. So take part. Get involved in whatever aspect fans the flames of your passion. Don't just sit on the sidelines disillusioned. On your feet. Get . . .'

'That's it,' Stuart shouted. 'Disillusioned. That's the word. How do I get rid of that?'

For the next two and a half hours, Stuart and Quigley remained locked in conversation. Stuart filled Quigley's pint glass, and they tried their best to clarify exactly what was missing from Stuart's life that had left him feeling so—word of the moment—disillusioned. Stuart told Quigley all about the girl—Jenny. Quigley said it was all part of the same problem; there was no meaning in his relationships with women. It occurred to Stuart that in the field of women, Quigley's theories lacked a little punch. It was approaching six o'clock by the time Stuart bundled a still excitable, but increasingly unintelligible, Quigley into a taxi outside the pub. By then, Quigley had lost his mystique but gained a little in the down-to-earth stakes.

Stuart checked his phone. Rachel had rung but not left a voice message, and two more messages had beeped in while he had talked with Quigley. The first message was from Owen and Christina, a joint message, from an unrecognised number he took to be Christina's. The concept of a joint text message held within it some of Stuart's worst fears. It was an overt surrender of all measure of independence, just like the joint Christmas card or wedding invitation, only worse; those were annual, or once off, and called for by practicality. But the joint text was an invasion of the everyday, an unconditional surrender of social and, most frightening of all, emotional independence. It signalled the standardisation of a relationship, stripping the individuals within the relationship of their nuances and subtleties. It may have seemed adorable to the senders, a show of unity, but it was plain creepy to Stuart—0832425665: HAD A GREAT LAUGH LAST NIGHT. WE SHOULD GO AGAIN—TINA. GOOD TO SEE U, STU. TALK SOON—OWEN.

The second message was from Rachel, having failed to get through earlier, explaining that she had tried to ring, and she would leave the car back around seven in the evening. The fourth message had beeped in around half past five, from his father. His father loved texting, because it meant he did not have to actually talk on the phone—'I'm a face-to-face man. Always have been.' He was letting Stuart know that they were having a dinner, and Sara was coming over with Kevin. He was requesting Stuart's company and letting him know that his mother would be calling him herself, later. The third text was from Jenny. He had been dreading this one, and had known that one of the alerts must have been her. It was a brusque text—JENNY: LUNCH 2MORROW. CHEZ CHEF AT 1. MUM AND DAD WANT 2 TALK. There was no question or choice involved.

He was standing on the street reading his texts, with Quigley safely shipped off, when the phone rang. MUM! MUM! MUM!

'Hi, Mum. How're you doing?'

'Good, Stuart. Thanks. We're having a family dinner tonight. Sara and Kevin are coming and I'd like if you were here. So wherever you are, just get in a taxi A.S.A.P. Short notice, I know, but your father was on to you earlier, I understand.'

'Yeah, he texted me,' Stuart said.

'Typical. I hate those awful texts. Dinner is at eight. You can deal with Owen, if you want, but I won't be expecting him.'

'Mum.'

'Yes?'

'Can I ask why we're having this dinner? I mean, I'm coming, and it sounds lovely, but we were only out on Friday.'

'Kevin wasn't though. It was Sara's idea actually. Now get a move on,' she said, and hung up.

MONDAY EVENING

Stuart paid the taxi man his money and got out of the car. He was still thinking about what had been said before the drink took control of Quigley's limbs and brain. Disillusion? Meaning? Vocation? Could all the palpitations, the sweats, the nausea, the anxiety, the lonely apathy, be down to job dissatisfaction? Did it all go back years, really? And if so, why had it come to a head now? Why not earlier? Why so suddenly? He walked up the driveway of his parents' exclusive house.

The Victoria hadn't always been their home. It was part of a secluded estate of one-off houses, hidden away near the summit of Killiney's low hills. The houses were detached and regally named. It was relatively modern, seventies sometime, and had been fully renovated before the Byrnes moved in, including a hideously out of keeping glass conservatory, added on a whim. They were nearly eight years in the house. Eight years ago, Owen had been missing from the family home for four years and Sara was a couple of promising years into her career as a journalist—she was freelance and had gained herself a reputation as a lippy voice in stodgy, political affairs, with a couple of features written for a fledgling and short-lived political magazine (she was the only thing of note to survive *Bust and Boom*'s single year in existence), and she also wrote reviews for one of the Sunday papers; her offbeat, metaphor-a-minute commentary on the contemporary Irish novel had made her popular with readers, and caught the eye of some savvy editors. She was long moved out of home, and engaged to Kevin.

Stuart had entered his fifth year at school. He was nearly seventeen and there seemed possibility abound. Only opportunity lay ahead, the brightest of futures filled by effortlessly realised dreams. But somehow, on reflection, despite all the success and the growth and record employment, Stuart now had a feeling of potential having gone unrealised; vague aspirations of adolescence never crystallised, never manifested themselves as a specific goal. He never had any actual dreams, nothing specific, and yet he still felt this awful sense of not having seized his opportunity, and of the very conception of his own dream being tantalisingly out of reach. Were the opportunities missed? Did they go unseen? Were they ignored? Were they ever truly pursued? Did they ever exist?

He felt alone, but it was more than company he required. It was a helpless kind of alone, filling him with feelings of insignificance, something like the kind of awesome smallness experienced when caught in the gaze of one of nature's enormities—Uluru, Victoria Falls, the Amazon or the Nile, the Grand Canyon. In the face of ungraspable, universal hugeness, it was meaning he craved. He stood before the biggest wonder of all, man's philosophical Everest, and felt tiny in the face of it, inadequately equipped to even pose the right question, never mind answer the great imponderable—the meaning of a single life in the greater scheme of the whole cosmic show?—and the chance of his freedom to ever explore it being swallowed by unwanted responsibility scared him, it brought a previously latent discontent to terrifying life. The fear of being embroiled in a life he didn't choose accelerated the process of realisation, a process he had, until Jenny, been plodding blindly through.

But this was a recent phenomenon. Weren't there happy memories too? Surely all his memories weren't tainted by an undercurrent of misery and dissatisfaction; had he been unhappy all along and not known? like some lunatic, rocking-crazy in an old chair in an asylum, with no normality with which to measure his insanity against? What were those happy memories? If only he could dredge up a couple, maybe then he could identify a pattern, a common tenor, that might reveal a sublime path to the grail of fulfilment.

He had already entered the final phase of second-level education, when the Byrne family took up residence at The Victoria, and had he not already chosen his seven subjects and settled in with a system and personalities he was familiar with, he might have been moved to a more prestigious school too, a school to match the new home at the illustrious new address; a move to a more esteemed educational institution, the fee-paying kind, would have been insisted upon by Elizabeth Sheridan-Byrne, had they been able to move into their new house a few months earlier, as she had planned. Although she pushed to be in the new house earlier and enroll her youngest son (her least ruined child, her favourite) in a reputable school, a school appropriately cultured and peopled, it had proved impossible, with busy builders working a multitude of sites, all trying to cash in while the going was great in an economy awash with cash. There were countless delays followed by excuses, but Elizabeth Sheridan-Byrne just could not understand why a house could not be built on schedule: foundations on Monday; floors and walls on Tuesday; roof on Wednesday; then send in the cosmetic people with their tiles and carpets and blinds and furniture.

The builder blamed plumbers, electricians, and logistics. He blamed the weather, which seemed fair in a country so meteorologically manifold. Patrick was summoned, late on a Friday evening in July, to rescue the project, placating the patience-depleted builder when he threatened to throw down tools and walk off site if, 'That woman,' rang him one more time. Elizabeth Sheridan-Byrne sat back and seethed in uncharacteristic silence—her mighty will and spite, her child-like impatience, bending to the desperate fear of her dream address slipping further into the future, too far to bear.

So almost eight years ago, with two children of three moved along into the real world, the Byrne family moved to a house with an extra bedroom and two extra bathrooms. More space for less people. To a bigger garden, a grander house, and a quieter estate, in search of space and privacy, went the family who cried out for intimacy and shared burdens.

Snowie lifted her old head off her paws and twitched her nose. Her dark, out-curved eyes were deep with a lifetime of memories and strained to see the figure as it approached. Her ears pricked up and her mouth opened, a sliver of tongue sliding out and to the side as she began to pant, slow and heavy, to the jangle of Stuart's keys: the familiar musical rattle of an owner's return. Stuart approached and put his hand out to pet her gently on the head. 'Hey, Snowie,' he said, in that gentle voice of affection we save for our pets. She forced a little bark that never managed to sound more than the chesty cough of a decrepit old man. She pushed herself up and walked towards Stuart's outstretched hand. She sniffed at his hand and her tail began to wag with more ado than her tired limbs seemed capable of sustaining. Then she lowered herself to the ground again as he came up the final step and onto the porch. She lay happily at his feet, and he scratched behind her ear and patted her less firmly than he used. He could hear the silence of separate lives inside the house, and the approach of a car behind him as polished driveway pebbles crunched beneath its tyres. He turned to see Sara getting out of the car. He met her on the middle step, and they hugged each other tightly.

'Didn't expect to see you again so soon,' he said.

'Me neither,' she replied.

'Hey, Kev. How are things?' he called out, over her shoulder.

Snowie coughed up another bark for Sara's benefit, and she said hello to the old dog as she opened the front door and went into the house.

'Not too bad, Stu. Yourself?' He was toying with the car alarm. He turned it on and off a couple of times, checking the doors.

The dinner was cooking and close to ready. Elizabeth was standing at the island in the kitchen, pouring herself a glass of red wine and a fruit juice for Sara. Stuart and Kevin said hello, and Elizabeth put on her plastic smile and beckoned her son forwards into her arms for one of her lame hugs. Stuart guessed she had had a couple of glasses already. Then she kissed Kevin on both cheeks. Sensing safety in numbers, Patrick made an entrance and greeted everyone.

'I believe we'll be having the famous char-grilled chicken. I would say that we could bring you all in and sit you down for your starter, at this point. Perfect timing,' he said, and showed them into the dining room. The large, heavy-legged, mahogany table was set, and the wide French doors were open, allowing a cool breeze passage through the spacious dining room. The shadows of evening were just beginning to creep across the width of the back garden, at an angle across the lawn, as the sun dropped below the hills and trees, sinking into the western sky. On the table were two decanters of red wine, airing nicely, the perfectly unsmudged silver cutlery gleaming proudly from each place, five wine glasses, and a tumbler with two melting ice cubes and a dribble of whiskey. The guests took their places and Patrick organised the drinks.

'Wine okay for everyone?' he asked. 'Kevin?'

'Just water for me, thanks,' he replied. 'I've got the new *Dulles* outside.'

'Oh, I must have a look at her later,' said Patrick.

'Just water for me too, Dad,' said Stuart.

'I'll finish this first,' said Sara, oddly daring in tone.

'Sara!' Patrick exclaimed.

'Joke,' she said. Sara was a woman who knew her own mind, who spoke it with lucidity, and was never anything but surefooted in opinion. Nothing was ever said that wasn't thoroughly, even if thriftily, thought through. She had a sharp mind, analytical. It was clarity of thought, singularity of vision, that distinguished her in a family lost in an emotional fog. It was the unfamiliar, apologetic tone that seized his attention. 'And a whiskey for yourself, Dad. Yeah?' she said. This was a pointed remark, less question than accusation—the peculiar flippancy of her previous comment put behind her—and much more in keeping

'Ah, sure I'll get one in before dinner,' he said, not rising to the bait. 'No wine, son?' he asked.

'No. Just going to take it easy.'

'So we've got some big news, then,' Patrick said, looking between Sara and Kevin, tipping a generous measure of whiskey into the tumbler.

'We might wait for Mum, Dad. Do you think?' Sara said, even more sharply than before.

'Oh, yes. Of course, love. I forgot my etiquette again,' he said.

It was only then that Stuart took note of the champagne lolling in a bucket of ice by the drinks cabinet, where his father was now standing, replacing the stopper in a studded and squared jar of whiskey and placing it back on the top shelf. He looked at Sara. He knew at once. He recognised the expression. He knew what pregnant and unenthused looked like. He saw the guilty despondency of not wanting something she should be delighted about. He saw life seeping out, rather than radiating from her. Where was that special glow pregnant women were supposed to have? Where was the miracle? Her news appeared to be anything but good. She was irritable, she was flinging out uncharacteristic remarks and searching for an argument. How much they had in common right at that moment; he wanted to tell her about Jenny, so that she would understand that she was not alone with her despondency. Kevin was still smiling at the thought of his new car. He was ignorant to the tension in the room. He was oblivious to the situation, to the fact that his wife was suffering and that she had come to hate him.

'Hardly etiquette, Dad,' she spat out. 'Common fucking courtesy. And sense. It's not something to do with breeding, something you inherently have. It's about other people. An awareness of that. Consideration.'

'Alright, love. I'm sorry. I jumped the gun a little. It's exciting for me too though.'

'And who are the other people who are excited, Dad? You and who else?' she asked, looking to her crash-test-dummy husband, and raising her hands in limp despair as the punching impact of personal slight failed to register.

■

Sara remembered Kevin just before she pulled him from adolescent obscurity; he was short and nervous as she lured him in among the greasy, denim jackets and grubby duffles.

Owen was eighteen. Their parents were away at the wedding. Kevin was one of many friends to Owen present at the opportunistic teenage house-party, orchestrated by Owen in the absence of his parents—the kind of friend you have at eighteen and think you'll always know, one among a group, only to wake one morning when you are thirty and wonder, Whatever happened to him?

Sara's exclusion from the evening had been bought with ten pounds stuffed into her hand and a tone of proposal that clearly told her she wasn't welcome—'Do you want to go to the cinema tonight?' Sara grabbed the tenner, as if it was the chance she had waited for all her life, and skipped theatrically out the door, but inside, her heart broke, and once she was out of sight she cried, tears cascading down her cheeks and soaking the angular neckline of her jumper.

Arriving home late from the cinema, Sara pushed past an obnoxious school friend of Owen's—who was prone to making lurid remarks about her developing body—on the front porch, with some bleary-eyed redhead, who was smoking beneath the dim porch-light, seemingly unconcerned by the unzipping of her jeans. Music was pumping through the house. She said hello to a few of Owen's friends that she knew, most of whom were discreet enough to ignore her sudden metamorphosis from little sister to hewn, teenage perfection. Sara, a fast fifteen, had begun to look differently at Owen's friends too.

Still piping hot from earlier rejection, she grabbed herself a Manhattan glass and poured herself a spirit-heavy vodka and white lemonade. Four of these later, and still reeling from the pain of an acidic ten pound note, she began flirting with all comers. She was a montage of teenage sensitivities—hurt, alcohol, love, sexual awakening, rebellion, hate. She isolated the boys she knew who hadn't already got some young girl locked in conversation, or an upstairs bedroom, or a downstairs toilet, and threw at them all the allure she could muster from her inexperienced fifteen-year old soul. None were prepared to forsake friendship.

So she tried a few strangers, but recoiled in excited alarm when they jumped at her artless seduction; a few tongue-filled kisses cut short when she felt strangers' fingertips skimming the skin of her back.

She could see the future fatness in Kevin's stocky frame, but he was pleasant and timid—an easy target for a mischievous younger sister hell-bent on evening the score. So, Sara, sixth vodka and lemonade in hand, put out her cigarette and led a submissive Kevin under the stairs, by the belt buckle, into the coatroom. In the darkened coatroom they kissed—sloppy, lusty kisses. Kevin was a novelty, exciting to Sara because it made Owen uncomfortable, but the frenzied fumblings in the coatroom came to little more than a squeeze of bottoms, a hand up the top, over the bra, and a fruitless grinding of hips.

In the couple of years that followed, however, she returned to Kevin, sporadically, on nights when there was nothing better, or when her ego had been bruised. He was always there, skulking around in Owen's shadow, in the hope of the next chance encounter. She knew he was malleable; she felt his consuming need for her affection, and she exploited it.

Once she turned eighteen and began university, their chance encounters became less frequent, until Kevin was gone altogether, and she didn't even notice. They became strangers. Years passed. Then one evening Kevin gate-crashed back into her life. A new Kevin: improbably confident and assured. He pulled up a stool beside her in a bar, poured two flutes of champagne and insisted that they share a drink, insisted, now that he was a roaring success (co-owner and acting director of sCent, a company specialising in cosmetics for men—aftershaves, deodorants, facial scrubs, moisturizers) that he was good enough for her. She listened to his swashbuckling tale of business adventure—Man Rides Crest of Economic Wave—that seemed to be sprouting out of every cake-hole in the city at the time, made somehow less banal, made interesting, in fact, because this was a tall story about somebody she had once known, somebody she used to walk all over, and he clearly still adored her.

She had had few relationships in her life. She had loved only once, and badly, the wrong kind of love for a girl who needed the big romance to redress the balance; her reference points for love were unfortunate—loveless, embittered parents; and then the archetypal older man. He stole her virginity (literally hoodwinked her and lifted it) and spat her then naïve heart out onto the floor. He cut her open for all to see, with all her unmatured emotions spewing out. She was devastated.

She recovered though, more cynical as a result, but was left to cope with an emotional glitch and the unpredictable effect of such a gremlin on successive relationships, putting devastation down as valuable experience. Sara's history shapes her, protects her, inhibits her, drives her—all at the same time. Kevin is a testament to Sara's history. He was someone she knew. He was someone who had never hurt her—how could he? She didn't care for him in any specific way. And when whimpering submission was replaced by success and ostensive self-confidence, he seemed viable. Love had not worked out for her, and she had no faith in love out of the blue, or of finding it where she least expected; those are adolescent dreams, only possible in those psychedelic years, never realised, forever the source of real life disappointment. Settled. Yes, settled. That's what she did.

■

Kevin awoke from his motor daydream, and said, 'Excited? God, yeah, Paddy. I sure am.'

Sara downed the rest of her juice in one. 'I'm gonna need some wine there, Stu. Could you pass over the decanter, please?'

Neither father nor brother rose to it, but Kevin said, 'I don't think that's a good idea, Sara.'

Elizabeth entered the dining room with the salad starters to find Kevin blathering on about the new car, and the one he would have bought if he was completely frivolous. Ordinarily, Patrick would have indulged his son-in-law, not because he had any time for os-tentation or extravagance, but because it was the fruit of Kevin's labour, and hard work was something Patrick admired, and Kev-in's industry and application were to be respected and applauded. However, the exchange with his daughter had rattled him.

Stuart leaned over to Sara and offered his congratulations. He was hoping she would be unable to hold her feelings in, and that she would just blurt it all out and declare how much she dreaded the idea of another child, so that he could sympathise with her and puke up his own unpalatable confession. But she did not. She just smiled tiredly at him and patted his hand in recognition. Stuart wondered was she just letting off steam. Maybe this wasn't about being pregnant or not wanting to be pregnant. Maybe it was about trying to wind Kevin up, for some reason nobody else knew about.

Elizabeth Sheridan-Byrne took her place at the table and poured herself a glass of red wine.

'Do you want to do this now?' Patrick asked his son-in-law, and so brought an end to his tiresome recounting of his new car's accessories. 'Do you want to do it now, or wait till after? We all know now anyway. But should we make it official?'

'Stuart, when did you find out?' asked his mother, shaking her head. This wasn't how breaking news was supposed to break.

'Just now,' Sara said, glaring at her father.

'For Christ sake, Patrick!' Elizabeth Sheridan-Byrne shouted at her husband.

'Ease off the two of you,' he said. His capacity for joviality and good humour had reached an end. He was assuming his hard-nosed solicitor demeanour. He was braced to exert the pressure of the bully that was only ever just beneath the skin. 'It was an honest mistake. It's not like I spoiled it for everybody. He's the only one who didn't know, so let's not pretend like everybody's big surprise is ruined. I'm only in the door an hour, and I've had an earful of you two already. Pregnant or not, it stops here.' He was pointing and wagging his finger. He could not contain the impulses. He took another slug of his whiskey and poured a glass of wine from the second decanter at his end of the table.

The two women loaded their guns, but it was an uncoordinated attack, and Kevin's intervention was enough to diffuse the situation, for a while. 'Sara's pregnant again, Stu. As I'm sure you've figured out at this stage. So let's have a toast and start again. Cheers,' he said, only to realise that three of the five people at the table had no drink in their glasses. There was a flurry of activity as token measures of wine were poured into the empty glasses for the purpose of the toast. Everybody said, 'Cheers!' And they sat in silence as they ate their salad starter.

Stuart sat thinking about Jenny again. He thought, She can't have it. She'll have to get rid of it. It doesn't matter what her parents say, or what she thinks she wants. I'm not ready. There's no future in it. He thought of all the things he would lose out on. He thought about all the travelling he wanted to do (though he had never so much as picked up a brochure for a world tour, or showed any sign of broadening his horizons beyond package holidays in tourist paradises) and how he would have to move, have to buy an apartment, or a house (and although buying was something he was considering anyway, the idea of it being forced upon him stirred up resentment in him) and try to make child-support payments at the same time. He thought how he would have to change nappies instead of watching football or going for spontaneous pints—the best kind. Or just doing whatever he pleased.

He thought about Rachel, and wondered. He thought about how Jenny annoyed him. He thought about how when they were all in college he would try to jockey for position in the pub, so that he would not be left sitting beside Jenny for the night, bored out of his mind. He thought how he had slept with her at the reunion. He wondered why he did that after spurning her advances for three years of college. What did she think? Did she think it was the start of a relationship? How could she? How many times did he have to avoid her before she got the message? Three years of it had not done it, mind you.

He wondered was he the kind of man to run away from this. He could head for London, and Afroditie's, where he'd been happy, and just disappear. Or America. Or to Spain, to somewhere sunny and pleasant, and just start again. Or Australia—he hadn't done that yet, and it was just about compulsory to spend a year drunk and bloated under the Australian sun. He was thinking of himself and feeling hard done by. He knew it was of his own making but still managed to feel cheated. He knew Jenny was not getting rid of it. He would have to tell his family. There was too much going on, there were too many hypotheticals. He needed to talk. He needed to hear the words come out of his mouth. He could not make sense of any of his thoughts while they were all swarming around each other in his mind. He saw the dissatisfaction on his sister's face and, hoping for an ally, felt she might understand. He wished Jenny had looked like that when she had found herself pregnant.

Snowie had wandered round the back of the house looking for comfort in the familiar voices and smells. It was still too hot for her, even in the evening sun, with her thick, long-haired coat. She brushed heavily off the frame of the door and wobbled a little as she walked. She lay down on the saddle board with her head inside the room, in the shade, cooled by the evening breeze.

Elizabeth looked to the old dog and said, 'Seriously, Paddy, when are you going to put that yoke out of its misery? She can barely walk. She can't see, and I think she's gone deaf too.'

'We're not getting into this again, Liz. I told you once already today, as long as the vet says she's not in pain, we're going to keep taking care of her.'

Elizabeth Sheridan-Byrne began collecting the salad bowls to bring them to the dishwasher. She was shaking her head and muttering words about that not being life and about cruelty, subjects she knew plenty about.

'She's got really old, Dad,' Sara said. Patrick turned around to look at his old pet. He loved the dog and that was something worth holding onto, for as long as he could. He was not sure what would be left if simple love like that perished to nothing. Early retirement had left him with an awful lot of time with his thoughts, and now that he had time to have them, he found them of no particular comfort. They were all looking over at Snowie now. The dog seemed aware of the attention and she closed her deep, black eyes and snoozed contentedly.

'Yeah, I know,' he said. 'But as long as she's not in pain.'

'She's such a lovely dog,' said Stuart.

'I never really got the pet thing,' said Kevin. 'Now cars. And bikes. I get that.'

Everybody ignored Kevin and sat quietly remembering Snowie for a minute, as if she was dead already, only to remember she was not, and appreciate her as she dozed. Elizabeth took the dishes to the kitchen and made a check on the baby potatoes. The smell of the cherry tomatoes baking in olive oil wafted towards the dining room. She was ready to grill the chicken, and she could hear the conversation through the open door.

'So when are you due?' Stuart asked.

'February.'

'Have you told Damien yet?'

'No. I'm not sure when we'll do that. Soon though, I'm sure,' answered Kevin.

'Is he with Granny and Granddad Kelly tonight?' Patrick asked.

Kevin nodded, as Sara responded to Stuart. 'He's mentioned little brothers and sisters before, so we're hoping that will be smooth enough. I was thinking we would tell him over the next couple of days.'

'That soon?' Kevin asked, but seemed to have no objection. It just appeared to have caught him by surprise.

'We have to tell him at some stage. Might as well do it sooner than later.'

'Yeah, I just thought . . . we haven't decided how to approach it.'

'It's not that big a deal, Kevin. He's a smart boy. He'll be fine.'

'And will you be finding out the sex, or are you going to make it a big surprise?' Stuart asked.

'Maybe a surprise this time, do you think?' Kevin said, looking to Sara for confirmation.

'We'll know in advance,' she said. 'It makes most sense.'

'Am I missing something here, you two?' asked Patrick. 'You'd swear you two had barely talked about this.'

'We haven't,' came the marked reply.

'Not in depth anyway, Paddy. Not yet. I've been busy with work and . . .'

'The new car,' she added.

'And things in general. You know yourself, Paddy. But it's great. I think it's great, and I'm really looking forward to it now.'

'And sure you've done it before. There can't be that much to talk about, I suppose,' said Patrick.

'Well, you might still want to talk it over,' Stuart suggested. 'What if you didn't feel the same about it? You'd need to find that out. You can't always just assume these things.'

'What are you banging on about?' asked Kevin, in an agitated tone that suggested he had a fairly good idea and didn't like it.

'I'm just saying that these are complicated situations. Maybe Sara's not sure.'

'Don't be ridiculous,' Kevin said. 'Of course Sara wants the baby, and I'm perfectly happy with that.' He was angry.

'Not exactly a ringing endorsement,' said Stuart. He was feeling a little braver. He reached over and poured more wine into his glass. He took a quick drink and went for the jugular. 'Are you sure about this, Sara?'

'That's enough, Stuart!' said Patrick.

'Of course she's sure, Stu! Why are you trying to stir the shit? What's going on here?'

'Nothing. Sorry. It's nothing. I was just asking, but I'm sure . . . sorry . . .'

'And it's a pertinent question,' interjected Sara, before Stuart had time to sheepishly withdraw from further discussion the unhappily pregnant elephant in the corner. She was calm and sure-footed. 'Because I feel bloody nauseous at the thought of having this child. I'm as unsure as I could be. I'm so unsure, in fact, that I know. I know I don't want this baby.'

'I think we should talk about this at home. This is the first I've heard of this, Paddy,' Kevin said.

'You can't be serious about this, love,' growled Patrick. 'There'll be no abortions in this family. You're married. You've got a son already. And all you could want. Is this about your career? You're reading too many of those bloody women's magazines. That's it, I'm telling you . . .'

'You're telling me nothing. I haven't listened to you since I was fifteen. I'm not about to start now, you cantankerous auld git!'

'Don't dare use that manner with your father, in this house!' came the voice from behind. Elizabeth Sheridan-Byrne was standing, tea-towel in hand, listening and jumping to the defence of her husband, despite herself. 'This is our house. I raised you to show respect.'

'Oh, and you can stay right out of it, you spiteful cow!' Sara yelled back.

Suddenly everybody was going for each other; it was chaos. Stuart was trying to undo what he had done. Somebody was likely to say something unretractable. He was appealing for calm, for quiet, realising now that this was not what he wanted. He called for quiet over the shouting and dismay. He gave up rather quickly. He stood up and bellowed out, 'I also have a child on the way!'

'Now there's a reason for an abortion,' said Kevin, on the heels of an abrupt, stunned silence. 'I wouldn't give you a licence for a fucking dog!'

Everybody was sitting back down. Sara had gathered her purse and sunglasses, and sat to hear what Stuart had to say before leaving. Kevin had taken out his car keys and was twirling them around his index finger, shaking his head as if he empathised with the shock on everybody else's faces. In truth, it did not even register with him. He just wanted to go, and he was not going to say anything that might prevent this conversation from coming to a timely end. The two parents sat at opposite ends of the table, looking at Stuart. They all had questions. He took another gulp of wine. So did his mother. His father finished his whiskey and topped up his wine glass.

'Are you sure it's yours?' asked Patrick.

'What kind of people are they?' asked Elizabeth.

'Are you with this girl?' asked Sara.

'Yes. I don't know. And no.'

'Where are they from?' asked Elizabeth.

'Ballsbridge, I think. What does that matter?'

'Well, that's something,' said his mother. 'It could be worse. You'll have to be upfront with them. They'll be as suspicious of you, if they're well off, as we would be.'

'I'm still suspicious of her. How can you know it's yours for sure? Young people, the way they are these days, you couldn't be sure,' said Patrick.

'Get her to the clinic,' said Kevin, still twirling his keys around his finger.

'Shut up, Kevin. If there's anybody going to the clinic here, it'll be me,' said Sara, and he stopped with the keys. He reminded himself to keep quiet.

'You should arrange to meet her parents. Maybe we should come. A show of solidarity. We're all in this together now. What does her father do?'

'Nobody is meeting anybody till I've decided what to do. I'm just here to tell you about it. I thought it might help me to come to a decision. But you're not helping with pointless questions.'

'It's not that they're pointless, Stuart. It's that they're irrelevant,' Sara said. 'Their questions aren't without point. They relate to their own self-centred agendas, as per usual. But they are irrelevant in terms of *your* predicament. Which was, of course, the topic you had hoped to discuss.'

'Sara, this is not helping.'

'In heated situations like these, the accuracy of your language is critical if you want to reach a clear conclusion. If you do this when you meet them,' she said, looking to Stuart, 'you'll leave thinking you have decided one thing, and they'll leave thinking the other. I'm warning you, you must be precise with your language.' She stole a glance at Kevin, 'Clinical, even.'

Sara was lapping up a drama that was not hers, firing out in all directions, after everybody, and Elizabeth was imagining a suitable merging of families, when for so long she had feared he might end up with Rachel, or somebody worse. She feared her youngest son would follow his heart the first time it spoke to him, make an irreversible mistake, and regret not being more pragmatic in his choice of spouse for the rest of his life. Patrick had turned his solicitor's eye to the problem, examined the potential loop-holes, and decided the best course of action for his youngest and most able son. He put aside the prejudice of his pseudo-Catholic morality and allowed himself to be guided solely by the cold hand of paternal instinct.

'Kevin is right. He was a bit crude, but she's got to be sent for an abortion. You're too young to take the chance that it might be yours. If you wait for tests, it'll be too late, too far down the line to send her then with a clear conscience.'

'A few minutes ago there was no bloody abortion in this family. And I'm fairly sure that she'll have a say in this too!' a maddened Sara burst out.

'I think she wants to have it,' Stuart revealed.

Everyone went quiet again. The tide of questions abated. Then they gathered their respective thoughts and Elizabeth, grandmother-elect, was first to break her particular wave on the sand of Stuart's dilemma.

'Okay. I take your father's point,' she said, 'But if that's what she's decided, there isn't a whole lot you can do about it. We have to assume it's yours. So we've got to approach this meeting with her people in the right way. We want to start off on the right foot. We need to size them up too. A house in Ballsbridge is a good indication of what we're dealing with, but it doesn't guarantee anything. We've got to be optimistic, but at the same time tread carefully.'

'There's no marriage here, Mum. Never even crossed my mind. Not happening.'

'Don't rule out anything until we meet them, is all I'm saying,' she replied.

'You're not meeting them, Mum. I don't want this thing. I'm too young. I don't even like her.'

'You liked her enough to sleep with her,' said Sara.

'And you married him, and look where that got you,' he volleyed back. She accepted it silently. It appeared that Kevin didn't hear, but that was impossible. He hadn't heard Stuart's barbed retort? He hadn't heard Sara's awful quiescence?

'Just take your time, son. Make the right decision. Nothing worse than regrets in this life,' Patrick said.

'That's true,' said Sara. There was still no outward response from Kevin, just a blank absence, an implausible absence.

'Oh, here we go with the regrets. Give it a break, Patrick. We all have them. We didn't all bring it on ourselves though!'

Just then the charred char-grilled chicken smell hit their nostrils and a light smoke from the kitchen became visible. Elizabeth Sheridan-Byrne leapt to her feet and ran to the kitchen to save anything she could. It was a lost cause. Sara and Kevin took the chance to leave. They got to their feet and walked. Patrick bid them a considerably less than cordial farewell, and Elizabeth ignored them as they passed through the kitchen and out the front door, saying good-bye as they went. She waved a dirty tea-towel at the cloud of thick grey smoke rising above the char-grill pan on the draining board. Stuart sat at the table with his stewing father and topped up his glass of wine. Once her daughter and son-in-law were out and down the driveway, Elizabeth stood at the island in the kitchen, alone, and sipped on the wine she had left there earlier while cooking. She began to cry. She cried silently and secretly, for burnt dinners and wasted years, and unrequited love.

It was ten o'clock. Patrick was in the study in his armchair, in the snug of a bay-window. At his feet lay Snowie, sleeping peacefully. The study was lit by a small, low-watt lamp on the bookshelf. He was fairly drunk. He sat with an open book—*The Complete History of The Irish Free State, 1916–1949*—straddled between the narrow ravine of his legs. He looked as though he had not read any of it for hours, or at all. His sturdy block of an oak desk was tidy and unused. His swivel-chair was pushed into the desk and the PC monitor was covered by a black cloth. On the small round table beside him was an almost empty bottle of whiskey. In his hand, resting around his crotch, tilted towards the book on his lap, was a full tumbler of whiskey—no ice, no mixer. The top four buttons of his shirt were undone, and his trousers were pulled halfway up his shins to reveal his bare feet, tucked in under Snowie's body. He was peering through his whiskey.

Elizabeth had shed her marriage's last tear and was now in the master bedroom, dressed in a long white nightdress, propped up on five pillows, outside of the bed-clothes, and was watching TV. She had recovered the composure she constantly strove for, and sat stoically watching a hospital drama. On the bedside table, under the lamp, was an envelope with a carefully penned letter to a solicitor not her husband. She swung her legs off the bed, picked up the envelope, and stood up. The long nightdress and the gentle lamplight concealed the bumps and roughness of time; she appeared as she might have been thirty years before—slender, sleek, elegant, and graceful. She walked over to the chair by the dressing table. She turned and looked at herself in the full length mirror, and ran her fingers down the length of her hair. She was remembering herself as she was when she looked like her daughter, only before that, before she became hard and cold and destroyed two other people; her youngest was spared most of her spite, and he could still be salvaged, even at this late stage. In the mirror, she stared until she saw through her skin and bones to the rot inside. She placed the envelope in the zip-pocket of her handbag. Maybe some of herself could be saved too.

Stuart was sitting in an adjustable deck-chair taken from the garden. He had placed it just outside the dining room French doors, and was enjoying the cool breeze, as Snowie had done earlier. But

Snowie was at an end, she was preparing herself for death. Stuart was preparing himself for life. He was being railroaded into taking responsibility. He took another drink of wine. New messages had beeped in on his phone. There was another one from Jenny, demanding to know whether he was coming to lunch the next day or not, and there was one from Rachel. She had tried ringing, and calling by the apartment, and just wanted to let him know that she had parked his car in the underground car-park, and put the keys in an envelope in the letter-box. He just could not get the space and time he needed. He could not think straight. He decided on an unprecedented course of action.

There was music playing quietly in the study when Stuart entered. It was one of his father's old jazz records. Patrick had no real interest in music or arts of any kind, although he wrote secretly—structureless, indulgent poetry—but somebody had given him a couple of Miles Davis albums once, and they had found something in him that he had not known was there. Stuart carried with him a gift of appeasement, not realising that his father had that covered already.

'Can I talk to you, Dad?'

Patrick looked up from his lap and smiled sarcastically, 'If it isn't the phantom impregnator.'

'Oh, forget it then.' Stuart put the bottle of wine, the two glasses, and the corkscrew down, and turned to go.

'No,' his father called out. 'I'm sorry, son. Come in. Sit down. Have a whiskey.'

'I think I'll need it.' Stuart pulled up a smaller armchair and sat across from his drunken father, waiting for wisdom to be imparted, like a Greek before Nestor. He poured some whiskey into one of the wine glasses. His father straightened himself up on his chair, and his trousers slid back down towards his ankles as he did so. Snowie was disturbed briefly by the movement of his feet. As he manoeuvred himself on his armchair, with his free hand, his still broad shoulders and chest flexed under the grey hairs and unbuttoned shirt. He was older now, but Stuart could see in his father's muscular frame, that he was once young and powerful and fearless. Stuart was not like his father, he was not fearless. There was just so much to be afraid of.

'So what do you want to do with this situation?'

'I want it to not have happened.'

'Son, there's no value in that mindset. How you deal with this will be what defines the rest of your life. I made mistakes at your age too, and older. I'm still living with them.'

'If it was somebody that I even liked, well then . . . no, I just don't want it. I can't be with this girl, and yet this will tie me to her, in some way, for life. I don't want a kid. I'm too young.'

'We all find ourselves where you are from time to time, Stuart. The details are different, but we all have to choose between the "right thing" and the right thing for ourselves. And contrary to popular opinion, the "right thing" is often the easy choice, the choice of a coward.'

'I just want some suggestions. I need to clarify my options.'

'It's not easy. When we choose what we do, we make our bed. I think we all think we are doing what's best. But who knows what's best? And so young.'

'Dad, just tell me what you think I should do. Surely there's a right thing to do here.'

'The thing about choices is that they come with regrets stapled on the back. But you never read the small-print until something goes wrong. Or until you realise that something has gone very wrong. And it may just be that the "should do" and the "right thing" are not the same.'

'I don't follow, Dad.'

'I mean,' he said, but lost his train of thought.

'You were saying about doing the "right thing," and that sometimes being easier, not knowing what's best,' Stuart prompted.

The more he spoke the lower his voice sank, but his diction remained clear. 'Ah, yes. What I'm saying is, Do you love her? Now that's the question.' Stuart had never heard his father use the word in this context before. As a father, he had said things like, 'We all love you, you know,' or, 'I love you all,' but to ask about love, or speak of it in its romantic context, was unheard of. Strangest of all was that when he said those words, they didn't sound absurd or inapt. They sounded fitting and genuine, as if he knew what it was he spoke of.

'No,' Stuart said, sombrely. For the first time, the casualness with which he treated Jenny embarrassed him.

'Then,' his father said, looking at him, 'You must run.'

'I can't run away, Dad.'

His father looked back to his whiskey. 'Not literally. No. I suppose we can't. We are like trees in the wind. Rooted. We should just bend to it. There's no point standing tall in the face of such power. I loved once, you know.'

'Dad, what are you talking about?' He talked in a garbled chant. These were old, well-rehearsed monologues, perfected in the lonesome early hours of many a night spent drinking alone in his study, monologues overlapping and interwoven by common themes of discontent. Stuart felt he was only there to prompt, not for any benefit of his own, but he sat and listened. Somehow his father's need seemed as great as his.

'So did Elizabeth,' he said, looking grimmer than ever. Then he burst out in a short laughter that tailed off with sadness, and said, 'Just not each other, that's all. Or both of us not each other. I was a coward when it counted, you see.'

'What?'

'I loved another but married your mother. I had resigned myself to never loving again. I was okay. I was content. She loved and adored and mothered. But eventually the emotional chasm got to her, and she realised it didn't matter how many kids she had for me, or how much she loved me. It wasn't enough for both of us.'

'Dad, I'm not sure I understand any of this, or should be hearing it. I really don't want to hear it. It's not what I came to you for.'

'Oh, Stuart, my boy. You're so naïve. You always were. Life is far more complicated than right or wrong. Things come so easy to you, and now you don't know what to do. But you should know your mother was once a great woman. Not formidable, like now, but great. She was warm and beautiful and sexy.'

Stuart began to wish for the imprecision of the chant. 'Dad! Please.'

'You know, Lemass married in difficult circumstances. The in-laws didn't approve, apparently. I think it was hers anyway. Maybe it was his people. But it was a difficult union. Of course, his problems were external, in that sense.'

'Lemass, Dad? Seriously? Again? Still?'

'He was a great man, son!' he flared up. How dare an idiot son strike ignorantly at one of the pillars of his personal constitution? 'Architect of modern bloody Ireland! That's how *he's* remembered. How will they remember you, Stuart? Eh? RTE, Security Council at the UN. J-F-bloody-K!' he listed off on his fingers. 'A man of integrity; something the generations he provided for know fuck-all about. There'd be none of your cars, or sun holidays, or mindless sex, without the foundations he laid. All that shite, that's what you've done with the opportunities Lemass and men—men, Stuart—worked to give you.' He flung his free hand in the air, 'Idiots!'

'Us or them?' Stuart threw back facetiously.

'You!' he roared. 'You and your fucking brother, you fucking gobshite!' Rage and aggression are never far below the surface with the deeply regretful.

'This is nothing to do with a dead Taoiseach, Dad. This is about your family, it's about me. I was looking for help,' Stuart belted out, with the kind of precision of thought Patrick could never have expected of his youngest son. There was dumb silence—how many silences there had been, silences just like this: big, empty, telling silences—as Patrick slumped down in his own seething misery, and Stuart clenched in frustration.

'Yes,' his father said, resignedly, the argument defeated, both men still loafing about in the serene and spacious seconds between defeat and retreat. 'That's exactly it, I suppose.' There was a long pause. 'I couldn't love her. For that, we've all paid.'

Stuart was ready to leave. 'This really isn't what I was looking for from you, Dad. I know you're drunk, and I'm going to pretend

I heard none of this. And I'm going to go. If you think of any actual advice when you're sober, let me know.' Stuart began to walk out of the study, leaving his father staring into his whiskey and meandering to his derivative conclusion.

'But I've given you so much more than advice, son. I've given you a history. History can continue to guide long after the finite relevance of advice has been exhausted.' He had come like a Greek to the sagacious Nestor, seeking wise council, but received only the hazy riddle of a prattling old sphinx. He walked away with nothing revealed, and left the impotent sphinx to his potion.

TUESDAY MORNING

Stuart woke up on the sofa in his apartment. His phone was ringing. The vibrating alert had it bouncing off the glass on the coffee table. PRIVATE NUMBER! PRIVATE NUMBER! PRIVATE NUMBER! He stretched over for the phone, eager to stop the incessant noise, not necessarily eager to answer any call, never mind another private number. It could be Jenny, he thought.

'Hello.'

'Hi, Stuart. Tamara Beckondale here,' said that smooth voice he would forever associate with R&S Foods. It was her voice he remembered when he thought about the telephone interview he agreed to almost four years ago—the inviting softness, the promising tone, the disarming politeness. However, he suppressed these thoughts long enough to ask the questions: Why were *they* ringing *him*? And why Tamara? Why not somebody from his offices, or from HR?

'We were wondering whether to expect you back at work today?' she asked, ever so sweetly, not a hint of accusation. However, when

Tamara Beckondale, with her voluptuous vowels—you could almost see her cushioned lips pursing at the end of the line each time she pushed one of those broad sounds into audibility—said *we*, she meant *he*. A.S. Stanley was on the case; one of his well-paid starlets was taking the piss with sick days, and he needed to exert some pressure, let it be known that A.S. Stanley is always watching. He checked the clock on the stereo. It was 10:45 A.M. That's why they were ringing him; he'd slept out his own sick-call. Already late, and already in trouble, he might as well just be sick for another day. And there was the lunch with Jenny and her parents too. He could use another day. Just one more. He was preoccupied now, by that lunch, and he found it difficult to listen, though he knew he needed his wits about him with the deadly threat of the puckering assassin on the other end of the line.

'Sorry, Tammie,' he gushed, trying a bit of his own deadly charm, playfully referring to her as he did when they met in person and philandered shamelessly. Tammie was in her late thirties, some said early-to-mid forties, and every bit as deadly in the flesh as she was on the phone. 'I'm still really under the weather,' he said. He was trying to think on his feet, but literally and metaphorically he was thinking on his arse. He sat up on the sofa. 'The doctor advised me to take another couple of days, actually.'

'Is everything okay? It seems to be a bad dose you've got,' she said, still smooth and pleasant on the surface. 'What is it exactly?' And there it was. As if A.S. Stanley had asked himself—the question he had successfully fended off when dealing with the less dexterous minds of telephonists and low-ranking secretaries, with no interest in extending themselves beyond their limited brief. Stuart mentioned a doctor, and she was in on top of his story in an instant, trying to nail his career coffin with specifics.

It was a well-executed plan. The call caught him off guard, made not from general company lines but an undisclosed number, probably from the boardroom, and they assigned the defence-stripping Ms Beckondale to liaise for them. Skillfully she prodded, identified the weakness in the story, and when she saw the opportunity, she didn't hesitate, she just drove the nails in, swift and clean, and dusted off her manicured hands—all in the name of the company, in the name of A.S. Stanley, all for the corporate cause. She was having none of his false flattery. Who did this kid think he was?—trying to butter up a woman of her class, trying to compromise her professionalism, like she was some old lady who could be played with honeyed words and obsequiousness, just grateful to still be noticed. This was business. 'Em, not sure really. Not a hundred percent. Viral,' he said. 'I think . . . he said he thinks it's viral.'

'Viral? Oh,' she said. 'Okay, well Mr Stanley asked me to give you a call to see how you are. We hope you feel better soon,' she said.

'Thanks,' Stuart said. Taciturnity was for the best. He had already sounded his own death-knell—if he'd been to the doctor, a record of his visit would have to exist—there was no sense in digging the hole too.

'Listen, just one other thing, HR are going to need a Med. Cert.' He knew it. 'If you're going to be back in before the end of the week, you can bring it to us yourself, but if not, we would appreciate if you could post it.' If it existed, it could reasonably be asked for. 'Or if you're too sick to go out,' she said, still managing to sound deceptively considerate, 'a fax of the cert would do for the moment. I'm sure your doctor would oblige.' She was ruthless, Stuart thought. He had strayed from his meticulously prepared lie for one ill thought-out sentence; he had unintentionally offended her professional sensibility, under-estimated the value of it to her, with his gormless flattery, and she put him in his place, taught him a lesson, and kicked him in the crotch for good measure.

'Sure,' Stuart said, and fell out of fondness for Ms Beckondale.

'Thanks for that, Stuart. Rest up. See you soon. Bye.'

She was gone. He was left on the sofa in his underwear, the TV still on from the previous night, but muted at some disturbed point of sleep, having dozed off with it singing in the background. He had taken a taxi back from his parents' house and come straight home. Although he had broken his Monday resolution—abstention from alcohol—it had only been a minor breach. He hadn't been drunk, over the driving-limit maybe, but not drunk. He had come home, almost perfectly sober, pulled the duvet from his bed, and curled up on the sofa, with the Monday night, late movie—*North by Northwest*. He was exhausted. He tried to contemplate his many dilemmas. But it was too much. He was jaded. He changed the channel, unable to believe in Cary Grant, or even Eva Marie Saint—as hard as that is to believe. He just couldn't watch old films. He got bored with the way that they looked and the dated dialogue. He flicked over to the R&B Top 100 and drifted into a bling-induced somnolence with the charts at number 11: Aaliyah, 50 Cent, Chingy, Sean Paul, Beyoncé, Busta Rhymes, Lil' Kim, Ginuwine, R. Kelly, Ludacris . . .

There had been a note from Rachel waiting when he got home. He had opened it immediately, read it several times, and wondered about her before his wonder was beset by everything else. It was on the coffee table in front of him now as he sat up. He read it again:

Hi, Stu,

I'm just leaving your car keys back (as you can see if you're reading this—how stupid is that?). Really appreciate it, the car. I was sooo tired today at the shop. I had a really great night though. Hope you did too. I've been trying to get through to you. You're not avoiding me, are you? JOKE!

Is that Jenny one still hassling you? She must have it bad. I'll ring you tomorrow. I'll call over maybe. Let me know. I'd like to sit in with you. Watch some TV, take it easy—you know. Had a great night.

love

Rache.   XXX XX

She had, 'a great night,' she said. Twice she said it, and finished with it. One of them was, 'a really great night.' She'd like to sit in with him, too. She nervously—and how unlike her—joked about him avoiding her. What was wrong with her? He knew what was wrong, of course he did. And that, 'you know'? In different circumstances it might have gone unnoticed, an unconscious verbal tick, transferred to the page in a hastily written note of thanks, but now it was conspicuous.

He put Rachel away for the time being. He put the phonecall to the back of his mind too. There was nothing to be gained by worrying about it now, and there was enough to worry about today, without futilely taking on tomorrow's trouble. He texted Jenny—B THERE FOR LUNCH. SORRY BOUT THE DELAY. I WAS WITH MY FOLKS.

It was too late for breakfast if he was going to be lunching with Jenny. He felt he might as well take full advantage of the free feed ahead and skipped breakfast. After all, the situation was going to be excruciating, and the satisfaction of free food to a starving Stuart might help dull the pain of the experience, he thought. He hit the shower. He shaved and adorned himself with fresh fragrances, including a heavy sprinkling of *Recherché*, one of sCent's classic fragrances and one of many complimentary cosmetic products pushed on him by Kevin. After careful consideration, he concluded that clothes-wise, this was a semi-formal occasion. He put on a shirt and suit trousers, but not the tie. He folded the tie and placed it in the breast pocket of his jacket, in case it felt more formal when he arrived. He felt alert and alive and fresh, for the first time in days. He still didn't know what he was going to say to Jenny and her parents. There was still fear in him, but after two days—was it three now?—the absolute terror had dispersed. He was more prepared than before to face up to the situation. He was sober, hangover-free, only slightly paranoid—following his conversation with Tamara 'The Snake' Beckondale—and that constituted an almost complete recovery. He was in good shape to get everything back on track—no shakes, no anxiety attacks, no unfathomable disillusion. He was stable, emotionally and psychologically, and physically he was back in full control.

The phone began to ring, and he came out of the bathroom still brushing his teeth. It was Jenny. He had texted, he had said he would be there, he was primed to take the situation in hand, and still she wanted more. This did not bode well; there could never be enough for a girl like Jenny. He didn't answer. He finished brushing his teeth and zipped up his trousers. He was ready to go. In the hallway a message beeped in. It was from Jenny—HI. C U AT 1. GUD 2 HEAR UR PEOPLE R ON BOARD. X. They were hardly on board, but Jenny's propensity for reading too much into very little was ceasing to amaze him.

Stuart put his jacket in the car and rolled down the windows to let the air inside breathe. His *Perquisita 200* was one of the first corporate perks to come his way when he started working at R&S Foods. He loved it. Lately, following his promotion, before the meltdown was in full swing, he had been considering an upgrade; the new *Perquisita 300* was available. The second thing he had done upon his employment was to move into his apartment. He loved living so city-central, loved the concentration of people and venues—pubs, cinemas, shops, restaurants—and being able to decide to go out at nine o'clock on a Saturday night and find everything on his doorstep, not having to plan a night out a week in advance, not having to suffer the Nitelink home or hustle for a taxi. Now, as he stood outside, readying himself to attend a meeting that could change all of what he was reminiscing so fondly about, he wondered was he looking at his life from this perspective for the last time? He wanted to know where these pleasant memories had been when he needed them, when he was in the grip of anxiety and examining his life through a jaundiced looking glass. I must get back to Rachel, he thought. He could not let that go another day or it would look like he was avoiding her.

He climbed into his car and drove towards the city centre. Traffic was light and moving at first, but soon slowed to a crawl. The windows were rolled down and the radio was up high. He was singing along to 'Hotel California,' rhythmlessly tapping his fingers on the steering wheel, creeping along in the slow, city traffic. At times, progress came to a complete stop, as trucks and vans delivered to the pubs and shops, pulling in and out of loading areas, and blocking the road as they manoeuvred for every inch available. He was early, so there was no hurry. A couple of cars ahead, a small truck backed out of a narrow alley in front of a car. The driver of the car, in a rush somewhere, was shaking his head and cursing out the open window, barely perceptible over the traffic and honking of his horn. On the passenger side of the small truck, a man in dusty overalls had his elbow out the window, and was looking over his shoulder, shouting back, equally annoyed. As the truck crossed the centre-line in the road, impeding progress on both sides, more horns began to blare and blast. A passing pedestrian, an elderly man with a rolled-up newspaper, remonstrated with the men in the truck and was met with abuse. He shrugged his ancient shoulders and gave up. On the radio, the DJ introduced the second of the morning's two classics from the Eagles—'Life in the Fast Lane'—which was coming up after the ad break, along with the Black Eyed Peas and Christina Aguilera, later in the hour. Stuart switched stations. It was all ads as he edged towards the lights at the junction. The dry, dusty, fuming heat of the city centre under day-time traffic was in his throat. He was thirsty.

Hi, this is Abbi from 4Ever. When I'm away travelling on tour we don't get much time. But staying healthy and trim is important to me, so I always have a Slimnut snack bar handy. Hmm, that's better. And healthier!

Stuart heard the first ad of a new campaign for the first time. He thought, As radio goes, that's not too bad. It's hard to do much else with food adverts on that medium. It has to be shameless celebrity endorsement.

When Stuart arrived at R&S Foods they were already in the process of developing a healthy line of snack food. They saw the growing concern in medical journals, and warnings from the health boards about obesity, lifestyle, and junk food, and anticipated a future backlash. They were determined to have the best PR when the issue blew up, and be ready to wheel out their healthy alternatives. The low-fat crisps had been launched three months previously. While many of their competitors were making defensive noises and sending out diversionary statements, linking diet to personal choice, rather than junk-food producing companies and their marketing campaigns, R&S Foods had rolled out their ready-made alternatives—just to show they cared. It was proactive, it anticipated the market, and it saved them from a lot of bad press, took the sting out of it, at least. Their healthy-alternatives campaign was a masterstroke in strategic marketing—releasing the products at the right time, supporting the products with well-placed, well-timed ad campaigns, choosing the right people to endorse the products—it had been a big success, and he'd been part of it. Stanley knew that; he would not lose sight of that fact.

He began to feel like quite the Regional Marketing Manager again, sitting in his beloved company car, dressed sharply, making his way through a thriving city with an ad for one of his products airing on the radio. It's not a bad life, he thought. Then he thought briefly about his life since the previous Thursday, the last day he was at work. He decided he would just come clean. He would say he took a few days off because he needed to think about his future. He would tell Stanley that he realised that pulling a sicky was a mistake, but that he was sure now, he had his priorities straight, and he knew that this was what he wanted. In his mind he worked up the bones of a little sales pitch for Stanley. He would tighten it up later, when he got home. He would knock on Stanley's door, nice and early the next morning, and show him he was back, with an early start, a clever pitch, fresh as a daisy; Stanley respected action, decisive action. He parked his car.

It was time to turn all his attention to Jenny and her parents. He reached Chez Chef fifteen minutes early. It wasn't the first time he'd been to the restaurant; there had been a couple of work lunches, and a date once with a Swedish girl he met in a hotel lobby while checking out after a golfing weekend. It was an average sized restaurant with well-spaced seating. The oval tables were planted in high-backed leather booths. It was not cramped, though. It felt more private, intimate even, than cramped. There was plenty of leg room in the booths, and although everybody could see each other and feel part of the same table, you were not on top of each other.

With fifteen minutes to pass, he went to the small bar. He was not feeling particularly nervous until he sat down. Arriving a couple of minutes early gave the impression of being punctual, which was good. But arriving this early gave him time to think. What would they see when they walked in? What kind of face and posture should he be wearing? He was concerned that self-assured might suggest carelessness; it might hint at triviality and moral frivolity, when what was called for was seriousness and rectitude. He squirmed in his skin. He ordered a pint, just one to settle the nerves.

Soon after, his phone rang and vibrated in his pocket. He answered immediately. 'Hi,' he said. Not a private number this time. 'Where are you? I'm just at the ...'

'I know. We can see you,' she squeaked, like a mother playing hide-and-seek with her infant child.

Stuart turned and hung up as he did so. Standing by the door, waiting to be shown to the table, was Jenny, smiling with inappropriate joy and warmth. She was flanked by a tall, burly man with a well-trimmed but thick, grey beard. His hair was mainly grey too, though there were still flecks of black. He wore a dark suit, tie tight around his neck. On her other side was a petite, skinny, dyed-blonde woman. She was caked in make-up and her face looked older than the man's. She was dressed elegantly though, in a woman's cream suit with a loose blouse. Her parents looked steely and prepared. Jenny walked over to Stuart as her parents sat down at the first booth. It faced the large, clear-glass window that looked out onto the street and the passers-by at lunch time.

'Hi,' she said, and took hold of his hand. 'Are you ready for this?' She was still wearing the ridiculous smile.

'Jenny, this is a discussion we're having, not an announcement we're making. I hope you understand that.' She dropped his hand. 'Yes,' she said, turning to lead the way, 'I know.'

'Dad, Mummy, this is Stuart. Stuart these are my parents, John and Carmen.'

'How're you doing?' said Stuart.

'Okay. Sit down,' grunted John. Carmen said something to John in what sounded to Stuart like Spanish, but may have merely been heavily accented English.

'I just need to run to the ladies,' said Jenny, and left Stuart standing over the table. John and Carmen were sitting close, occupying one curve of the oval table. Stuart would have to sit down on the edge, and stand up again when Jenny returned, to let her slide in. He did not want to be hemmed in on one side by Jenny, and on the other by her parents. He sat down.

'It's nice to meet you, Mr and Mrs Cumberton,' Stuart began, attempting to make as best an impression as possible. 'Even if it is under such,' he was going to say unfortunate, 'difficult circumstances.' With the reality of his future staring him in the face, he began to get scared again, and desperately began to wish for a way out, the morning's mature fostering of answerability up in smoke. He hoped, with enough flattery and salutation, that they might absolve him of responsibility entirely. He was aiming to dazzle with charm—the same charm that had dazzled girls from Sweden, England, Spain, Carlow and Donegal, Castleknock and Cabinteely, Cardiff and Nicosia, New York and Perugia, the same charm that made their daughter want to have his child. Of course, it was also the same charm that had fallen flat on its face with Tamara Beckondale.

Carmen spoke again, her eyes looking nowhere in particular, her hands making elaborate gestures that made Stuart think that maybe she was Italian. But again, Stuart could not understand what was said. All he caught was the name John.

'I'd like to say the same, but that's neither here nor there. Do you want this child?' John asked, in the thickest Dublin city accent; it echoed and elongated its gruff vowels, and indiscriminately cut consonants from the ends of words; he was a complete contrast to his high-toned daughter. Stuart was surprised, first by the accent and then by the directness. He expected Jenny's parents to be different. He expected them to be, well—frankly, he expected them to be better-spoken, his expectation a mark of his sheltered suburban up-bringing, a mark of his southsideness, where the only time he really heard an accent like John Cumberton's was passing junkies on the street in the city. Even in his adult life, where he brushed shoulders with people from all walks of life, he couldn't resist the ingrained proclivity to associate a given accent with a given stereotype. Jenny was so privileged and spoiled. She had had sun or skiing holidays on practically every week off from college, and she was one of the few car owners while they were students, and not just any hunk of metal, but a proper, spanking-new car. She had never worked, other than a few hours at the Dublin Horse Show every year, or on promotion work for her father—an afternoon handing out flyers with a smile. He couldn't see how an accent like John Cumberton's could raise a little princess like Jenny. Stuart was surprised by John Cumberton. Evidently, John Cumberton wasn't surprised in the slightest by Stuart; Stuart seemed to him exactly the kind of jumped-up cock artist he'd expected. John Cumberton would be calling a spade a spade; charm was defunct, proved useless for the second time in half a day.

'I . . . eh . . . I think it needs to be thought about carefully. I think we need to look at this realistically.'

'So you don't.'

'Well, I didn't say that exactly,' Stuart said, and immediately regretted it. It was a defensive statement, blurted out because he was not prepared for this level of bluntness, and he was thrown by Jenny's poorly timed toilet break. What he carelessly said, despite excellent sibling advice the previous evening, had left space for discussion of possibilities and options. Just then a waiter arrived to take the order.

The waiter looked at John Cumberton and said, familiarly, 'Mr Cumberton, what can we get for you this afternoon.'

'Two Caesar salads and a roast beef. And you'll have to ask this boy what he wants.' Boy? John Cumberton wasn't here for a friendly chat.

Stuart fully expected the waiter to now address him as 'Boy,' but he remained professional. 'Sir?'

'What's on this afternoon?' Stuart asked. Jenny was still not back.

'He'll have the beef too,' John cut in.

'I don't really like beef actually. I'd prefer . . .'

'Get him the beef, Tony.'

'Sure, I'll have the beef then,' Stuart said, but Tony was already gone.

John Cumberton was eager to get down to the business at hand. It seemed he wanted the whole deal wrapped up before lunch was on the table. He was an indomitable personality, a little like Stuart's mother in his bare, unflinching expression, but not unlike Stuart's father either, with physical aggression always perilously close to the surface. 'So you're considering fathering this child?'

■

John Cumberton was a man of similar vintage to Patrick Byrne; they both had a core toughness of character that seems synonymous with men and women of that generation—growing up in the forties and bleak fifties, cutting their teeth in an exciting but ultimately unpredictable sixties, enduring the epic lows of the late seventies and early eighties. He was the type of man you expect to be one of twenty-six children, the only one not to go to prison.

He was similar to Patrick Byrne, but not the same. He too had worked his way up and shared the values of hard work and optimism, but there were distinct differences. John Cumberton loved where Patrick Byrne endured; he was content where Patrick was regretful; he was a man of sober conviction to Patrick's drowning procrastination.

John Cumberton's had been the tougher journey, for the Cumbertons—violent, alcoholic father and all—had no friends worth turning to for a social leg-up. John Cumberton had no formal education, and his comparatively saintly mother was just happy to get from one end of the day to the other without loosing a tooth, or an eye, or a clump of hair; she was a gentle soul, preoccupied throughout her life by her own survival, necessarily, but at the cost of her children's welfare.

Essentially, he was alone from the beginning. Aged eleven and long given up on school, he convinced a local grocer to employ him. By the time he was fifteen, he was working at the grocer's six days a week and at a local pub on Sundays. He picked up extra nights where he could at the pub. By the time he was twenty, he was managing the pub and had left the grocer's entirely, bar odd days when he would repay the favour of a lifetime and work for the grocer on his day off, for nothing. He owned his own public house at thirty and was married to Carmen Ó Braonain, an elfin Kerry girl, whom he had employed as a barmaid after discovering her crying on the platform at Heuston Station, just arrived from Dunquin and with nowhere to go. They soon had a child, a girl.

Upon meeting the seventies, he left for England and the building sites, leaving his wife and sister to manage his pub. After several years traipsing around England—laying bricks, plastering, digging holes, driving diggers—and travelling backward and forward to home twice a year—a week at Christmas and two weeks in the summer—he met an Irish-American entrepreneur from Boston in a dirty, old Irish bar in Kilburn, one Paddy's Day. The Boston philanthropist took a shine to the no-nonsense grafter, and offered him work managing one of his bars in Boston.

In the States, he made his fortune and flew his family over to live a couple of years later, third girl of three on the way, Jenny. After a further six years, they all returned home, homesick and wealthy. He bought three more licenced premises for himself and his family. Then he bought a house in Ballsbridge, the kind of neighbourhood he couldn't afford to be seen in when he was a kid. With the turn of the decade, he decided to add a new business to his empire and went into auto-trading too. It didn't seem like a brilliant idea at first, until the nineties took off and made it look prophetic.

John Cumberton was a man of decision and initiative. While the country of his birth, 'sat whining in its own shite,' as he put it, feeling sorry for itself and content to fail, he just got on with things. Those dark decades never had the same resonance with John Cumberton as they did in the popular consciousness of the country. When business slowed, he upped and left. He didn't say, 'I'm a bar manager, things aren't as great for me here as they might be.' He asked, 'Where are there jobs?' and said, 'England, eh? That's where I'll go then.' He didn't say, 'But there's no jobs for bar managers there,' he just asked, 'What work is there?' and decided, 'Building sites, eh? Okay, I'll labour then. I've got a family to take care of.'

It was precisely that work ethic that his Irish-American benefactor liked in him, no doubt seeing something of himself in the ever-positive grafter. And when the opportunity to go to the States opened up before him, he didn't freeze, in awe of the goose with the capacity for laying valuable eggs, he didn't say, 'But it's too far,' or, 'What about my family,' or, 'What about my pub at home, and this labouring money is fairly safe.' He said, 'Sure thing. I'm in. I'll work it out somehow.' It was never not going to work out, because there was no such thing; situations arose, problems were dealt with or alternatives were taken—there was no such luxury as things not working out.

Life was just about doing whatever needed to be done; he had three daughters and a wife to love, as he did enormously, and their every need to tend to, anxious to spare them a moment's hardship. And there's no value in pointing out, to fathers like him, the irony of having worked to provide your children with everything, and protect them from hardship, only to discover that they have reached adulthood having learned nothing from life, more importantly, having learned nothing from the hardships of your life, and are incapable of fending properly for themselves; real lessons are learnt first hand, something John Cumberton knew well, but was never able to square with a father's instinct to provide and protect. He had no sons; every last drop of masculinity and testosterone must have been needed to sustain his insatiable desire to provide and protect his girls; there was nothing to spare to go into fathering a boy.

Everything he was, Stuart wasn't. That wrangled with him as much as anything: the fortuitous timing of birth; the inherent good-looks; the casual relationships; the lack of character-defining struggle; the self-indulgent, therapy-sofa, poor-me approach to life.

Had he known of Stuart's career crisis, he might have lost his head completely. The obsession that society had developed with the notion of 'career', as if that's all we are, and the way people used one they didn't like as an excuse for not giving the best of themselves, drove John Cumberton to distraction. He couldn't understand, 'the myth of career', and the idea that happiness was somehow dependent on what you did to pay the bills—all that mattered, surely, was that you gave it your best; satisfaction and fulfilment, he knew, were gained not by what you did but how you went about it. The pampered generation expected when they needed to earn, collapsed in listless exasperation when what was needed was for them to put their shoulder into it. He didn't see that the problem was society having lost its soul, or the moral deficiency of his children's generation—he was no moralist—it was that they had lost sight of the fact that the party isn't life itself, it's a celebration of life, made valuable only by having lived. John Cumberton had always known, with a certainty only men of his kind can have, that satisfaction is in the living, whereas Stuart, and his own spoiled daughters too, mistakenly believed satisfaction to be in the reward; a false god, a spineless constitution, exposed for its failures by the whining little maggot in front of him, trying like he's never tried at anything before, to get out of the way of life and responsibility. He's running, John Cumberton thought to himself. Like a coward! He's running from the very thing that he needs.

■

'I'm considering all our options, sir,' Stuart said, hoping some deference would calm the foul mood.

'I'll tell you something about fathering my daughter's child, will I?' John was leaning in towards Stuart, and though he wanted to, Stuart knew it was inadvisable to pull away. He was just paying homage to the gods of interior design, for the spacious booth and the width of the oval table, when Jenny arrived back. Stuart moved to let her slide in the other side of him, but she insisted he slide down the booth instead, allowing her to sit on the outside; he was right in it now, surrounded—it was practically an ambush. John began to take a different line with his daughter now present. 'So what are the options you two have?' he asked, with less hostility.

'You know what I think, Dad. I really feel we should have this baby.' There it was again, the move from 'I' to 'we' in a single sentence. 'Sure, it's a shock. But I'm twenty-five, not sixteen. I can deal with it, and I think Stuart would be a great dad.'

Stuart was stunned. She was like a runaway train; she couldn't be derailed. He thought his first words to her had brought her down to earth, harshly but necessarily—the way she dropped his hand, the dissatisfied pout as she led him to her parents. But she just couldn't be deterred from her hurtling fate—a fate that could only end in more tears. She ignored all the signs, she refused to yield to impossibility.

'Jennifer tells me that you've talked with your parents about this, and that they're okay with it.'

'I've talked to them, yes,' Stuart replied.

'And they're okay with it?'

'They're shocked. Like all of us.'

'Do they think it's a good idea?'

'They have questions. Just like yourselves.'

'Questions? Like what questions?' It was developing into a rally. Jenny was pushed to the sidelines as Stuart and her father desperately tried to force the other one to say 'abortion.' Neither wanted to be the principal villain.

'They wonder, at our age, if we really know what we would be getting ourselves in for. They wonder do we know each other well enough. They wonder, financially, have we thought about it.'

'Jennifer tells me you've got a good job, that you got a promotion.'

'Yes,' said Stuart. He didn't recall ever telling her that; he must have been really pissed.

'What is it you do?'

Carmen Cumberton had sat without a word since her earlier unintelligible mutterings. Suddenly, she burst into hysterics, clearly not as steely as she had first appeared, and clearly nothing but window-dressing in this show of parental strength. There were two tears, exactly two tears, and they only just made it over the ridge of her bottom eyelashes, cemented as they were with mascara. The rest of her trauma consisted of wails of tortured pain.

'You better go out and get some air, my love,' John said, putting an affectionate arm around her and handing her a napkin. She seemed tiny, enveloped in his monstrous wingspan. She wailed louder.

'I'll take her, Dad,' said Jenny. Jenny stood up and waited as her hysterical mother shuffled out from the booth, her father standing to let his wife out. She wailed as she shuffled, never breaking for breath, and just before straightening up, she wagged an angry finger at Stuart, gestured to Jenny, who was already standing, ready to comfort her, and blubbered something in what Stuart was convinced had to be another language; he could not understand one word of her whining allegation. They left the men to each other; angry father to lily-livered womaniser. John Cumberton took up his position opposite Stuart again, leaned in again, closer this time, straining to arch his upper body over the widest point of the oval table, and talked into Stuart's face.

'Listen here, you little pansy,' he said, 'I can't figure what you're up to here. But I am warning you now—no more mistakes. If she has this child, you're going to be there. If you're not, you're going to tell her, right here today, to go and do what's got to be done. That's not going to be left to me.'

'So you think that's what should be done,' Stuart said, relieved to hear what he believed was a consensus.

'No!' John shouted, and slammed his fist down on Stuart's fingers as they lay on the table, pointing at him on the upward bounce, stopping in line with Stuart's nose so that his finger was almost sticking up his nostril, and grinding his teeth. Stuart yelped and snapped back his hand, holding his aching fingers in his other hand. John sat back, withdrew his finger and dropped his closed fist to his lap, and forced an unconvincing smile as he looked around—like a maniac trying hopelessly to blend innocently into the crowd. Not many people in the restaurant had sight of them behind the high-backed booth, facing the front window. A passing waitress glanced their way but went quickly back to her work.

'What are you doing, you crazy old f . . .' Stuart strained through a whisper.

'No!' he grunted again, leaning back in. It was a livid response to an unasked question. 'No!'—it told Stuart to shut up, told him to forget trying to worm his way out, it told him to face up to the situation like a man. It was a completely disconnected riposte; he had no interest in what Stuart had to say. 'You selfish little wanker. What I'm trying to make clear to you is that my daughter gets notions into her head, and right now the notion she has is of cottages in the country, happy families, and white picket fences, just like in the books she reads. Now if you can't provide any of that, even the bloody fences, she needs to hear it.'

Stuart was angry, but he was intimidated too. 'I'm not proud of the . . . the untidy way this has worked out. It was a mistake, but it was a mistake that doesn't have to affect the rest of our lives. So I agree.' John Cumberton's eyes widened, and his arm began to move slowly. His still-clenched fist appeared from below the table, where it had been resting on his lap. He detested the implication that he was complicit in anything that could hurt his daughter. 'Sorry. I take that back. My mistake is nothing to do with you. I think that getting rid of the baby might be the wisest course of action.'

John Cumberton did not know what to feel. He wanted to inflict incredible violence on the gutless little Tiger Economite before him, for the cheapness with which his daughter had been treated. But he needed the same man to prevent his daughter from ruining the rest of her life. He was afraid that unless the words actually came from Stuart's mouth, that his daughter would dig in her considerable heels, and have her baby regardless of consequence.

The possibility of the scene descending into all-out violence was brought to an end by the return of the two ladies. They stepped aside as the waiter arrived with the food and laid the plates down on the table. Carmen Cumberton had recovered herself sufficiently, and was ready to sit down for lunch. She dabbed at her eyes with a mascara-stained napkin. Jenny stood consoling her, arm around the shoulder, as they waited on the waiter to finish.

On the other side of the glass window that looked out onto the busy street was a man wearing bicycle shorts and a T-shirt. He had a small rucksack on his back. His goggled sunglasses were bound tight around his head by an elasticated band, looping round the back of his curly, blond hair, holding them in place. He looked like a courier. He was shifting his head from side to side on his shoulders, waving frantically, until finally, he rapped on the window with his knuckles. It caught a few people's attention in the restaurant, but when they did not recognise the man they went on about their food and ignored him; nobody wants to become the focus of a lunatic's wild attention. The noise eventually caught Stuart's attention and his heart sank. Trouble had arrived on top of crisis. It couldn't be worse. The man outside locked his bike to the lamp-post, and entered the restaurant. Before anyone knew what was happening, Gary was standing beside Jenny and her mother. The waiter left. Stuart was petrified—anybody but Gary.

'Hey, Stuey. How you doing, pal?'

'Gary, this really isn't a good time.'

'Why? What's going on? I'm sure your friends here wouldn't mind if I joined you, would you? I was stopping for a bite anyway.'

'It's kind of private, actually,' Jenny said.

'Oh, okay. And who are you gorgeous?' Gary gave her a wink.

'Jenny,' she said, and offered her hand to be shaken. 'And these are my parents, but this really is private. So if you don't mind.'

Gary shook her hand gently and winked at her again. 'Gary. Lovely to meet you. But I can take a hint. I'll head across the road for some lunch. Parents,' he said, nodding their way, 'nice to meet you too. Enjoy.' He turned to go. It was all okay. Then he stopped. 'Drop in before you go back to work, Stu. Ring in sick again. We'll make an afternoon of it.' That was not the kind of thing prospective grandparents needed to hear about the father of their future grandchild—that he's the kind of man to skip work and go drinking instead, and that such an occurrence might be more than a once-off—and certainly not the kind of revelation to win over a man like John Cumberton. Stuart could have done without it, but under the circumstances he was breathing a sigh of relief; if that was to be the extent of the damage, he could live with it. Could have been so much worse, he thought. 'By the way,' Gary said. He hadn't finished. 'Are you the Jenny from college?'

'Yes,' she said, looking pleased with the recognition.

'Oh,' Gary sighed, feigning discomfort. 'Sure I'll take you if he doesn't want you. Don't take any rubbish off him, now.'

Jenny's eyes welled up before he had even stopped talking. Her mother began to build towards a wail, and John Cumberton, standing now, began rounding up his family like sheep and ushering them to the door. Gary stood there with his hands out, bemused. Stuart called after them.

'He doesn't even know. You don't understand. He doesn't even know.'

John Cumberton returned with Tony the waiter and spread his hands wide on the table, leaned over and put his face right up to Stuart's—Stuart was sure he was about to get thumped—and said, 'Don't ever come near my daughter again.' Some spittle from his frothing anger sprayed onto Stuart's face, but Stuart didn't flinch, didn't dare dry himself off. John Cumberton straightened up, and rubbed his beard with the back of his hand. 'Tony, give this pansy the bill.'

'What's going on, Stu? What did I say? Hey, you want to watch who you're calling a pansy, you bearded bollocks!' he shouted after Cumberton.

John Cumberton stomped heavily out of the restaurant, subjecting the floor to the kind of pounding he was surely dishing out to Stuart in his mind.

'For fuck sake, don't,' pleaded Stuart. 'You don't even know.' He shook his head. 'You're such an idiot.'

'Easy, Stuey. Whatever you've got yourself into isn't my fault. I'm only here a minute. Even I couldn't cause a scene like that in a minute. You must have done a lot of groundwork before I arrived.' He took a drink of water from one of the glasses on the table, and slid into the side of the booth vacated by the Cumbertons. 'Sorry, Stu. I can't take responsibility for this one.'

Stuart had his head in his hands at the table of food for four. The bill was unpaid and his lunch partner was an obnoxious playboy in cycling shorts. This was not how he could ever have imagined Tuesday lunch. 'You're such an idiot,' he said again.

'Stu,' said Gary, and he started to laugh at the slapstick moment. 'Come on. Whatever it is, it can't be that bad.' Stuart lifted his head from his hands. He felt like screaming, or crying. 'So I messed something up with that Jenny bird. You didn't seem too keen anyway, as far as I could make out. And okay, it was complicated by her parents being here.' The penny dropped for Gary. He put the pieces together. 'Are you trying to marry her? Was this an engagement-type thing?'

'No. Definitely not. You sound like my mother. It was the exact opposite.'

'A divorce?'

'No!' Stuart snapped. 'It was an unwanted pregnancy type thing. I was trying to be tactful, until you came along and made a balls of it.'

'Didn't look like you were doing such a great job of that, in fairness. Pregnant, eh? Shit one!'

'Why did you say, "Oh," and look like . . . you made it look like I'd been talking about her.'

'That was an instinctive reaction, Stu. You can't blame me for that. I mean the way you hit the drink on Saturday after talking to her. It was the natural thing, what was I to think?'

'And the, "if he doesn't want you . . ." bit? What in the name of sweet Jesus was that about? What kind of a thing is that to say to anybody?'

'I don't know,' said Gary, shrugging his shoulders. 'Hey, can I dip into one of these salads, if you're going to be paying for it anyway?' Gary lobbed his grimy handlebar hands into the salad bowl and picked out a crouton. He popped it into his mouth and crunched down on it.

'What kind of thing is that to say to anyone? Seriously?'

'I don't know, Stu. Relax. It's just something people say. Like "Don't do anything I wouldn't do," or . . . I don't know. I didn't mean anything by it. I was just filling a void.'

'You're the only fucking void round here, Gary.'

'Who got her pregnant, Stu?'

'What?'

'Who got her pregnant? Wasn't me. I don't think I can be saddled with this one. I'm a bit-part player, a walk-on role. I'm an unknown extra.'

'Hardly. Your contribution pretty much brought the house down.'

'Maybe,' Gary said. He reached for a fork and lifted the salad over in front of him. 'But it was a house of fairly flimsy cards. And I wasn't the builder.'

Stuart had had enough of the mixed metaphors, and was too exasperated to argue any further with a man who had nothing but time for this measure of inanity. Gary ordered a bottle of wine and they had a Caesar salad and roast beef each.

TUESDAY AFTERNOON

It was half past three. They were now lodged in Laughin' Murphies, across the street from Chez Chef. Stuart had texted Owen, he wanted to let him know what was happening—Jenny, Sara, his job, Rachel—and he was on his way. Gary had rung Anna and she had already arrived. They sat outside at a round table, under a parasol. The sun had come out again and the city began to look young and sexy, as the parting clouds unveiled the young, well-heeled population of Dublin looking awfully busy, on their way to and from conferences, meetings and junkets.

Anna was a short and stunning-looking Londoner. She was attractively skinny. She had shoulder length, jet-black hair. She was wearing a black vest-top and an above-the-knee, denim skirt. Her smooth skin was tanned. Her features were sharp, and in the long breaks between drags on her cigarette, her suburban London accent bobbed along melodically. She was open and flirty, and best of all, she was prickly and feisty when challenged by one of Gary's many conceited observations. She was a welcome tonic for Gary.

'Your round, pal,' Gary said.

'How do you work that out?'

'I got the bottle of wine. By my calculations you owe me at least two pints. And that's being generous, 'cause I think you had more than half the bottle.'

'But I got the food. I paid for four lunches,' Stuart contested.

'Food's different. That's nothing to do with booze. Separate issue.'

'So when will the food bill be settled?' Stuart contested further.

'You give me half the money for the food, and then I'll go to the bar.'

'Stu, you know meals are different. You get one, I get the next one. Although, that said, this is slightly different. I wasn't actually part of that meal. I just got lucky and wandered in on leftovers. So really, I don't owe anything, which means—uncontestably—it's absolutely your round.'

'They were entire meals. There were no leftovers.'

'As I said, I got lucky. You can't expect me to pay for that. It would be like taxing luck. It would be like punishing me for my good fortune. And that would be wrong. It would tarnish the beauty of blind luck.'

'Oh, shut it, Garr,' Anna said, looking up from her gossip magazine that was draped over her crossed thigh. She took a final drag of her cigarette, exhaled, and stubbed it out in the ashtray as she stood up. 'I'll get the drinks, and this can be the start of the round. You two girls can argue about it another day, on your own time.'

'That's as close to diplomacy as you'll get with this bird,' Gary said, winking again.

'What do you want, mate?' she asked Stuart, sliding off her sunglasses to reveal dark, beautiful eyes, and laying her hand on his shoulder and giving it a gentle squeeze, as she passed around him to enter the pub.

By the time the round was due to be completed by Gary, Owen had arrived. It was five o'clock. They were still outside.

'Now how's this going to work?' Gary asked. 'I'm going for my round, but I can't exactly leave Owen out. But that messes with the fundamental equality of the round system.'

'How're you, Gary? Long time.'

'Not too bad, old boy,' he said, and got up to lean across and shake Owen's hand. 'Owen, this is Anna. I don't think you've met before.' Owen and Anna had their introductions and Stuart resolved the round situation.

'I need to have a chat with Owen, so you can buy Anna a drink, and skip me, and end the round, you miserable . . .' he said, but did not finish. Stuart and Owen went inside the dingy pub, ordered a drink, and started to talk. Stuart coughed up everything. He told Owen about meeting Jenny at the reunion and sleeping with her, about avoiding her after, about the history of avoiding her in college when he knew she was interested, but didn't like her; he told him about the dinner at home and Sara's news; he told him about the lunch with Jenny's parents, and he told him about work. Talking and thinking problems to death was not common practice for Stuart, and yet in the last few days it was all he seemed to be doing. Usually he swept things under the carpet and hoped they would be forgotten about. He needed to talk now though; he was compelled to share the burden, unable as he was to just ignore it. All the little things, his once tiny difficulties, seemed to have congealed into one massive, undissectible, nauseating knot in his stomach, somehow all connected by an invisible thematic thread. His earlier buoyancy was a distant memory now—back to square one, the pub, and making the same mistakes all over again.

Owen listened carefully. He probed at appropriate times and made sure Stuart kept his train of thought; after half a bottle of wine and three pints, Stuart was talkative, free of verbal inhibition, but had begun to tend towards tangents. He was not expecting advice from Owen. It was merely a case of keeping the wayward brother in the family loop, and exercising his new-found need to discuss and consider.

When he had finished talking, Owen offered something that could be considered, by any reasonable standards, advice. He told Stuart there was more than one way to live a life. He said just because Stuart could not envisage different kinds of lives for himself, beyond what he had at the moment, was not to say that different lives and lifestyles would be miserable. 'Don't panic,' he told him. 'See what comes of the situation. Let the girl make up her mind and work from there. And when people ask you, "What's going on?" it's okay to say you're not sure at the moment. Find answers in your own time.' It was all insipid, but it was comforting in a way. Owen, successfully holding it together for once in his adult life, and for once the least troubled member of the Byrne family, was on a roll. 'And as regards your job, Stu. Sounds to me like a definite case of corporate queasiness. Disillusion.'

'Dis-a-fucking-llusion! You're the second person to float that boat.'

'It's "i"-llusion, not "a"-llusion,' he said dryly. 'You must be hanging out with wise people.'

'Or arts and humanities folk. Is it curable?'

'Afraid not, little brother. You're screwed now. You're realising that the swanky city apartment, the ten suits, the stereos and the widescreen TVs, and the cars, don't mean shite, when it comes right down to it. The excess and waste is cluttering your personal space, and you can't breathe, the capitalist gorging is smothering you. You're surrounded by images, and images of images, but you're low on tangibles. You've got ideas about life, misconceived ideas, but very little actual life. You can see the serious stuff coming down the line and it scares the shit out of you, because you know you're not prepared for it. But I'll let you in on the big secret, you're never ready. I expect you'll be singing protest songs and writing metaphysical poetry by the end of the month.'

'Do all you freeloaders read the same books, or something?' He paused. 'I love the car. The car can't be just nothing. It's not hurting anybody.'

'Burn it all and move to the country. That's the only thing for you now,' Owen said, mimicking a washing of hands.

'There's one other thing,' Stuart said, suddenly serious.

'There's more? You have been a busy boy. What else could you have done lately?' Owen invited him to continue, but Stuart changed his mind.

'Christina seemed nice. I liked her.'

'Good,' said Owen. 'And what about you?' He was aware Stuart had not unburdened himself completely.

'Me? I've got my hands full being, as Dad put it, "The phantom impregnator."'

'And you're sure it's yours?'

'Yeah. I don't think she'd make it up. She's nuts, but she's not the scheming type. Funny though, that's what Dad said too.'

'Forget it then. I must be way off. Have you told Rachel?'

'No. No way. I don't think I should. Why would I?'

'Because she loves you?'

'Don't start, Owen. I don't need it.'

'She does.'

'Come off it, Owen. I don't do this stuff.'

'It's not like that, Stu. It's just that it's helpful sometimes to talk it through, and hear your own thoughts out loud. See if they hold any water, you know what I mean? And hear somebody else's perspective. Didn't it feel good to just get all that other stuff off your chest?'

'Not so much. I mean, nothing's changed—what about Jenny?'

'Maybe you need to talk about Rachel too.'

'And Jenny? Don't you think that's more important than this schoolyard shite?'

'There's nothing schoolyard about it. Not for Rachel anyway. She looked great the other night,' Owen said.

'What's this now? You trying to appeal to my shallow side?'

'Just saying she looked great. She's a good girl. I wouldn't like to see you mess the whole thing up. A girl like that won't keep hanging on, Stu. The next fella to come along may not be such a dick.'

'Can we talk about some other part of my life, please, or something else entirely, in fact?'

'You're very touchy.'

Stuart ordered two whiskeys in shot glasses. He threw his down the hatch while Owen sniffed cautiously at his. 'I slept with her,' he said, finally. Owen let the four words hang in the air, not for his own ingestion, but for Stuart's. He let Stuart sit with what he had said. Rachel wasn't going to have to wait, after all.

TUESDAY EVENING

When Stuart and Owen had finished inside Laughin' Murphies, they returned to Gary and Anna outside, and sat down with them for a drink. By now, Gary was properly drunk. He was slurring and he was on the phone every two minutes trying to arrange a place to meet up with some other friends. Anna had already stated she had no intention of going anywhere with him in his current state. Gary declared he was more than happy to have a night out on his own. He wished Anna good luck with her own mates, if she could find any. Anna's caveat, 'I've never had much trouble picking up a friend when I need him,' sounded like an empty threat, at the time.

Before long, Gary had unlocked his top of the range mountain bike from the lamp-post, and was propped up on the saddle like a string puppet with four of its eight strings severed. He had his feet on the pedals and was balanced by his hand on the lamp-post. He was laughing stupidly and gave the table of three a final wave before swerving off down the street. He zigzagged erratically over the first stretch, almost creating student carnage as he caused a group of teenage Spaniards to yelp and jump clear of the drunken lunatic on a bike, swerving without warning from one side of the street to the other. He narrowly avoided bouncing off various obstacles as he rode towards Grafton Street, and a whole host of further danger. By the time he reached the end of the street, his brain seemed to have gained ground on his feet, and they were close to working in harmony. The last they saw of Gary, a middle-aged man was taking a few angry steps after the escaping bike, having very nearly been spun into the air like a matador clipped by a rampaging bull, and shouting after him.

Owen's exit was more dignified. They had all moved inside the pub after Gary left, and Stuart excused himself to go and make a call, leaving Owen with Anna. He rang Rachel.

The conversation flowed easily, no awkward tension. He apologised for the not getting back to her sooner, and she said, 'Don't be silly.' He said he was busy, and she said, 'I understand.' He asked could she pick him up, and she said, 'Sure, as long as you don't try to jump me again.' It was reassuring. Nothing changed? The sex had not complicated anything, he thought. Except that it had. How could it not? He hung up the phone and set the alarm for 7:30 A.M.; he had one eye on his planned meeting with A.S. Stanley the next day. When he returned to the table, Owen was ready to leave. He was saying good-bye to Anna and heading off to meet Christina at the cinema: a new French film, all subtitles and brooding unconventionality.

'Not my cup of tea now, Owen. But you enjoy.'

'Thanks. I will.'

'Sounds interesting,' Anna said. 'Nice to meet you.' She stood up and kissed him on both cheeks, as if the thought of France and all those subtitles brought out the cultured European in her. Owen indulged her. It looked gauche on his behalf, but she managed to get away with it.

■

Theirs was an immediate friendship. They were both seventeen. Gary was the new boy at school and he took a seat beside Stuart in a cramped classroom. This was the time when Stuart's platonic relationship with Rachel was at its most confusing, and a period when he withdrew from her, finding it too difficult to see her cooing at her then-boyfriend, and in need of a surrogate, and temporary, new best friend, he latched onto Gary, both of them finding comfort in each other's ineptitude.

Stuart was handsome (though he hardly knew it then) and Gary's privileged disposition was inherited (and how well he knew it); between them, they were dynamic in their youthful appeal. Stuart's modesty, combined with his chiseled adolescence, worked in perfect tandem with Gary's not unattractive features and the arrogance of his received fortune. Gary infused a spirit of improvisation into Stuart's previously predictable existence. He was a partner in crime, an inventive and effusive partner, who opened doors that Stuart alone would not have bothered to push at.

Until Gary, Stuart had only one friend, the girl he had known since infancy, even before he knew he knew her, sharing a street with her. Stuart and Rachel were drawn together (and how many times in life we are surprised by the odd couple, not knowing what it is that makes one person love another, resorting to quasi-scientific analogy—opposites attract, I suppose—to explain that which we are ignorant of) by some unquantifiable force. They eyed each other cautiously, at first, Stuart standing on the driveway as his little, blue ball ran down and away from him, bouncing into the closed front gate, rattling the hollow iron frame, while Rachel spun around in circles on the lawn, on the other side of the low wall that separated the neighbours' gardens, and fell dizzy to the grass, laughing and wheezing with delight.

Then one day, she stretched up on her tiptoes and offered him a jelly over the wall, both standing in their respective flower beds, like two inmates learning to trust each other through the bars of a cell, exchanging tiny luxuries for companionship. When the time came they walked to school together, holding hands, talking all the way, lost in their tiny world. The hand-holding persisted for longer than anyone could have predicted, through infancy and the lower primary years—when the differences between boys and girls first make themselves known, and cavorting with the intriguingly different enemy leaves you open to ridicule and ostracism—through the tree-house building era—two planks of old wood nailed haphazardly to a tree, at a slant between two branches, as uncomfortable a seat posing as a house as ever there was—through to the stage when Rachel humoured Stuart by pretending she was interested in *Ninja Turtles*—figures and models, games of battle and conflict—and although she was unable to feign interest when Stuart's obsession became sport—football and golf—the hand-holding continued.

Their teens sent them to different schools. But the friendship endured, even through the confusion and pain of first kisses and boyfriends and would-be girlfriends. Their friendship muddled through, somehow, and although the early years of their teens made it feel like they were drifting reluctantly but necessarily apart, the joys of underage smoking and drinking (in that order, I'm told) won back for them some much-desired common ground. However, the common ground was surrendered almost instantaneously when sex was added to the list of teenage misdemeanours; under the influence, Rachel confided in Stuart that she had slept with her then-boyfriend, and although Stuart absorbed the information stoically, he was wild with jealousy and fury, and it pushed him, probably a little too soon, into the bed of a slightly-too-old for him floozy who lived next door to Gary.

Gary had only just announced himself on the scene, and it was as much Stuart's estrangement from Rachel that pushed those two together as it was a fusing of comparable, if uncomplementary, personalities. It was a period when Rachel seemed to have given up on Stuart, for all the infatuation that once consumed her; Stuart only realised Rachel's importance when he discovered what she was doing with other boys—the balance of power had shifted.

When college began and Gary was no more than a contentious footnote, and there was an array of new friends for both of them, they drifted back together again. It was during their college years that the hangover recovery routine was developed: calling into each other, watching TV together, having afternoon pints—pints that often turned into too many, the way it can when you're young and in college and can still function the next day with a head full of booze and a belly full of gas.

It was a more mature friendship, though the jealously was never spoken of even then. Every one of Rachel's boyfriends roused barely concealed revulsion in Stuart. Rachel was more elusory, claiming Stuart's exploits didn't bother her, and telling herself that she was happy for him—during periods when she had a boyfriend—to be out sleeping around, never settling for longer than a period of weeks. And maybe she was happy, secretly, that he was as he was; maybe she thought that meant there was always a possibility of Stuart. Maybe she never put the whole of her heart into anybody else, always holding something back. Maybe that's why none of them worked out, maybe the tacit desire for each other was a kind of self-fulfilling prophecy, thwarting the chances of all other relationships. They had spent years dancing around each other, an elaborate mating ritual, waiting for the other one to make the first move. And when Rachel dumped Seb (finally acknowledging the extent of her desire for Stuart, to herself, regardless of consequence) at exactly the point when Stuart was compelled by crisis to ask questions of himself that were always likely to come to restful conclusion on Rachel's sweetest face, the inevitable was in motion. The only question then was, that having waited so long for the right moment, had they missed it?

Stuart and Gary were on the brink of early adulthood when they met, but very much at the mercy of adolescence and uncertainty, both adversely affected by garden-variety familial dysfunction; nobody was abused, or left wanting, or forgotten about. Gary's parents showered him with gifts, which they called love, and left him to his own devices, which they called freedom. Stuart, with a father whose already significant success grew exponentially with the city's, and a mother who kept an impeccable house and had family dinner on the table every evening without fail, had little to complain about, it seemed. Both of his parents were giving of their time and their awkward affection, they showed an interest, undoubtedly, but there was an empty space between them, a space that seemed to contain infinite pain and nothing at the same time.

It was on Stuart's fifteenth birthday, when his parents presented him with his birthday presents that that awful, cold space became discernible to him. It wasn't something he noted consciously, it was just a feeling, a skewing of the way he viewed the world, a tilting of his emotional axis, that happened in a moment, without him realising. But it was something that affected him deeply enough for him to carry it around for ten years, unaddressed, unconsciously festering, and something that just poured out of him with the rest of his tale, as if he knew it was intrinsically linked to everything that happened to him since, even though he couldn't quite explain how, or articulate how he knew it to be so.

His father swung a brand-new set of golf clubs into his arms—the glinting silver shafts free of finger smudges, and the ridged face of the clubs clean of grass and muck and course experience—by the thick, leather shoulder strap. 'Happy Birthday, son!' he said. 'Now you can stop sneaking off with mine when I'm at work, and I can stop pretending I don't know. Get some practice in, we'll have a proper game soon.' His father clapped him on the shoulder and stepped aside.

His mother stepped forward with a card. She handed it to him, leaned rigidly forward, hands to elbows, the way she did, and kissed him on the cheek. 'Happy birthday, darling,' she said. 'My present is upstairs. In your room. I think you'll like it.' And he did. It was a black Santo stereo system he had been looking at and talking freely of for months: fifty-watt speakers; five-disc CD changer; remote control; coloured digital lights indicating volume, bass, and treble levels. It was brilliant, the best present ever, he recalled, but it was brutal, too; the brilliance was overstated.

As his mother creaked back from rigid affection to her usual stiffened veneer, he noticed his father slung against the sink, like a bruised banana skin against a wall, staring down at the glass of water held at his navel. He was dressed for work, and as soon as his wife had finished, he stood up, swallowed back the last drop of water as if it was a shot of whiskey, and said, 'Right, I'm off to work. Have a good day, son. See you later.' He put the empty glass down on the draining-board and was out the kitchen door, in an instant, not a word to his wife. His mother walked over and opened the fridge, busy in her own morning.

So what? you say. I don't get it. What's the problem? It's hardly the stuff of Dickensian neglect and abuse, you say. What about the kids in the inner-city flats? What about the abused, the crippled, the ones whose parents never buy them presents at all? Well, yes, but this is not a comparison, it's an explanation. I am extrapolating backward from what I know in fact, in search of an answer. Suffering is not relative, it's a totally subjective experience, and knowing the man down the road has two broken legs doesn't make your one broken leg any less painful; Stuart is not exempt from suffering. I know there are people out there in the world with far greater problems, but that is not to say that Stuart's don't count. All I'm doing is painting a picture, looking for motive or cause, though I know they're essentially useless straws to grasp at, given the inescapable legacy of consequence—the bed we make for ourselves.

I feel compelled to explain, you see, to tease out a coherent narrative from the series of events placed before me; it is the narrator's lot, perpetually compelled to justify the story, always looking to round off the rough edges, tying up its loose ends, adding colour and definition to the roughest pencil sketch. It's tragically simplistic, it's pop-psychology, but I need to believe there is a link between the parents' dysfunction and Stuart's emotional retardation, which I believe is the root of his immense and ostrich-like stupidity, because I won't believe in the innately bad—Stuart can't be this self-absorbed, this disengaged, this dismissive of the needs of others, merely because he is. There has to be more to it than that, I need him to be fucked-up with good reason. I need his deplorable inertia to be diagnosed and explained, because then it can be treated as something *other* that has invaded the person, and not something innate that can never be removed and never be forgiven; after all, it's such a short hop from innately bad to evil, and if evil exists, if nature ultimately prevails over nurture and culture, then what chance have we; how can we face into tomorrow knowing we can never win?

So, in my tidy narrative, it was at the precise moment that Stuart was spoiled by the best birthday presents ever that his belief in love was warped; what he received were two different presents, from two different people, both trying to make him feel loved, but separately. Both parents wanted him to know they loved him, uniquely, and irrespective of their relationship to each other, but what they failed to understand was that the love of two separate parents, no matter how devoted, can never adequately compensate for the shattering illusion of our parents as a single bank of love from which we can forever draw. We demand that our parents exist together, we demand it for stability's sake, for comfort, as a frame of reference for love and companionship which we can continually revert back to when times get tough, and when we lose faith in the world.

It's a social construct, of course—the model for familial harmony could as easily have been two parents and a golden retriever, had that been what we'd settled on in the first place—but the construct is in place now, and failure to square with it creates feelings of inadequacy and loss. Maybe it would have been easier for Stuart if he'd known all along that his parents were broken. But he didn't; he found out. And it is here that I would say his story began; this was the emotional, psychological, and constitutional birth of Stuart the man.

Stuart doesn't know what love is, and is rightly exacerbated and mistrustful of it. That was the consequence of exploding the illusion of his parents—disillusion. Disillusion deflates us and wearies us, it makes us turn away from that which we once swore by, it's an assault on the essence of our convictions. And it doesn't happen in an instant; disillusion is a slow-burner, it's a cancerous growth whose conception can go unnoticed for years, only discovered when it's gone too far, only realised when it's wormed its pervasive way throughout our system and has us dangling from its meathooks. There can be years and generations and lifetimes between illusion and disillusion; the illusion is by its nature a deceptive appearance of being, and the destruction of the illusion, the disillusion, the realisation that the whole thing was not only no good, but untrue, is only arrived at over time, and it is utterly debilitating. We can recover from disillusion, but only in the way a manic-depressive, or a chronic alcoholic, or the victim of a mental break-down recovers—somehow half the person you were before, life's joys dulled and its lows cushioned, so that you live in a perpetual state of sepia-tone emotion, Ritalin steady, braced for disappointment, as afraid of vibrant thrill as black and white disappointment.

Stuart and Gary, dysfunctional in their own moderate ways, did all the things teenagers are advised not to, all the things adults know they really should, because there's just nothing like them when it comes right down to it: enjoying the company of nubile girls; the thrill of inebriation; experimenting with soft drugs; lazy afternoons playing Pitch and Putt, sometimes long golf, or down at the snooker hall, instead of studying; listening to music and watching TV, poring over the perceived greatness of their generation's mediocrity, worshipping mere potential as if it was already realised—the best band, the best singer, the best song, the funniest show, the greatest this and that—when they should have been in class.

They slept too much and read too little. They both learned to drive in Gary's red *Absentu*, a seventeenth birthday present from his parents, who were holidaying in the Caymans at the time. Both lost their virginity on the same night, in the same bed—Gary's parents' eight-foot, four-poster—half an hour apart; Stuart with the aforementioned floozy next door, and Gary with her long-forgotten friend, after meeting them while sitting on the pier drinking illicitly acquired bottles of beer.

The world seemed there for the taking. Their freedom was never curbed, both sets of parents caring little for how the solid but unspectacular academic performance was eked out, and although Mr and Mrs Byrne, as a matter of routine, suggested that there was more in Stuart than he was showing, and implored him to do better, their reservations never manifested themselves as a withdrawal of Stuart's freedom to come and go as he pleased.

The end of the boys' carefree alliance began the night before their Leaving Cert. exams, when Stuart and Gary met two girls in a Dalkey pub. They were cutting loose from the perceived pressure, in a restrained way, with a single pint before the start of their exams, when they caught sight of two girls, more ludic than giggly, sitting at a nearby table. These were classy girls, real Dalkey—all smooth, tanned skin, expensive clothes, salon hair, and large sunglasses. They looked slightly younger than Stuart and Gary, but not much, and a year hardly mattered when it came to girls of this caste.

Gary initiated a conversation (asking for a light, how else?) and before long Ali and Amanda (seriously, you can't make this kind of alliterative coincidence up) were back in Gary's house with the two boys (and if we accept that Stuart's fifteenth birthday was the beginning of Stuart the man's story, then this episode, nearly three years later, was an equally critical point in his development, a point where it still could have gone either way). Ali and Stuart were in bed getting to know each other before the last drink (they had decided on more than just the one, having met the girls) had time to hit the brain.

Ali was gorgeous. She went to some posh school or other—all girls, a convent school. She was tall and slender, genuinely blonde, and bewilderingly well-spoken. She was one for posterity; this was a girl to tell stories about and remember fondly. Even then, with so little experience, he assumed this would be his peak, still believing that appearance—good looks—was a definitive attribute, an irrefutable measurement, something that could be quantified, a master formula from which all our values could relatively be determined, still in the dark with regard to the random fancies of mutual attraction, the impalpable force that draws any two people together. This was a beautiful girl before he realised he had a knack for beautiful girls.

In the morning, he leapt out of bed, but only because it was eight o'clock and Stuart had an exam to get to. She didn't, she had another year to go and was on her summer holidays. They arranged to meet up later in the afternoon, after his two exams, and Stuart was already getting carried away.

Gary and Amanda, having been left choking on the dust cloud left by Stuart and Ali's exit to the privacy of the bedroom, decided to make the most of the night, and enjoyed some more drinks and each other. And, in the morning, although Gary seemed less than enthused by the prospect of taking the night any further, he agreed to play the willing side-kick to Stuart's dashing hero, and the girls were invited back to Gary's again that night. The rest of exam-time June, nearly three weeks, was spent at Gary's. Gary's parents were in Argentina, horse-riding and eating fine steak for the month. They left Gary to take responsibility for his own exams—'You do the study, you get the results, you get the rewards,' they said.

Gary's parents' house was a luxury study hall, a place of exam focus and tranquil concentration: whether Mr and Mrs Byrne bought into any part of that deception is a moot point, they made no attempt to undermine it (perhaps they had their own problems to worry about, maybe marriage had them on their knees and they were happy to have their son out of the way). During the first week and a half, exams themselves occupied most of the mornings and afternoons, with short cramming sessions in between, before, and after. Towards the end of the second week of exams, with the compulsory and more popular subject choices behind them, mornings, afternoons, and entire days were freed up by gaps in the exam timetable. The boys sat at home, studied in thirty-minute bursts, barely able to maintain interest with only a subject or two to go, and the honing pressure of the first week done and dusted. They survived on toasted cheese sandwiches, and wondered who in the name of Jesus would take on a subject like Applied Chemistry?

In the evenings, their efforts at study were usually abandoned in favour of drinks, fast-food, and the girls. It was a dream existence, a kind of living that neither of the boys could have envisioned even a couple of weeks before; it was happenstance at its most poetic—Gary's parents' holiday, meeting Ali and Amanda, and even the heightened pressure brought to bear by the exams helped: it stopped the situation going stale, gave them all another focus, and made the relief of their escape into hearty pleasure all the sweeter each night it arrived.

Ali and Amanda moved in too, more or less, which was not entirely to Gary's liking. Like Stuart, the girls returned home once a day, changed clothes, and made excuses for each other each night. During the day they went their separate ways, the boys to battle in the exam hall of St Christopher's, the girls shopping, or to tennis, or hanging around the yacht club. Usually they went shopping, buying clothes and cosmetics, both provoking what seemed a disproportionate level of excitement in them.

On the middle Friday, Stuart returned home to Gary's from a gruelling Biology exam to find Ali standing outside, holding a paper bag. More clothes, Stuart thought. 'I've got you something,' she said. When she pulled out a baby-pink T-shirt, Stuart began to fear for the future of whatever it was they had. His brain went into overdrive, he was back-pedalling as quickly as he could, he was frantically looking around for a way out—the way we do when we see an embarrassing social faux pas unfolding before us. After watching him squirm for a minute, she said, 'Only messing,' and smiled (the augural naughtiness evinced in the strange pleasure she took in his discomfort might have been noted). 'I actually got you this,' she said, suggestively holding out a black-lace bra and matching panties. She raised a blood-rushing eyebrow, 'You want to come and help me try them on?' These were the ways that the girls amused themselves during the days, as Stuart and Gary went off to jump through the hoops of state education.

As exam-time June wound to a conclusion, Gary and Amanda's alliance of venereal convenience began to show signs of being the fraud it was. The atmosphere changed in the house as they bickered more and more, not like the proverbial old married couple, but like the couple who never liked each other in the first place. Stuart, on the other hand, began to look further than the next fuck, letting his heart get ahead of his dick, in a manner that is far more common to adolescent boys than nervous parents of teenage girls would care to admit. There was symbiosis between heart and penis, as sex thumped on tables, squelched and squirted in the shower, bounced on several beds, and, on one occasion, even fell to the kitchen floor. Every minute they were left alone, Stuart and Ali were nipping and tearing at each other, swept along by the newness of it, excited by the freedom and opportunity before them, finding out for themselves the puerility of the adult world's approach to teenage sexuality; the birds and the bees, the facts of life, physical love, agony aunts. The excitement is in the unknown, the dangerous, the lurid, and the explicit, in all the aspects you can't read about in the *Parents' Handbook for Sexually Active Teenagers*, or the unfortunately titled, *Sexual Education in the Classroom*, and they immersed themselves in the extraordinarily primal joy that parents and teachers are afraid to talk about. Stuart ignored the spite of Gary and Amanda, preoccupied by Ali. She could have been the experience that saved him, the one that reaffirmed that which his parents had pulled asunder. But perhaps that's unfair of me, too much to have expected of her, she was only seventeen, after all.

Stuart's final exam was Economics. It was a Wednesday afternoon and it was warm and sticky—reliably uncomfortable and demotivating exam weather. He faced his final hurdle with relief rather than nervousness. The finish line was near. He flew through the paper, and it seemed to him that love (yes, he thought it might be) was conducive to academia. With fifteen minutes to spare and feeling relaxed and confident, he strolled out of the exam hall for the final time. He thought to himself, That's it, I'm done. I've given this all I'm willing to. I'm passed or failed, but I'm done. It was a quarter past four.

He passed all those old-style Victorian desks, moved to the hall for the month of June, striding down the aisle between them, with pupils' exam numbers going grimy and upturned on the corners, and past some students still writing frenetically, the minutes ticking past like seconds, trying to put everything they knew, relevant or not, onto the paper in the allotted time. He took one look at the clock above the door before emerging into the foyer. It was sunny now, and outside the exam hall was bright and hopeful. He continued on, stopping for nobody. He was gone out of the foyer door, dropping his red and blue pen in the bin as he passed, and out the school gates, and away home without the slightest pause for sentiment. He was done with school.

Plans had already been made for later. He was meeting Ali and then they were heading for the city with Gary and Amanda. Gary had finished his exams the day before and claimed he was going to spend a day with his thoughts, considering his future. Stuart took this to mean that Gary was going to have an eccentric day out with himself, maybe take a hip-flask of vodka and red lemonade to The Zoo, or a hashish-yoghurt lunch. Stuart didn't feel like going home to the post-exam interrogation with his mother, when all he wanted to do was forget about the exams, and with the spare key to Gary's placed oh-so-imaginatively under the flower pot, and most of his clothes there too, stopping in to Gary's for a shower and change, before going out, seemed like a sound plan.

Stuart was hot and thirsty by the time he reached the top of the hill on Johnstown Road. He stopped in at the petrol station for a cold drink. He came out and sat on the red-brick wall by the service area, watching the cars chug past. He guzzled down the first can of ice-cold *Orangizzz*, and his head went a little light with the cold relief. As he cracked open the second can, he saw a guy he knew from school coming round the corner towards him on his racer, a Stephen Roche special, handed down by an older brother. He was in Stuart's French class, and sat beside him for two years in English, but they had not seen each other since the opening exam. Stuart liked him, though they hardly knew each other, except in the oddly intimate way you get to know somebody you sit beside and work with for two years; you share a few jokes and a few problems related to the task at hand; you swap notes, and a peculiar closeness is found. It's like sleeping with somebody and never finding out their name, liking them but not wanting any more than you've already taken.

The guy was weaving in and out, from the wall on one side of the path to the curb on the other. The pedals were rotating effortlessly; the bike must have been in seventh or eighth gear. He was moseying along as carefree as you like. Stuart thought, He must have finished up too. As he came close, Stuart could see that that the guy was smiling.

'Hey, Stu,' I said. 'What's up?'

'How're you doing, Tom? I just finished,' Stuart said. 'You?'

'Yeah, yesterday afternoon. Fucking relief, eh?' I said. 'That French was a bitch though.'

'Tough enough, yeah. What about English? I haven't seen you since Paper One.'

'Alright actually,' I said. 'I thought it was good. Loved the *Gatsby* question. I'll miss that book,' I said pretentiously. I was perched up on the saddle of my bike, one foot on the red-brick wall and the other on the pedal.

'Yeah,' said Stuart. 'What about *Othello*? I thought it was okay.'

'Yeah,' I sighed, in muted concurrence. 'As long as they give you a question on Iago you're alright. There's just nothing to say about any of the other half-wits, other than they're fucking stupid. And you just don't get the grades for three-word answers like that.'

'What're you doing tonight then?' he asked, chuckling at the earnestness of my concern for fictional characters.

'Oh, nothing much,' I said. 'There's a few parties I'm considering, you know the way.' I lied. I had already decided on a celebratory jaunt to the cinema, alone, for a good film, a giant popcorn, a jumbo hotdog, and a quart of coke. 'You?' I asked.

And off he went, he just opened up, unnecessarily and unprompted, allowing me a brief but privileged glimpse into his intimate world, the same way he would seven years later in Cloud Nine, the Departure Lounge bar in Dublin Airport. I don't know what it is about me that makes him swing open the doors to his soul, but I can assure you it's no gift of mine; it's not a congenital mark of character, or an acquired skill that I can use to open up just anyone for the benefit of my own whims and fancies. He is thoroughly unthreatened by me, to the extent that he feels he can tell me anything (and here I am, putting him up to ridicule and judgment, picking him apart one fault at a time, hanging him out to dry in a narrative in which he is granted no meaningfully independent voice, and no opportunity to make a riposte; all I can say in my defence is that I never asked for his story; he came to me, desperate to tell somebody, like a budding glamour model to the red-top journalist she met at a sleazy party, dying to divulge the details of her sordid night of titillating filth with a moderately talented and half-famous Premiership footballer). He told me all about his time with Ali, because it was just too brilliant to keep locked up inside.

'So then I'm meeting up with Ali, and then the other two are joining us and we're heading for town. I'm just on my way to Gary's now, actually.'

'Where's he living?'

'Oakdene.'

'I can give you a cross-bar that far, if you want?' I offered.

Stuart had become accustomed to the luxury of Gary's red *Absentu*, but he was not keen on the walk and there was an element of seizing the spirit of the moment in his decision to hop onto the cross-bar of my bike, steering our course, as I sat high on the saddle, hands on his shoulders for stability, and pedalled dementedly. We cut a fifteen-minute journey on foot down to three or four minutes. We swerved up onto curbs, braking suddenly, almost losing our balance, and ramped back off the path, avoiding everything from cars and vans to buggies and a hyperactive dog. We navigated the busy entrance and exit of the shopping centre, before negotiating the treacherous roundabout, scarcely avoiding the bumper of a small van as we jumped without stopping from the path to the busy road, and off up towards Oakdene.

At the entrance to the estate, Stuart hopped off the teenage taxi and thanked me. He asked me, as I set myself to go, feeling obliged, if I would be interested in joining him later. He suggested with certainty that Ali could bring another friend. I understood, but had no intention of playing the pitiful charity case; I had my heart set on the cinema, where my pride would remain intact. I declined the offer graciously and we said our good-byes, neither of us wondering when we would meet next, or aware that it would be seven years—and quite a few memory-ruining pounds on my side—before we would once again stand before each other saying good-bye.

Gary's car was parked in the driveway. He had obviously decided on the inebriated tour. Stuart took the spare key from under the flowerpot and let himself into the house. As he walked in, the smell of the previous night's Chinese food rushed at him. All the curtains and blinds were still pulled over. The place badly needed an airing. He walked around, drawing back the curtains and raising the blinds, and opened as many windows as he could; a draft swept through the downstairs and cleared the air of its staleness.

Then he collected up the leftovers and tipped them into the curry-sodden, paper bag, and eased that into a plastic bag, before pushing the whole lot into the already overfilled kitchen bin. He emptied the dregs of the wine down the sink and lined the empty bottles of beer up on the draining-board before going over to the fridge and opening it up. There were two well-chilled beers left from a six-pack; he wondered how they had escaped unopened. Maybe Gary had a few before he went out, he thought, or maybe they had been drunker than he remembered. He took one out and snapped off the lid with a bottle-opener.

He made his way back to the living room and sat quietly on the sofa, sipping his beer, totally content in the moment, with nothing on the horizon to worry him or detract from the pleasure of his present. After several harmonious minutes, the muffled hum of music became audible. Beneath the hum were some barely perceptible voices—unfamiliar, at first. But the harder he listened, the more kinks of tone and rhythm held his attention.

He rose from the sofa and slipped softly across the floor, like a cat in slippers, towards the hall and the stairs. At intervals, through the amalgamation of voices and music, vaguely recognisable peaks and troughs of inflection became distinct. With each step on the stairs he listened harder still, and the closer he got the better he could distinguish that which was somehow familiar from the unfamiliar blend of music and voices. He reached the landing and stood for a second, bottle of beer still in his hand, listening. He walked across the landing and stopped outside the bathroom door. Van Morrison was playing. With his breath held, he placed his hand gently on the door-handle and stood listening—confusion and apprehension contorting his face—before flinging open the door and taking a few steps onto the white, diamond tiling.

There was a soundless exchange (for what words are there?), and to Stuart it seemed that time slowed down until the component parts of the scene were freeze-framed, and the conclusions irrefutable; much of life is spent in uncertainty, having opinions and theories and suspicions, but rarely do we experience absolute clarity, a moment where we have no doubt, and where we can categorically affirm that there is no explanation for what we see before us other than that which we know in that instant. Stuart had come upon one of these moments. Gary and Ali were sitting facing each other in a ceramic pond of bubbles. Gary had to look over his shoulder to see Stuart standing just inside the bathroom door. Ali was sat with her hand resting on Gary's bent knee; one of her breasts was concealed by the bubbles, but the other was exposed—naked and brazen. Her blonde hair was all wet and swept back and down onto her shoulders; her beautiful, confident smile was halfway to startled (though not ashamed or embarrassed)—it had not had time to readjust from whatever betrayal she had been indulging in the moment before Stuart burst through the door.

'Stuart!' she gasped, before regaining composure where it seemed improper. 'Look, Stu . . .' she said, hinting that whatever reaction he was about to have was bound to be an overreaction.

'Stu,' said Gary, interrupting her. 'Shit, Stu. I'm . . .' Gary was leveraging himself up out of the bubbles. Stuart took a few steps deeper into the bathroom and Gary lowered himself back down, leaning away from Stuart and looking up. Stuart kept coming forward until he stood in front of them. Gary looked stunned. Ali looked at Stuart as if to say, 'So you caught us, so what?' Stuart looked at the CD player on the floor and the four empty bottles of beer around it. He reached out towards the wall and unplugged it, bringing an end to 'These Dreams Of You.' He extended his arm, looking Gary directly in the eye, and tipped the rest of the beer in his bottle over smug Ali's head. The beer mushroomed into froth on her mop of wet, blonde hair, and flowed over her forehead and down the sides of her nose, and then down her back and chest; she screamed. She was still screaming as Stuart dropped the empty bottle bobbing into the bathwater and walked out of the bathroom, down the stairs, and out of the house.

■

So, when Anna—sexy, feisty, English Anna—dropped her hand to Stuart's upper and inner thigh beneath the table inside the pub, you can understand why he did not dismiss what seemed more than mere sexual innuendo at once. He gave the situation more than a second thought.

'Listen, Anna,' he said.

'We're not married, Stuey,' she said. 'You don't mind if I call you Stuey, do you? I have a half-brother called Stuart, you see, who we call Stu, and it feels a bit weird.'

'The fact that I'm your boyfriend's best friend, maybe his only friend, isn't weird, no?' Her hand still went unreprimanded on his thigh as he spoke, and her fingers stroked provocatively.

'We're both young, Stuey. Gary goes off, like tonight, and meets up with his crowd, and I'm sure he's . . . you know, doing whatever takes his fancy. And that's okay. I turn a blind eye, and I do my thing. Doesn't mean I don't care. I'm just not the jealous type.'

Stuart's ego was enjoying the massage, and he still had not moved her hand from his thigh. He leaned in closer and began to talk in a low voice, as if the place was full of people he knew and the whisper would protect him. Anna took the leaning and the whispering to be encouragement, and she slid her stool across the floor until she was almost nose to nose with him. She left her hand where it was and propped her head up on the other, chin and cheek cupped by her palm and fingers, elbow on the table. She looked into Stuart's eyes. Her lips twitched as if she was primed for kissing. Stuart wanted to kiss her. But it was not only long-awaited sweet revenge that had Stuart's heart and loins pumping now. He wanted her smooth legs, her delicate arms, her slightly too big for her skinny body breasts, her cushioned lips, and her reckless promiscuity. 'I can't, Anna. Sorry. Not that I . . . you know. But I can't.'

Anna drew back slightly. She looked surprised. 'Even though he fucked your bird in the bath all those years ago?' she said. 'You still can't do it? Even after that?' Stuart was surprised by her aggressiveness. The rawness with which she used the F-word slightly shocked him. It was rupturing with salaciousness, carnality, and belligerence—the way she said it. He wanted to say, 'You know about that? I can't believe that's a story he tells! Bastard!' But there were things holding him back from what he wanted to say and do. He was furious with Anna, and he wanted to strike back at her for her effrontery, but he ached as well. He wanted to hurt Gary too, because the memory needled, and there was one sure way to do them both in one stroke. But would that hurt her? And had he not had enough action for one week without adding his friend's girlfriend to a nameless plump girl, a pregnant one-night stand, and complicated sex with his oldest friend? Surely he had had enough for now. Anna leaned back in, closer again. He could feel the faintest tickle of her bottom lip brushing off his. As she spoke, she cupped and squeezed him with the final throw of the die. 'Are you really sure?'

Stuart was sure. The unexpected squeeze was like a jolt free from hypnosis. 'Yeah,' he said, and sat back against the wall, leaving Anna pouting, chin still on hand, and with her other hand now looking awkward at full stretch. 'He did that, and that was then. I've got enough on my plate without getting mixed up in this. No offence.'

Anna withdrew her hand from his leg, straightened up, and took a drink. 'None taken. It's admirable, I suppose. The morality of it.' The audacity of the girl, she just shrugged the rejection off and was ready to resume as if nothing had happened.

'Look, I'm staying for another drink. Rachel is picking me up around 8:30. Do you want one?'

'Is that the girl you got pregnant?' asked Anna.

'Ah, for Christ sake! He only just found out a few hours ago.'

'He told me while you were in talking with your brother. Speaking of which, how's his moral fortitude? I liked him.'

'He's the loyal type. You wouldn't click. And no, Rachel's just a friend.'

'Have you ever slept with her?'

'Do you want a drink or not?'

'Yeah, why not? Some kind of spirit and mixer. Bacardi and something. You choose. You know, nobody has ever turned me down before.'

At half-past eight on the button, punctual as ever, and looking good enough to knock the intrepid wind out of English Anna's sails, Rachel entered Laughin' Murphies—another grand entrance.

'Hey, Rachel. You remember Anna from the other week.'

'Yeah. Hi. Gary's girlfriend, right?'

'Yeah. Hi,' said Anna, boredly.

'Where is he anyway?' asked Rachel.

'He headed off about an hour ago.' Stuart said. 'Owen was here too. He's only just left.'

'Oh,' Rachel said. 'How is he? Did he enjoy the other night?'

'I think so, yeah. He's fine.'

'Christina seemed nice, actually. Didn't she?' Anna had not spoken since her brief introduction, and Stuart couldn't have been happier with that. He hoped she would leave soon.

'Owen seemed nice. That's what I think,' Anna said.

Rachel noted the obviously hostile, though ambiguous, comment. 'Yeah. He is nice,' she said. 'And like I said, so is his girlfriend, Christina.'

'There you go—two nice people being nice together. Lovely,' Stuart said, but Anna was not finished.

'That's right. You did say that. The thing is, nice girlfriends don't always have the nice boyfriend they think they have. He might be nice all over town.'

'I can see why you're with Gary. You seem, what's the word, em—suited. Yeah, that's it. Suited.'

Anna washed down all pretence of restraint with the last of her Bacardi. 'Don't presume to judge me, princess. I know you. A little brunette Barbie with half an education and no idea. Look at you running around after this empty tin, jumping when he says jump, limping hurt and dejected back to your no doubt girly-pink bedroom when he ignores you. And you just keep coming back for more. Because what you really want is for him to drop to his knee, marry you, implore you to give up your job, and fill you up with babies.' Anna was standing now, straightening her skirt and top, cigarettes in hand. 'But you're in for a shock, because somebody got there before you. Little Jenny posh-tits is trying to strong-arm him.' Earlier when Anna asked was Rachel the pregnant girl, Stuart felt Anna was flexing her retaliatory muscle. Now he knew she didn't waste time with idle threats. She had known exactly who was who, and when the disclosure of that information would do most damage. 'She's got herself pregnant and trumped you.' Anna put a cigarette between her full lips, lit up, and breathed in deeply. She tilted her head and exhaled fully. 'You kids take care now.' She blew a quick kiss at Stuart and headed out the door triumphantly.

In the wake of Hurricane Anna, Rachel was trying to piece together the details and find her place in Stuart's drama, and Stuart was wondering exactly what Rachel knew already, and how to fill in the gaps. The chronology of events was what was going to do for him.

'I'm sorry, Rache.'

'When did you find out?' She wanted to hear it for herself. She wanted to be positive she hadn't overlooked some vital detail that might alter her perspective, something that might redeem her peerless Paris.

'Saturday, I suppose. But I kind of blacked-out on it. I didn't remember it till she told me again on Sunday. I'm sorry, Rache. But Sunday night . . .'

'Fucking hell, Stu!' Rachel rarely swore. 'Why now? All these years. There were times when you wanted to, I'm sure. I know there were times when I did, but we didn't. And then you decide when you get somebody else pregnant that that would be a good time to go for it.' He had expected her to storm out. He had expected her to clam up, raise the defences, and walk away from it. He wished she had. The postmortem was painful. He wanted to say that it took two to sleep together; he wanted to say it was not entirely his fault, but he knew the lameness of that; in the dark and sweat of Sunday night, when formerly respected boundaries were gloriously transgressed, only one half of the alliance knew that the spirit of Jenny Cumberton lay between them, impatiently tapping her spectral fingers on her fertile belly.

'Look, Stuart, I'm not going to flip out,' she said. 'I might later, but not here. I haven't had time. But I'll drop you home, because I said I would,' she said, as if that was the point of the whole thing; her word meant something.

The car ride home felt long. Stuart sat slumped, fairly drunk, in the passenger seat. As Rachel drove, she went over and over everything. She knocked off the Otis Redding CD that had been playing in favour of the radio. She did not want an album ruined and stolen from her by an awful associative memory. She left Otis sitting on the Frisco Bay, and chugged through the evening traffic to the sound of trite, formulaic pop. There were bland cover versions of songs whose emotional import had been sabotaged by danced-up backing tracks and vanilla vocals. Who stole Tracy Chapman's soul? was a question that occurred to her. Other songs were festering with throwaway lyrics and cliché of the most obscene kind. Whatever happened to Bob Dylan's kind of love, love that broke, love like a corkscrew to the heart? But despite its awfulness, she was glad of the chance to attach such disappointment to the outpourings of commercial radio, rather than a precious album holding twelve tracks of her life.

Stuart did not know what to think. He just sat and wished himself home. He wanted to sleep. He wanted to get up in the morning and start over. Work? He had a plan. Jenny? Who knew? It was all up in the air. Rachel? He wanted it back the way it was before. Rachel pulled up curbside and put the hand-brake on. The engine was running. She turned down the radio.

'Here you are,' she said.

'Thanks, Rache. I don't deserve you.'

'You certainly don't.'

'Do you want to come in for a while?' Rachel snorted and shook her head. 'Sorry, you're right.'

'Do me a favour, Stu. Stop saying "sorry." I get it. But "sorry" doesn't change anything. I believe you're sorry, but it doesn't make it any better.' A chastened Stuart got out of the car and walked to the steps of the apartment. He turned to see her brake-lights flicker as she slowed for the corner, before taking off round it and away.

WEDNESDAY MORNING

While Stuart slept, the city flared up in a rash of criminal and domestic violence, as it does from time to time, just to let us know that the glossy, modern shop-fronts, the booming business, the O-New cars, the designer sunglasses, the soaring house prices, the pre-packed lives, and the complacency of our tame little tigers, is always threatened by the neglect and ensuing rage of the wild cats—the systematically impoverished, those excluded from the salvation of a nation. There had been a high-speed crash on the motorway involving a youth in a stolen car, a drugs raid in the west of the city, a murder of a Nigerian man, an arrest of a concussed man (struck by a frying-pan during a domestic), and both police and civilian casualties following an arson attack in a run-down housing estate.

Stuart slept soundly. His alarm went off as set, at 7:30 A.M., but he went back asleep. He understood the possible consequences, but the comic-tragedy that his life had descended into had broken his spirit. Stark reality was all that was waiting, so he decided to keep his eyes closed, like the petrified child in the dark who hopes that self-imposed sightlessness will somehow protect him from the danger he cannot see.

The city awoke from its tumultuous night to find it had overlooked the assault of a French tourist, whose story would have to wait for the evening papers. But life went on, unstirred by the night's upheaval, for the people who populate this story—they buttered their toast, and brushed their teeth, and took their vitamin supplements, and listened to morning radio on another pleasant summer's morning, just like any other. Only the usually insular Elizabeth Sheridan-Byrne took note of events that didn't put the slightest dent in their lives—'That kind of violence is a disease of the miseducated and the poor'—but she had no more time than that for the less fortunate, and she had a letter to post. She had held that letter for a day, not wishing to be impulsive. She had given Patrick Byrne every opportunity to make amends. Now she would give him his name back in exchange for half his fortune.

Patrick Byrne was sitting in a room cum tiny office space, recently leased under the pretence of keeping himself occupied, but really just using it as a private getaway. His feet were up on the desk, and he was munching on a jam doughnut and sipping his franchise-outlet coffee from a cardboard cup. As a rosy pearl of jam oozed out and dropped onto his tie, he thought of what he would do if he was free of responsibility, just like he used to when he really worked, before ill thought-out early retirement. Every morning before he began his work of dotting *is* and crossing *t*s, and making plain English out of legal gobbledygook for people who just wanted a roof over their heads, or a new roof, or a bigger roof, or a roof in a better neighbourhood, he liked to sit down and imagine his life without his family. He imagined what it would be like had he been strong enough to not propose to Elizabeth; they had gone together for nearly two years, they were both of marrying age, the expectation was there, as was a certain degree of pressure, and she clearly loved him then, her younger heart endearing her to him, in a manner, even though his heart was no longer his to give, and the best he could offer her was human decency.

He was imagining what it would be like to walk out now, imagining all the things he could do with freedom; the kids were grown up and independent, after all, and any fondness he had for Elizabeth when she was open-hearted and in love, was long since disappeared. He imagined retiring to the sun, though in his imagination he was a younger man, leaner and lighter of face, and relaxing with a beautiful woman he had once loved—she still looking as young as the day he watched her leave—and the dinners they could have with the sun setting on the ocean behind them, and the life they could lead with his money already made: golf in the mornings with his retired friends, and occasionally younger men who come seeking his advice; lunches by the Marina; swimming in the clear water in the afternoon; sipping whiskey in the twilight on the veranda, writing poetry about the exotic and his muse.

The soothing illusion (some illusions sustain life, like a ventilator—it's that or nothing) came to an end as his cardboard cup of coffee ran dry. He swung his legs down from the desk, straightened up, replaced his dreamy demeanour with furrows of earnestness and regret, and got back to the blank page he could never fill with all his contrition and naff couplets.

In the passenger seat of a people carrier, Sara was drying her eyes as Damien climbed out of the vehicle, jersey, shorts, socks, shin-guards, and football boots already on, and barrelled across the grass towards the Clubhouse with impish enthusiasm for World Cup Camp. Kevin, having taken a day off to save his marriage, was sitting in the driver seat. Sara did not wish to repeat the mistakes of her parents; but how to get over her dislike for her husband, and the unasked-for child, and not lay the foundations for further resentment and disharmony later in life, and not cause structural damage to the inchoate nature of their living, breathing son?

Meanwhile, in a dank bedsit, Owen and Christina were lying wrapped up in each other, and Christina was about to rubber-stamp her efficacious impact on Owen's life. 'I've got some news for you,' she said. 'Oh, lord,' he said, and asked her was she pregnant too. She was not though, not yet, but she had been beavering away on his behalf, part-time personal assistant and part-time muse—the envy of the father, if only he'd known. She had found him a prospective publisher for his agonised poetry of self-reproach and redemption. 'He'd be really interested to talk to you,' she said. 'He said it's raw. Beat-like, he said,' she said. 'And by the way, I think you should give up this place and move in with me,' and his dislocated heart popped back into its socket. 'This is love,' he replied. 'This is why people endure their childhoods,' and he enveloped her with joy. By the miracle of human resolve, Owen's gallant naïvety and inherent innocence proved indomitable in the face of unyielding parental stricture, clinical melancholy, and his insistence on sentience in a fiscal world unable to estimate his value.

As his family in their various roles acted on once idle threats, daydreamt oblivious to it all, navigated another loveless marriage, and finally found a place of warmth and support in the world, Stuart slept tight. He slept all the way to eleven-fifteen, when thirst caused him to get out of bed and make his way to the tap for some cold, healing water. The end had begun and he did not even know, just like he had missed the beginning. Stuart has compounded one mistake with another, and time is getting on. We're nearing the end. I will get back to it, back to what we are all here to see—the fall of Everyman, Faustus all over again: greedy, lazy, cowardly—divine reprisal is surely on its way.

He woke up dehydrated. And once again, after a pint of water, downed in one, he found in himself the resolve to salvage his career at R&S Foods. His cause would have been best served by an early start and a show of enterprise. That opportunity to impress Stanley had been squandered, it was too late now, the initiative had been lost. But he couldn't afford to wait for another call from Ms Beckondale. He needed to show that he had come round in his own time, he needed to return to his job of his own volition, not be ushered back to it in humble gratitude, ever grovelling and indebted to the second chance afforded him.

But what if there was no way back? Had he failed to take his final opportunity for professional redemption? Stuart liked his city flat, his *Perquisita*, his expensive suits, his no-strings lifestyle, and

after an extra-long weekend of uncertainty and tactless manage-
ment of his personal life, he craved normality. He just wanted to
go into work, do a good job, and be forgotten. He wanted to be a
faceless worker in the city. He wanted to be a simple statistic. He
had been happy just being like everybody else. He wanted to be
let alone to recover, to regroup. The only way he could envisage
achieving that was to go back to work. That way his career would
cease to be a problem, and he would be left with, in order of importance, Rachel and Jenny.

'Rachel?' I queried. 'Still trying to dodge the issue, Stuart?' I suggested. He had, of course, been avoiding the inevitable from the
moment he found out—black-out drunk with Gary and sleeping
with a girl whose name he could not remember; lunch with Rachel and ignoring Jenny's calls as he sat safe, head in her metaphorical bosom; drinks with a customarily troubled brother followed by imprudently timed sex with Rachel; the subconscious
seeking out of Quigley, as if he held the answer, simply because he
empathised in a general way, with a maybe real, maybe not, indif-
ferent emotional mien of a generation caught between excess and
emptiness; the relief with which he eased into the middle of his
sister's marriage at crisis-point, happily allowing her problems to
distract him from his own; the refusal, even in the aggressive face
of direct question with a rightly incandescent Mr Cumberton, to
address the issue of the pregnancy, to answer a straight question,
to really look at himself; another piss-up and the distraction of
Anna, yet another beautiful girl; bestowing on Rachel the responsibility of saviour—all ways of not thinking about what simply had

to be realised—and sooner better than later. Stuart, though, just wanted it gone. He wanted the situation to disappear. He wanted his phone to stop ringing.

He had slept through two calls, one from Jenny and a private number. Could have been from anybody, he thought—work, Owen, his father or mother, or Sara, or from Jenny again, trying to trick him into answering. There was no message from either call. That surprised him. He expected Jenny to leave a message, blubbering down the phone, still thinking it could all end in happy families. As he placed the phone down on the counter, it rang again. This time it was his mother. He looked at the screen—MUM! MUM! MUM! He left it alone. Whatever she wanted would have to wait; parents always have to wait while their children soak in self-pity.

Stuart dressed in one of his light, summer suits. He had shaved and showered. He was going to meet A.S. Stanley. When he was ready to go, he picked up his phone and dialled.

'Good morning. Ramsey and Stanley Foods. How can I help you?'

'Hi, this is Stuart Byrne. Can you put me through to Al Stanley's office, please?'

'Certainly, Mr Byrne, just a moment.'

'Good morning.' Stuart's knees nearly buckled beneath him. She still had it. 'Mr Stanley's office, Tamara speaking. How can I help you?'

'Tamara, it's Stuart.' There was a pause and nothing emerged. 'Stuart Byrne.'

'Oh, Stuart. Hi. Sorry, you're the last voice I expected.' She went no further. She let Stuart begin, before interrupting again.

'Sorry, Tamara, can I please . . .'

'How are you? Are you better?'

'Yes, I am. Thanks. I'd like to talk to Alan, if that's possible.'

'Well, he's very busy, as you know, Stuart. But I think he'd like to talk to you too—now that you're better. But he's not here right now.'

'Okay, how about early afternoon? Will he be back?'

'I'll schedule you in for 1:30. He should be here, and he has half an hour then before his next meeting.'

'Golf again,' Stuart joked, looking for levity.

'Half-one, Stuart. Thanks. Good-bye.'

Stuart gathered up the necessaries—wallet, keys, and phone—and left the apartment to walk into the city. The car could sit in the car-park, where he'd left it overnight, until after his meeting with Stanley.

The tone of the phonecall with Tamara Beckondale had shaken his confidence a little, and weakened his resolve. Was she acting on Stanley's orders, or was she harbouring some secret grudge? Stuart could not imagine what grudge she might bear, so he had to assume that Stanley had ordered her to be tough with him, and that he had been the topic of unfavourable conversation among the company's hierarchy. All the more reason for going in and being straight with Stanley, and holding his hands up, coming clean, and getting back to what he was paid to do—meeting with TV, radio and print media people and talking over future campaigns, or problems with existing campaigns; making sure ads were shown and heard at optimum times; meeting celebrity endorsers, and making sure that they knew what was contractually required of them, without making them feel like they were being used; ensuring the marketing campaigns remained innovative and capitalised on cultural phenomena (planting ads during the most popular reality TV show, picking the right celebrity for the right product); anticipating changes in the market. That was normality, and it had to be better than what he'd endured since calling in sick the previous Friday, he thought.

Stuart walked the canal again, this time preoccupied and unaware of his surroundings: the passing cyclists, pedestrians, the many signs of city life floating in the shallow canal—traffic cones, an old rubber welly-boot, a milk carton, stained Styrofoam—the rusted, blue bike chained to the railings, the postural swans drifting in single, obedient file, the diving ducks, feathered asses to the sky, and free that day of the haemorrhaging hate of red-haired kids with freckles and filthy manners.

It was approaching noon as he crossed over the canal, towards St Stephen's Green. The uneven tarmac beneath his feet became perfect square slabs of pavement. He followed the grey paving, and although he noticed it becoming speckled with rain, it wasn't until he felt cool raindrops on his head and his neck that it occurred to him to run for shelter. The sky turned suddenly black overhead and the power-shower clouds hosed him down; a flash shower bucketed down for a hundred and twenty seconds. Conscious of being in his suit, he made a run for the café he had been in for breakfast on the Monday.

It was too late. By the time he got there he was soaked, and the rain was easing off. He stood in the doorway of the café looking out at the slowing rain. Inside, behind him, the gentle waitress was getting a tongue-lashing from her intemperate boss. Stuart didn't notice, though the sound of the shouting was loud enough to reach his ears, and he stood waiting for the peeping sun to make a meaningful hole in the greying clouds. People began to slope out from under doorways, and shake off umbrellas, and look mistrustfully up at the mercurial sky. The streets around the Green repopulated steadily, until the buzz and hum of urgency had returned to its aspired level. Stuart walked into the Green in search of a bench. His phone rang. It was Gary. He ignored it.

When he reached the centre of the Green he stopped and dried off the bench with some tissues he found in his breast pocket. The sun was out in force again. The manicured grass and the array of colourful flowers glowed surreally. It was a Willy Wonka garden, unblemished and resplendent. The flowers in their vibrant colour possessed a lambent quality, glistening slightly with a coat of still-fresh rain. The peaceful centre of the Green provided a break from the busy city and the traffic. It was peopled by elderly couples, young mothers and fathers come to feed the ducks with infants, and workers on early lunch. It was peaceful.

Stuart sat hunched and pensive on the bench, letting it all wash over him. With his elbows on his knees, he stared straight ahead of him at the iron foot-rail that traced the border of the flawless green grass. Lives passed by unnoticed and unaffected. A young girl in a wheelchair spun past him and he looked up for a second. She had a plastic supermarket bag, overflowing, sitting on her lap. She felt his attention. He smiled at her, and she smiled back self-consciously and spun off on her way to wherever. There was a homeless guy asleep on the wet grass under the lurching, leafy branches of a great big tree. He was wearing a tattered old suit. It was black and faded. It was badly frayed at the bottom of one leg. There was a rip at the elbow of his jacket, his grimy elbow protruding—crusted, dried blood to the air. The soles of his old navy runners were worn down to a pair of slippers. He looked like a tramp from Beckett's imagination, still clinging to his once dapper but now dilapidated suit, as if it was the very essence of his dignity. He slept with his head on the varicose root of the tree and curled up on the wet grass. A small dog went over and sniffed at him, and he swatted it away with a tired hand.

Stuart began to notice the pains in his own body. He felt thirsty. His back ached. He had the beginnings of a headache and his stomach was making dissatisfied noises. His shoulders and his neck ached, and his thighs throbbed delicately. His five-day bender of self-discovery was cashing in its chips; the house always comes out on top.

Somebody stopped in front of him. He thought, Another homeless guy begging. These are the ones who upset us; the ones who want to interact. Stuart noticed that the shoes looked fairly new, and as he raised his eyes he observed the heavy, polyester trousers.

'Stuart?' A pallid man with shoulder-length, black hair stood in front of him, looking to him for confirmation. The man looked like somebody Stuart used to know. But this man was more filled out in the face, still Iggy Popish, but healthier looking than the man Stuart once knew. He was wearing a suit, his tie hanging low around his neck and the top button of his value-pack shirt undone. He was the reluctant employee of the city office. He was the guy who hacked away at the keyboard in the offensively bright office block, processing data, all the while hating every minute, and imagining the world tour his under-rehearsed, talent-defective band should be on. The suit did not suit him. Whatever job he was doing, he needed a new one. 'Stuart Byrne?' he asked again, the way you might if you just pulled up to a celebrity hiding under a baseball cap and a big puffer-jacket in a record shop, and asked, 'Are you who I think you are?'

'Yeah,' Stuart said, tentatively. The man laughed. An unmistakable, rowdy laugh.

'Dave? What are you doing here?'

'Having lunch.'

'When did you leave Brixton?'

'About a year ago.'

'Shit,' Stuart said, shaking his head disbelievingly. 'Of all the people. How are things?'

'Good. You?'

'I don't know. I've had a few nights out. I can't think straight at the moment.'

'Do you mind if I sit down?' He sat down on the other side of the bench and unwrapped a tuna and cheese roll. From his jacket pocket he took a bottle of lemon-flavoured Bucks. Stuart nearly heaved. 'You want some?' Dave asked, with his mouth stuffed full of tuna, cheese, and bread. Stuart declined. 'So how are things, Stu? To be honest, I only noticed you because you looked like one of those boys that jump from pedestrian bridges onto motorway traffic. What's up?'

'Women. And me. And work. And . . . mainly me.'

'More than one? Fair play to you.'

'Huh?'

'Women. You said "women." That's more than one. And work, tell me about it! I've been corralled up in an office block punching codes into a computer for the last nine months, for Mintocorp. So what's it you've done then? Married someone, dumped someone, killed someone?'

'Well, I'm on the verge of being sacked from a really good job, for starters.'

'Not the end of the world.'

Stuart continued, 'I've got one girl pregnant, slept with my best friend, and been cracked onto by a friend's girlfriend. All in the last week, or less even.'

'You've had a busy week, then. And, if you don't mind me saying, that's some fast-acting sperm you've got.'

'Oh, yeah, well I only found out about that part.'

'And I trust your best friend is a bird.'

'Yeah. Rachel.'

'So, what are you going to do, if that's not too broad a question?'

'I'm not sure,' said Stuart, unaware just how broad the question was.

'Well met,' replied Dave, sarcastically. 'All my question deserved, to be honest.'

'I've a meeting with my boss in an hour or so,' Stuart went on, deaf to Dave's teasing sarcasm. 'And I'm going to try and rescue my career.'

'Is this the same job you left London for?'

'Yeah, same one. And it's good. So, that's first off. The meeting with the boss. After that . . . I don't know. How come you left Brixton for Mintocorp? I thought you loved it over there.'

'I did. But I'd had enough. Too much of everything. I turned thirty-nine a few months ago. I wanted to get out of London. I couldn't breathe there.'

'IT work doesn't seem like you.'

'My mam's sick. I did a couple of shitty courses and got a job. You do what you have to. And it's hard enough to get into the nine to five world at my age, and with no experience. I had to, duty came calling.'

'I didn't know your mum was sick.'

'She's not got too long,' he said, matter-of-factly. He was resigned, but not morbidly so. 'She has days when she's in a lot of pain. Death's not so daunting when life's like that.'

'Sorry,' Stuart said.

'It's okay. I was gone all those years. It's my time now. And job aside, it's been good to be home. I'll miss her.'

'Lordy,' Stuart said. 'And I thought I had problems.'

'Hey, listen now, we all have problems, and I wouldn't swap mine for yours. You're always better off with your own, kid. When Mam's gone there'll be nothing here. I'll go my own way. I fancy a bar in the sun somewhere. A Greek island, maybe. But there's plenty of time for that yet.'

'Get a tan while you work,' Stuart said, and they both laughed.

'Yeah, that's it. Palest man on earth, working in the sun. I'm burning up just sitting here.'

They talked for another ten minutes, reminiscing about the shared London months. In the course of their reminiscence, Stuart's phone rang twice. There was one call from Owen and another from Jenny. Stuart did not answer either of them. Stuart found Dave's presence reassuring. Dave finished his roll and guzzled back the last of his Bucks Lemon, screwed back on the bottle top, and tossed the empty bottle into a nearby bin. He stood up and lit a cigarette.

'I've got to get back. It's good to see you,' he said, exhaling after his first drag.

'You too,' said Stuart. He didn't want Dave to go. 'We should meet up for a few drinks sometime. Give us your number?'

'I don't have one. Sorry. Landline's been cut off too. Missed a couple of bills. But I usually have a few in Casey's on a Sunday afternoon, if you're ever around. Drop in.'

'You don't have a mobile?' Stuart could not believe it. It was like not having socks. 'Why not?'

Dave thought for a second. 'I like to eat my lunch in peace, I guess,' he said, with a sagely grin. 'See you around, Stu.'

'Yeah, see you, Dave.'

Dave stopped and looked at Stuart sitting crumpled and damp in his suit. 'Decide what you want, Stu. If you want your best friend, tell her. Rachel, isn't it?' Stuart nodded. 'And if you don't want her, tell her. And if she's upset, tell her I'll take her.' Dave nodded his head emphatically in the pretence of seriousness. It reminded Stuart of Gary's comment to Jenny; Dave managed to make it sound so much kinder though. 'And this bird with the baby. If you don't want it, say so. That's not the kind of thing to be arsing around with. They're just decisions. They'll take you one way or the other. Don't be afraid of them. You've got your face up against the glass right now, that's all. Everything is distorted. Clear mind, above all, Stu.'

Stuart watched Dave traipse back along the winding paths of St Stephen's Green to a job he hated but accepted had to be done. He watched him merge and finally disappear into the lunch-time crowd and the foliage. It was five to one. It was time to head for the meeting with A.S. Stanley.

As he walked, he texted Rachel—SORRY RACHE. I DON'T KNOW WHAT TO SAY. SORRY. He finished his text and turned off his phone. Maybe Dave was onto something. Maybe the mobile phone was the source of all his confusion and woe. Was being ever reachable a twenty-first century assault on the sanctity of mind and soul? Was there any room for peace, in the quiet, detensifying sense of the word, in this day and age? Had the possibility of escape and recuperation from the invisible strain of our humdrum lives been stolen from us by radio technology, electromagnetic waves hungrily hunting us down and seeking us out wherever we might run? Stuart hoped Dave's calm and clarity would instantly be his the moment the screen faded and died. He walked slowly. By twenty past one he was standing outside the R&S offices, ready to ascend the four stone steps to the big, yellow, Georgian door.

Ms Beckondale showed him into Stanley's office; there were no pleasantries.

'Stuart, take a seat.' Stanley gestured to the swivel-chair in front of his desk. He sat behind his desk, on his padded, leather armchair. On his desk was a telephone, and in front of him a closed booklet, a report on some survey or other; R&S loved their customer surveys. Ms Beckondale pulled closed the door as she left. Behind Stanley was a wooden cabinet with glass doors. In the cabinet were a number of expensive bottles of spirits, brandies, and whiskeys. On the counter surface below the cabinet was a photograph of Stanley and a whole hoard of other Stanleys, Stanleys of different ages and sex, all variations on his genetic vision—wife, children, and grandchildren, mostly round-faced and well-dressed, all peering out at Stuart like real life Larrabees; it had never rained on these people because they just wouldn't stand for it.

Stanley was a smallish man, round, clean-shaven, balding but hairy. He was not a handsome man, but he was well-groomed. Today he looked stern, but Stuart had known him to be vivacious and dominate a room with the intensity of his conviction. His conviction was that R&S Foods was the best run business around, and that its products were better quality and more competitively priced than anyone else's. He believed completely in any marketing slogan or gimmick they contrived. As soon as an R&S Foods initiative came into being, it established itself in Stanley's mind as an absolute truth, an incontestable fact. His faith was unshakable, his jargon indigestible.

'You look like you slept in that suit, Stuart,' Stanley growled.

Stuart sighed, exhausted again, irked by the capricious cruelty of chance; another opportunity to rescue his reputation undermined. 'I got caught in a heavy shower on the way in.'

'You didn't drive?' Stanley asked, quizzically.

That was something Stuart had no intention of trying to explain. 'I apologise for my absence, Alan. I'm good now though. I want to come back in and do my job. I want to get back on top of everything.'

'There's no need to apologise for being ill, Stuart. You were ill, weren't you?'

'I think so.'

'Because if you weren't ill and you missed three and a half working days, just went AWOL, I'd have to be looking at taking some serious disciplinary action.'

'I was ill,' Stuart said, unconvincingly, not in tone but in tense. 'And I was confused. But I'm back now.'

'Are you absolutely sure you're ready to climb back on board? The R&S Express doesn't wait about for ditherers.'

'Yes,' Stuart said, trying to be more assertive.

Stanley was sitting with a wrinkled, pit-bull moue, when not speaking, with his fingers interlocked and his thumbs twirling round each other. 'Because if you're not ready, if you don't believe in us, we can't believe in you, Stuart. You've been with us nearly four years now. You're damn good at your job. I'll be honest with you, when your mother first rang me up and asked me to find a place for you, I was sceptical. But it turns out . . .'

'Sorry?'

'It turns out that you're really quite talented, good with people. Your team are always positive in their feedback about you. You're good with our clients, especially the big egos. And there's no bigger asset . . .'

'No, sorry. Not that, Alan. Excuse my interrupting you, but what is this business about my mother? You two know each other?'

'Oh, I see,' he said, sheepishly. 'She did ask that I keep her influence quiet. But I expected you would know by now. Anyhow, it's irrelevant how you got the job. The point is this, it turns out that you're five-star, top-drawer, and we want to hold onto you, but only if you're still the animal you were.' All sorts of things were falling into place. Faded memories of his mother, during his degree, mentioning that she had a friend who could get him straight in at the lucrative end of marketing, returned to him now. He remembered how he had reacted irritably to that offer, wanting the chance to cut his own place in the world.

It was obvious now; narrative threads were sewing together what had previously seemed no more than random turns of fortune. Everything had been too easy, the transition from college to a reasonable summer of freedom, to the return home and career that could have been handpicked by his mother, and whose rewards satisfied his father's desire for one successful son. It was all too smooth. No months of looking for a job, no failed interview experience, no mounting debt as he waited for work appropriate to his talents and training. It never occurred to him that others were pulling the strings. How smug he had been with college friends who found themselves in badly paid, short-term, post-college jobs, declaring how he had earned everything he had himself, advising others to, 'Seize your moment when it comes,' as if he had succeeded in this endeavour and they had somehow failed, when all along the difference was who your mother knew.

Stuart was sunken. What was he here fighting for? A job that filled him with such indolence that he could not roll out of bed, and now it turned out it was bought by friendship or favour. It did not matter which, or who put what where. The only decent things he believed about himself were untrue. He had achieved nothing. The things he thought he had earned on his own steam had been laid down beside him, like a framing murder weapon, carefully placed at the scene while he slept, ready to incriminate him and strip him of all credibility further down the plot line. He was gutted and angry. He just wanted to get out from under Stanley's overbearing gaze.

'I don't believe this,' he said. If he stayed now, no matter what he achieved, it would always be qualified by nepotism. How could he find satisfaction in something he had not earned? 'I was sick,' he said, not really talking to Stanley. 'I'm still sick,' he said, correcting his tenses.

'Listen to me carefully, Stuart, I want you to stay. Your mother and me go way back. There's nothing untoward here. You got a leg-up, that's all. Our clients like you. You're a real general, and there are big rewards in it if you can pull yourself together. You should be thankful. We both know you weren't sick, but I've got a company to run. You're back with us now, you're running with us, or you're not. One hundred percent. That's what I need from you—one hundred percent certainty, and one hundred and fifty percent effort.'

'Al, Alan, big Stan, I'm two hundred percent out of here.'

'Nothing impetuous now, Stuart,' Stanley warned. 'You're good, but so are a million other guys out there.'

Stuart stood up. He was thinking more clearly than ever. He felt his shoulders ease out of their tense contraction. 'Al, the big A.S.S.-Hole, I hate this fucking job! It's pointless. I won't thank you, you understand. Good-bye.'

My heart skipped a beat as he recounted this episode for me. I began to think there was hope for him yet; he was throwing off the shackles, reacting honestly, with genuine emotion and real conviction. He was waking up. And with that he walked out, past Ms Beckondale's desk, not a second's regret. He reached the street exhilarated and relieved. He wanted to see Rachel. Forget Faustus, this was Phoenix.

He turned on his phone, and as he did so he heard Ms Beckondale calling after him, unusually flustered. 'Excuse me, Stuart! Excuse me!'

'Yes,' he answered, keying in his PIN code.

She caught her breath. 'We'll be needing . . . Mr Stanley sent me after you to let you know that we will be needing your keys—car and office—and your laptop and printer, and your phone. Company property, you understand.' He took the car and office keys off the key-ring, tout de suite, and handed them to Ms Beckondale. 'We can pick them up. It doesn't have to be right now.' He gently pushed her hands away from him, and handed her his phone, too. 'Take them,' he said. 'The car's parked in Stephen's Green.'

'Thanks.' Ms Beckondale spun round and bounded inside like an obedient lapdog. Some of the consequences of his actions were beginning to dawn on him, but the exhilaration of the freedom opening up before his eyes fizzed through him. He took off towards Pearse Station. He climbed on a DART and rode it out to Dalkey, in the general direction of home, because home, no matter how dysfunctional or imperfect, is what we know, and it is to the familiar we return to settle our nerves and set a new course.

WEDNESDAY AFTERNOON

The DART creaked into Dalkey Station around a quarter past three. He walked through the small town without stopping at any of his favoured spots for a drink, anyone of a half a dozen pubs. He crossed over the potholed tarmac outside the DART station and on up through the town. In no particular hurry, he began to notice everything else the town held, besides a string of pubs. There was a jeweller's, several gift shops, a boutique, arts and crafts shops, take-aways—a Chinese and a chip-shop—a bank, a building society, countless restaurants, a mini-market, a pharmacy, a bakery, a butcher's, the public library, a mortgage and property adviser's, a newsagent or two, an Internet café; local pride was right, it was more than a village.

Despite its narrow mainstreet, that would seem to discourage traffic, it was quite busy. He was through the town, end to end, in minutes, before turning up Dalkey Avenue. The avenue wound narrowly upwards, past a series of modest houses—a semi-detached and some distinctive terrace houses grouped together in twos or threes—and then some exclusive estates. When he reached the top of the avenue, he saw the long, concrete path, rising up in a snaking S to the foot of Killiney Hill Park, and started up it.

Stuart remembered learning to drive, practising hill-starts on the motor ramp that runs alongside the path. Over his shoulder, and over the tops of the trees, the harbour was becoming visible. The woods loomed above him as he pushed on up the pathway. The dirt track towards the quarry veered away into the trees, but he stuck to the path. Up ahead, the wood waited there for him, with all the wonder and magic of childhood lingering in its sessile oaks, beeches, sycamores, and Monterey pines, and the mysterious heather and the hybrid Dalkey ragwort.

The walk to the car-park was hardly the stuff of Shackleton, but for Stuart, in his suit and shoes, and having outgrown such pursuits, it felt like a hike. The climb became less severe as he neared the car-park. There were nine or ten cars parked, and a family of four—Dad, Mum, son, and daughter—came out of the woods after their silken-coated collie, gleaming in the sun as he bounded out beyond the shade of the woodland. There was a rock-climbing instructor running through the equipment and safety procedures with a group of first-timers.

Stuart felt the shady cool of the wood come over him, and the unevenness of the ground with its dips and mounds, fallen twigs and branches, bored in at his feet through his thin soles. The floor of the wood was flecked with random patches of luminous sunlight, ricocheting down through the leaves and branches, into the soft shadows of the wood.

Comforting memories of childhood visited him; it was wilder then, the whole of the hill was, in the days before the coarse undergrowth and overgrowth was cut back to reveal the obelisk. He remembered how his imagination had run away with the idea that behind all the thick heather and nettles—for only the tip of the obelisk was visible then, and in his childish imagination it was a great palace—that there was an honourable King, or a beautiful Princess, trapped. He imagined how he, the hero, would be the one to battle through and save them from their fate, dreaming then of being a hero, a hero who could defy fate and fight the epic battle for the lives and love of an ancient noble-folk. Curses that held them captive were broken, and fantastically vicious enemies were slain. That was the story of the obelisk, but he was not going there today. He walked further into the small wood, drawn to his right by a natural parting of the trees. He could see the footpath that ran alongside, and he was only calling distance from it. After a minute, he came onto a less densely populated wooded area. Here the Monterey pine needles covered the floor, and although they looked in their crispy brownness like they would break and crackle underfoot, the spongy give in them always came as a pleasant surprise. This small plot of wise Monterey pine's ran up along the ruined wall, towards the Telegraph Tower, away from the spellbinding obelisk.

Here, Stuart used to be Robin Hood, running up and down through the pines, or along the steps towards, what was to him, Nottingham Castle, at the top of the hill. He would rescue his band of merry and idealistic men from the clutches of the Sheriff, save the poor from their helpless misery, and get the girl. He wondered did everybody else just play hide-and-seek, or did they imagine themselves to be medieval heroes, too? He remembered being here with friends—friends of early childhood, long since left behind—and losing himself in his private game, forgetting the time as he crouched in a hollow behind a fallen tree, and how annoyed they were when he returned, and how they blamed him for ruining the game because you had to come out when time was up, when you were called, when the person who was On, or It, had done their hopeless duty of trying to catch the other three on a wooded hill of uncountable hiding places. But he had not heard them. He was lost inside, awed and delighted by his exploits.

He scrambled up a bank, his unsuitable shoes slipping and sliding beneath him, and he had to take hold of some protruding roots to haul himself to the top. The perfect blue sky glowed almost white with brightness through the wrinkled trunks of the pine trees along the gradient of the dipping hill. Over towards the bouldered wall, he stepped through one of many collapsed openings, out of the pine area, and onto the path and steps, a quarter of the way up. He began the short walk towards the Telegraph Tower. Panting a little, hot and sweaty in his suit, he took off his jacket.

The path up was interspersed with steps. Much of the path was worn away, with roots from the trees growing over, under, and in and out of the ascending stony track. A short way up, a clearing revealed an awesome coastal panorama. He stepped out into the clearing and stood for some moments. There were a couple of small pools of water held in the rocks from the earlier rain. He looked out over the shrubbed and wooded slopes of the cliff-side, onto the shingled crescent of Killiney Bay, a bay nostalgically compared down the years to the Bay of Naples, the surrounding place names—Vico Road, Sorrento Terrace—reflecting a kind of pretentious pride in that comparison.

The dark clouds had dispersed. The rippling surface of the sea was a slightly darker, less vibrant blue than the perfect sky. The currents of the sea brushed pale blue rivulets onto the dark blue undercoat, with one bending all the way round Bray Head, in a single brush-stroke. The sea seemed to be caressed by the breeze, with the gentlest flutter, like a bed-sheet on a clothesline. It rippled and shimmered, frosted white and blue waves, glittering and sparkling beneath the sun, one hundred and fifty metres below. Sailboats dotted the filmy surface of the bay. The line of the horizon seemed as if it had been traced by a grey marker, dividing the defining blues of the sea and sky.

The sweet, syrupy smell of the leaves and bark, and the wild flowers and the fresh, sea air, lingered for seconds at a time, before being blown clear by the breeze. The feeblest drone of passing cars at the foot of the hill could still be heard, but was being becoming less audible the higher he climbed. Stuart felt an exhilarating sense of the world's enormity, of nature's potential, of freedom's possibilities. He turned back onto the path, to see two cream-coloured butterflies flapping up towards the branches of an overhanging pine, fluttering around a low-hanging, sickly cone, and away.

He brushed past an older lady on the steps, greyed but still spritely, out walking her dog. She was talking to a young woman who spoke with a European accent, while the terrier scuttled around their feet, up and down steps, in and out of the undergrowth. He heard the older lady lament the awful violence of the world today. The girl nodded apologetically, as if assuming personal responsibility for her generation.

Soon he was at the top of the hill, and he leaned on the high wall that ran the perimeter, his elbows up above his chest, like a genie, and ignored the ugly radio beacon behind him, just as he had ignored it in his childhood when it stood inconveniently modern over his imagined world. He looked at the Dublin and Wicklow Mountains, and the faint, wispy-white clouds that hovered at their peaks. Just below him was the quarry.

Unsheltered at the heights of the hill, the breeze became more of a wind, and it was pleasantly cool and came in gusts. Sometimes it scratched, rising to a Perspex wobble on his eardrum, before snapping like a wet towel in his ears, and blowing back his hair and making him squint his eyes. He walked around towards the dilapidated Telegraph Tower, and onto a tiny plateau at the edge of the cliff-side. The whole coastline lay before him, visible from a single vantage point.

He had been here before, often enough for it to be powerfully familiar. It is at its most perfect around five A.M. on a clear morning in summer. The birds can be heard tittering, the grass is dewy, and the sun rises to look you directly in the eye. First, it sprays the horizon from below, and any low-lying cloud, with an orange you can only see at dawn, and then, as it arches its tangerine, balded head over the horizon, an ever widening funnel of orange spreads across the viscous blue surface, until it reaches land, and climbs out of the water and scales the cliff-side. For maybe half an hour, or forty-five minutes, this incredible orange irradiates the waves and currents of the monstrous sea, as they flex and release in slow tidal contractions, like the immense sinewy body of a most powerful beast at rest.

Once upon a time, Stuart had watched the snoring sea basking in the sun of one such Wellsian dawn, while sitting huddled on an old blanket, taken from the family shed, with Rachel by his side. They were twelve, maybe thirteen, at the time, and used to sitting outside on the streets in the mild summer nights with the other kids. As one by one all the others would disappear or be called in, Stuart and Rachel remained. They sat side by side on neighbourhood walls or curbs; they walked back and forth to the late night shops for popcorn and crisps; they talked and laughed, and touched awkwardly in moments of clichéd sweetness—'You're the only one I can talk to, you know.' When a late-night video turned into a sleepover, and they were still awake at daybreak, Rachel set her heart on sharing her first sunrise with her first love. In a moment of spontaneous romance, they climbed the hill and greeted the dawning of the day, together.

Stuart laid his jacket down on the grooved, coarse surface of white rock, pointing out towards the east and the sea, over the cliff-side, like an elongated, ancient finger of a fallen giant. He slipped off his shoes and socks and sat down on his jacket. He rolled up his sleeves and stared soberly out at the sea; seagulls swooped and hovered over the water in the distance, and the sun blazed down on the brow of the hill. He sat there for hours, mulling everything over, going round in circles, unable to shake the hypotheticals—what if Jenny hadn't got pregnant? what if he hadn't slept with Rachel? what if he had gone to work on Friday, and Monday, and Tuesday?

Eventually, there came a decision. From the uninterrupted tranquillity came the only decision he was ever likely to make, not because of fate, as he would have you believe, but because all his other options required degrees of courage and subtlety of mind. This was the only one that alleviated his anxiety—a clean break. Any future with Jenny was imponderable. There was no way back with Rachel, he felt. No way back with Stanley either, even if he wanted it. The blazing sun, the parching hangover, and the exacting emotion of the last five days caught up with him; he felt exhausted again. He had given up, conceded defeat, believing he was powerless in the face of predestination. He needed sleep and more quiet. He descended the hill, decision made (I should have known, despite my earlier optimism following his barnstorming performance at Stanley's office, that he hadn't the fortitude for difficult decisions), and shuffled back into Dalkey, where he hailed a taxi home to his apartment. Once home, he readied himself. He had retired to bed, wasted by his week, by eight in the evening.

THURSDAY MORNING

He slept soundly for thirteen hours. He was woken by the sound of knocking on the door of his apartment. The intercom had buzzed to no effect. It was the unusually persistent rapping on the door that woke him. He grabbed a T-shirt from the floor of his bedroom and made his way quickly towards the impatient knocking.

He felt refreshed, clear-headed after some restorative sleep, and he was resolute in his decision. He did not pause to think who it might be; it didn't matter now. He opened the door, and there stood a choked and downtrodden Rachel. Her burnished, chestnut hair was tied up and fed through the back of a baseball cap, and she was wearing a bulky hoody, and faded jeans and canvas runners. He wanted to wrap her up in a comforting hug, but it was no longer appropriate.

'Hi, Rache,' he said. 'Come on in. Please. I've wanted to talk to you,' he said, but he didn't. That was the last thing he wanted.

Somewhere in his cowardly heart he had hoped he would avoid seeing her.

'Thanks,' she said. Her head lifted as she thanked him, but dropped again, eyes protected beneath the peak of the cap. 'Been out in the sun then?' she asked. Stuart's forehead, nose, and cheeks were sunburnt, the tender red of the Irish on holiday. She walked in and sat down on the sofa, hands together, tucked between her knees. She noticed that the television was plugged out. So were the DVD player and stereo.

'I did a lot of . . . walking. Yesterday,' he said. 'Do you want tea? Or water?'

'Tea, please,' she said.

'Sure.' Stuart filled the electric kettle and returned to the living area.

'So Jenny's pregnant. I didn't think people really got caught in that trap, Stu. We have condoms these days, you know.' It was testier than she had planned.

'I know. I don't know what happened. I used.'

'Oh, right. Sorry,' she said, not sorry at all. 'I just assumed. Because my experience of you led me to believe that you don't use contraception.' This was not going at all the way she had hoped.

'Look, Rache, I don't know what happened. Just fate, I guess. I didn't . . .' He could not finish because it all sounded trite. It sounded like sales-speak—hollow and dishonest.

'Fate? A faulty condom? Unfortunate, maybe. But you did have the choice of fucking her or not, regardless of quality control. And it's not like I raped you, you had choice there too. You do have a say in how things work out.' He felt obliged to take whatever she wanted to dish out. It would be painful, but it would be over soon. 'So what are you going to do? Is she having the baby?'

Stuart knew his favoured non-committal answer was not enough here. Rachel demanded better than that. 'I don't want the baby. I've no feelings for Jenny. In fact, she annoys me—a lot.'

'Those are feelings.'

'You know what I mean. I don't want the baby. But that's out of my control now, there's nothing I can do.'

'Will you ever love anybody, Stu?' He could not answer that, though what he wanted to say was, 'Never again.' She continued. 'Because, I love you, Stuart.'

'I love you too, Rache,' he said, verbatim.

'No! Not like that, you idiot! Not like that. I love you,' she cried, glaring at him.

'Sorry,' he said. 'I just . . .'

'You know, Stu, I do have real feelings. I know I've always played up to this myth you have in your mind. This illusion that I'm so laid-back and secure, and that I'm not needy like "other girls." But you know what? I am. I am fucking needy. I'm awfully fucking needy. I have fat days, and ugly days, and lonely days. I get premenstrual. I eat big fat bars of chocolate to comfort myself, and all I want is love, you know. I want a whole lot more besides, for myself and from life, but all I'm asking from you is to love me—and I thought you did. Maybe I was wrong. Maybe I should just piss off back to my crap boyfriends and my stupid heart. This great girl you have in your head doesn't exist. This is it. There's just me.'

He wanted to say, 'There's nothing "just" about you,' and, 'I do love you,' but the guilt in his bones, the uncertainty of Jenny, and decisions already made, would not let him. 'You know I think you're great, Rache,' he said.

'That's just it, I don't! What if it was me who was pregnant? What if . . . ?'

And all the panic in the world came over Stuart. Oh no, he thought. Don't tell me her too. Please, he thought, I can't be this unlucky. 'You aren't, are you?' he asked, stupidly. Oh my Christ, what do I do now? What do I do now, he thought.

Rachel started to cry—another illusion busted. She had managed to bring the matter to its crux. As hypothetical questions go, it was the most important question of their lives, and when they were most in need of certitude, Stuart was procrastinating. He was like a prince now, not the hero prince of his childhood, but a Danish prince—flawed and spinelessly indecisive—and she like Desdemona, baffled by the change in a man she believed she knew, a mishmash of Shakespearian tragedy, a plagiarised, mongrel drama, lifted—fittingly—from the archives of the Bard.

She had come to Stuart knowing that the situation was woefully complicated, aware that it would take a monumental effort on both sides to carry on; she would have to let go of the selfishness and deception he had treated her to, and if they were to make it that far, he would have to grin and bear the pain on her face every time Jenny rang or visited with an update, and there would be the birth itself, and the family occasions afterwards—Christening, birthdays, Christmases—and her painfully superfluous role in those events. And what about the day his first-born burst in the door screaming, 'Daddy, Daddy!' and jumped into his arms, saying, 'Hi, Rachel,' but never, 'Mammy'? What could she do with that, and would he be able to overcome the guilt, or would it eat away at them until they had to give up, too old and too damaged to be any use to anybody, life over before it ever really got going. It would be a long process of forgiveness and understanding, and there would always be a living, breathing, talking reminder of it. And there would be no guarantees.

His response, as off-the-cuff as it was, clarified what she had come to find out; he hadn't the stomach for it. Rachel stood up and walked to the door, tears meandering round her nostrils and into the corners of her mouth, so that she had to lick her lips to relieve the miserable tickle.

She stopped when she got to the door. He was walking after her. The kettle was boiled, and the flick of the switch seemed to echo through the apartment. She lifted her chin and looked at him properly for the first time, and, in contradiction of her tears, spoke in a strong, defiant voice: 'After twenty-five years doing whatever pleased yourself, don't go ruining your life now by acting out of obligation on the first decision that really matters.' As she finished speaking she saw the packed suitcase propped against the wall, behind the door, with his passport placed on top. She realised that Stuart had already made his decision. 'When you didn't answer my call, I rang your office. I thought you were just taking another day off, with all that's going on. I didn't realise . . . Where are you going?' she asked. Somebody else might have thought this was just a holiday suitcase, somebody taking some personal time to think things over, but Rachel knew better than that now.

'I don't know.' It always came back to that eventually.

'Somebody who cared about you might ask questions like—What about your job? What about Jenny? What about your family? What about your responsibility?' She paused. 'You'll regret turning your back on it.' She shook her head. 'It was hypothetical, Stu. You know? I wasn't looking for you to drop to one knee. I'm not,' she gestured towards her stomach. 'I mean how could I be? Already? How would I know? But you're safe, don't worry.' There was a knock at the door. Rachel opened it and took the opportunity to leave, pushing past the man standing in the doorway. She left Stuart to his stupid fate, and to a stranger in navy overalls. She was glad she was gone before she realised he would have been anyway.

'Stuart Byrne?'

'Yes.'

'Morning. I'm from MuchHaste. Courier service. I'm here to pick up a laptop and a printer for R&S Foods. I have a docket here you need to sign, and there is a letter here from R&S Foods that I need you to sign for too.' The man handed him the envelope, and a clipboard so he could sign for the pick-up and the receipt of the letter. He signed and pointed to the laptop and printer in the corner of the room. 'Thanks,' the man said, and proceeded towards his cargo, placing the clipboard on top and gathering the two items in his arms.

'No problem,' Stuart said, and he closed the door behind the courier as he left. The letter stated that Ramsey and Stanley Foods were disappointed that Stuart Byrne had decided to leave the company, and that they would appreciate if he could return the outstanding company property in his possession, as listed in the letter. They asked him for written confirmation of his resignation, and informed him that any remaining salary and bonuses would be paid to him as per the conditions of his contract. He had never read his contract, but he presumed that meant he would be paid till the end of the month. It also advised him that he could pick up any messages from his company phone by dialling the provided access number, and using his personal PIN. Messages were to be saved on the message minder for a two-week period, at which point his account would be deactivated. The gravity of being jobless hit him again, and hardened in his mind the correctness of the decision.

Stuart had messages from everyone he could have expected. Owen had phoned to see how he was, and to tell him that he was moving in with Christina: 'Hey, just ringing to see how you are. And to tell you I'm moving in with Tina, so call around, don't be a stranger. Oh, and I might have a publisher for my poems. Tina again. Who'd have thunk it? Talk to you later.'

Sara had called too, to ask about Jenny: 'Hi, Stuart. Sara, here. So what's happening with this girl you inadvertently knocked up? Don't let her blackmail you with tears. Be straight with her. Give me a call if I can do anything. Oh, by the way, Kevin says, 'Hello.' He's trying to be more aware of other people or something. Whatever. Listen, I'm sure it'll all work out. Talk soon.'

His father had called too, just to say: 'Hi, son. I texted earlier. Thought I should call though. Call me. If you want. Bye.'

Then, as he should have by now expected, there was Jenny with the utterly unexpected: 'Hi, Stu. Look, this is the fourth time I've rang. It's twenty past five, Wednesday evening. I don't know if you're avoiding me or something. Look, all this stuff has been so emotional. We all made mistakes. I just want you to know that I don't hate you. But you'll be sorry you didn't pick up earlier when I tell you this—I got my period this morning. It's never been this late before, but I've been totally stressed lately, and, well, phew! I mean, what a relief, eh? Sorry about the mix-up. Don't hate me. Maybe we could meet up for a drink sometime. Anyway, sorry.'

He placed the receiver back down and fell onto the floor. More than anything he was euphoric. He knew when the rush of palpable relief was gone that he would have questions, angry, disbelieving questions—had she put him through all this over nothing more than a late period? had she not gone to a doctor for confirmation, or done a pregnancy test, at the very least? was she really fucking serious about wanting to go for a drink? But for the moment, he lay on the carpet, breathing heavy with speechless relief. He shed the weight of burden he had been bench-pressing for the past five days.

The electrics were all plugged out, his bags were packed, and he was mentally prepared to take flight, only to find he was safe. He was free, a last minute reprieve, he was free to pursue whatever life he wanted. He should have been free. Having flung his perspective-inhibiting albatross from his shoulders, he could see how Jenny's lie (he was adamant that it was a lie, not a mistake), and the panic it had subjected him to, had coloured every decision that had been made since. He was in the clear, but his life had been changed in the time between Jenny's fabrication and a couple of minutes before when he retrieved his messages. If only he had been able to get his messages earlier, he thought. Was that what she was calling to tell him yesterday, the missed call in the morning and the one he didn't answer before he went to meet Stanley? Why didn't he pick up? How differently the conversation with Rachel might have gone with the knowledge that Jenny was not pregnant? 'Fucking fate!' he screamed. And, 'Jenny!'

THURSDAY EVENING—DUBLIN AIRPORT

His old life was gone, the good with the bad, all unsalvageable, and it was all fateful Jenny's fault.

'All? Like how?' I asked, when he told me this, feeling he was losing all sight of personal accountability. Quitting his job?—this was not Jenny's doing. I reminded him that he had sat on his bed unable to face work, so full of lethargy that he barely had the strength to stand up, long before Jenny broke her lie (he really insisted on this word), and that he said he was disillusioned with his work anyway. And Rachel? 'I just don't see how Jenny can be held responsible for you sleeping with Rachel, when you knew Jenny was pregnant,' I said, indicating my sympathy for Rachel, and by doing so, implicating him.

'But she wasn't pregnant!' he exclaimed.

'But you thought she was,' I said. And the manner in which he dealt with Rachel after that, I put to him, was that not a reflection of something other than Jenny—himself, say?

He was getting really agitated. 'It was a . . .'

'A lie, I know. A lie,' I said, trying to appease him so that I could get my point across. 'But would she have slept with you if she had known about Jenny?' I asked him. No response. 'Do you have a different answer for Rachel now, a different answer to the one that pumped her eyes full of tears, do you really?' I asked, pushing him further.

'I couldn't think straight. With Jenny's bloody lie popping around my brain twenty-four hours a day!'

'But you're still leaving,' I said. 'If it's Jenny's fault, why do you need to leave? If you have limited responsibility, you don't need to run.'

'I'm not running.'

'Well, if your life before Jenny's lie was so good, and she's responsible for most of what has happened, and you want your previous life back, why are you leaving?'

'Because . . . I can't unmake the decisions. It's out of my control. The gods are against me.'

'Which decisions? Your job? You hated it anyway, there's no reason to unmake it. The only decision to unmake is Rachel. Now she really is a priority, now that Jenny's not pregnant. Why are you leaving her?'

'I'm not leaving *her*, I'm just leaving!'

'But why?'

'Because there's nothing here for me.'

'Rachel?'

'How could I go back to her now? What could I offer her?' And there it was, he missed the point. She never wanted anything but him, she'd have taken him jobless and with a child that wasn't hers; she'd have taken him and his fate, and loved them all regardless.

'What would I say?'

'Well, you'd have to think it through. And to be fair, you probably deserve a little time in purgatory, thinking things over.'

'Who made you God?' he flung back at me, quite correctly.

Indeed, who am I to moralise? encouraging his candour only to be judgemental with him later. That's beyond the call of the narrator, though I'm afraid I've strayed across that line too often already, not to mention it was beyond the call of one school friend who hasn't seen the other in over seven years. Our conversation was coming to an end. I went too far. He didn't want advice, he wanted a yes-man. He was annoyed with me, but still polite, as he stood up to leave.

I met him in Cloud Nine. He did not recognise me. I am probably twice the size in the face that I was when we last met, me cycling towards him as he sat alone on a wall after his final exam of the dreaded Leaving Cert. At the waist, I am barely squeezing into a thirty-eight these days, and the extra weight makes me appear a couple of inches shorter. I feel sure this is just the perception-altering effect of fat, and that I am still a nearly average five-foot-nine, but I am afraid to measure, just in case.

I watched him for a few minutes as he supped on a pint. He has never been to where he is going, I thought. He kept looking up at the screen information, and out the massive windows at the planes. I took my coffee from the bar and walked over to him, coffee balanced on the saucer in one hand, and briefcase in the other. He was still tall and athletic looking, though his facial hair was darker and thicker than I remembered, and his face was beetroot. He looked his age, which was something I could not say about myself.

I said, 'Hello. Sorry to disturb, but—Stuart?'

He looked back at the fat suit before him, the angry skin beneath my rolling chin flared from a recent shave. He looked at my small, stained teeth, lost in puffed cheeks, and at the wire-frame glasses stretched to the limit around my temples, and said, 'Yeah.'

He did not look impressed or happy. The first of these, at least, I took to be down to me. 'How are you? It's Tom. Tom Kilbane.' He still looked lost. 'From St Christopher's. English class, and French class. *The Great Gatsby*,' I tried. 'Or, *The Halfwit, Othello*.'

'Oh, Jesus. Tom. I didn't . . . you've changed,' he said, but was polite enough not to tell me how. 'How are you?'

'Not too bad,' I said. 'Do you mind if I sit down.'

'Sure,' he said, unfailingly affable. 'Just a coffee?' he enquired. 'Not having a drink?'

'No,' I said. 'I'm watching my . . . It's a bit early for me.'

We talked for a few minutes, just vague conversation about the weather and where we were headed. I told him that I was on my way to London to interview Hanif Kureishi for a Sunday paper magazine, and that I had not had a girlfriend since I was a thirty-two inch waist. I embellished slightly, in that I was on my way to London to interview a newly famous soap star for *Fame & Shame*, and I had not actually had a girlfriend since I had a thirty inch waist. It did not matter, because he didn't know who

Kureishi was (asking, 'Was he something to do with 9/11?'), and he had absolutely no concept of the direct and proven relationship between your waistline relative to your height (your area squared, if you like) and having a girlfriend. Even my lies lacked mystery. Instead of being envious and enthralled by the news that I was on my way to interview one of my heroes, and being disarmed by my self-deprecating wit, he nodded inattentively, took a scrap of paper from a pocket, and asked could he borrow my phone.

'Hello. Elizabeth Sheridan, speaking.'

'Hi, Mum.'

'Stuart. Where are you?'

'Mum, I'm phoning because I want you to know that I quit R&S. I know you got me that job. I suppose I should have realised all along. But I'm not angry with you. I'm just ringing to tell you that I quit and that I'm heading off for a while. I don't know where.'

'Stuart, slow down. What did Alan tell you?'

'He thought I knew. He was trying to persuade me to stay. How do you know him anyway?'

'And you left. Well, the old fool didn't do a very good job then, did he? I've known Alan years. Old friends, that's all. Nothing seedy in it, so don't get high and mighty with me. There's an excellent career there for you, Stuart. I'm sure you could fix this. Alan has big plans for you. I know that.'

'It's over, Mum. I'm not going back.'

'But, Stuart, listen to me. I could . . .'

'No, Mum. I don't want you doing any more. I'm finished with that.'

'And now you're running off. What about this girl? Are you going to just leave her to single parenthood? Sounds like something your brother would do.'

'It's nothing at all like Owen would do. And he's moving in with his new girlfriend, by the way. And he might have a publisher for some poems he's written.'

'Poets are poor, they never make a cent. If they're lucky they gain posthumous notoriety after killing themselves, and what use is that to anyone? The girlfriend's some tramp, no doubt.'

'Not at all. She's a regular citizen. He seems happy.'

'I'm sure he does,' she said, and Stuart realised that there was no generosity of spirit left in his mother for her second biggest disappointment. 'Now, what are we doing about this girl, Stuart?'

'Nothing. She isn't pregnant after all. Just a scare. I don't want to talk about it. I'll be in touch.'

'Wait, Stuart. Please? Where are you going?'

'I'm not sure. London first. After that, I don't know.'

Elizabeth Sheridan steadied herself. 'I'm divorcing your father.' Stuart could not say anything. 'I'm sure it's not a shock,' she said, and she meant it. But it was a shock to Stuart. He never believed his parents' marriage could actually end in divorce. 'We just cannot go on like we are. It's been long enough. And it hasn't all been bad, I suppose.' Her tone had softened to an unfamiliar pitch. She sounded hurt and disappointed, but not devastated. Stuart felt protective of her. She continued, 'But the country has moved on, like we all must, and I have options. It's not as if I was the first one in the door the minute they sanctioned it. I gave it time, I tried. But I'd be foolish not to use my options, now wouldn't I? Isn't that what this modern world is all about—choice?'

He forced himself to speak, feeling she needed to hear something. 'I don't know what to say, Mum. Are you okay?'

'I'm fine, darling,' she said, still gentle. 'So what does Rachel think of your leaving?' she asked. It was almost as if she was concerned for Rachel, referring to her by name, another unpredictable turn he couldn't comprehend.

'We had a bit of a fight actually,' he said.

'Your fault, I suppose,' she said, sympathetically.

'Yeah. It was.'

'I've always given her a hard time,' she said, reflectively. 'She loves you, Stuart. And love is not to be scoffed at,' she said. 'When reciprocated.'

'Mum, are you okay? Have you told Dad about this yet?'

'Your father has been divorcing me for thirty-seven years now, Stuart. I can't see any reason for him to be surprised.' Her old tone had returned. 'Go away, Stuart. Have a break and come back to us. We'll figure this out.'

'Okay, Mum. Bye.'

'Good-bye.'

Stuart conducted the entire phonecall at our rounded table with me sitting there trying not to feel embarrassed by hearing every word. It was not eavesdropping, but it felt like getting caught with an ear to the door. When he hung up and handed me back my phone, I had heard enough for him to feel there was nothing left to hide. So I ordered him a drink and we talked. I missed my flight to Heathrow—budding soap stars would have to wait. His flight wasn't ready for boarding for another couple of hours.

He had had a couple and he was chatty. He opened up for me again, like he had seven years before, when we were barely men. I had decided on a drink too, by this stage, but I drank slower, trying to keep the story in my head. I was already imagining the day when some want-to-be writer would be sitting in an airport lounge on his way to interview me, and when he arrived we would sit down and talk about Stuart. 'Whatever happens to Stuart?' he would ask. 'Did you ever think of a sequel? Stuart was so hopelessly flawed, but at the end redemption was there for the taking, Mr Kilbane,' he'd say. 'Call me, Tom,' I'd tell him. 'Stuart? Who knows,' I'd say. 'Still running, probably. What I mean is, he loved Rachel, everybody knew it. But he wasn't strong enough for grown-up love, love where you can hurt the one person you can't bear to. He wanted sanitised love, perfection, an isolated, uncontaminated, everlasting moment, like the night they slept together, with the rest of the world locked out. When that possibility evaporated, when he saw the pain in her eyes and envisaged the effort and moral balls it would take to stay and assume responsibility for that, he caved. No matter what the rewards, he wouldn't face the arduous journey. You know what they say about trust—hard-won, easily lost. He didn't have it in him, and if he didn't have it then, I doubt he ever would. So I'd say he's still running, from whatever rears its ugly head. In that sense,' I would correct my imagined protégé, 'I think you've misread my novel, or Stuart, at least—redemption was never likely, you see.'

Stuart's story landed in front of me, a godsend. In truth, I admit that I was more interested in Stuart's failure than his redemption, dramatically speaking, so I didn't try too hard to put him on the right path. But Stuart wouldn't listen to me anyway, not in reality and so not in fiction. You saw how he reacted when I asked questions, when I wouldn't servilely endorse his self-deception. You heard what he said—it's true. This is firsthand reporting; I'm my own primary source. I'm not extrapolating or taking narrative licence; there's no need for that here, because I heard all this with my own ears. He believed it was all fate. He believed that the perfection of him and Rachel was tarnished, and, therefore, pointless.

All that said, there was still a part of me that wanted to rouse Stuart from his somnambulistic passivity, from his habitually sleepy disposition. I wanted him to realise that it wasn't fate. Fate is bullshit. We are self-determining beings, always flying in the face of random disaster, adapting and coping like the predestined never could. Fate is just a four letter word, like shit, that people use to explain what happens to them when they're too lazy to take the time to stop and look at themselves, when they do not take the time to understand why they do the things they do, and how to change their circumstances. 'Fate is rubbish, Stuart,' is where I should have started, 'A way around personal accountability.'

But he also needed to have the paradoxical notion that it had been during the events of the previous five days that everything collapsed on him—family, career, love—dispelled. He needed to see that it was god-knows how many years of indifference that brought him to this juncture in his life, and just because something goes back years doesn't make it fate. I wanted to show him that he could have intervened at any time and changed the course of events, that Jenny couldn't have done all this alone, but the only example I could think of was the one that already infuriated him. I should have been tough with him. I should have said, 'There were other choices, Stuart, but you made the easy ones, every time. There's nothing wrong with Rachel, there are no virgin queens left, and she wasn't one to begin with. No perfect love exists. There are no happy endings that just stretch on for eternity, uninterrupted. There is no love like when you were eighteen and overflowing with hormones and utterly unafraid; that was an illusion, not a broken dream fated to fail. What is left is not second-rate. We are more interesting and profoundly complicated as a result of the pain we bore, wiser and more rounded for the moral indiscretions of our past relationships, and imperfect love, where we hurt each other and apologise, and spoil each other and feel self-satisfied, all within the confines of the same relationship, has always been more wonderful and complex, and enduring, than the jejune Hollywood ending.'

He was standing, ready to go. He was determined to leave and start afresh. I should have told him all this, told him to take his fate in hand (fate, because that's the word he seems so obsessed with, and the thought of being at the mercy of some already decided ending is what paralysed him to common sense, that and indifference), to stop running, stop thinking of what he was do-ing as 'the decision,' and start realising it was *his* decision, *his* to make, *his* to reverse, *his* decision of *his* life. I should have told him to turn around, run back to her, and beg for forgiveness. But what I said, off the top of my head, was, 'Onwards and upwards, eh! Without Rachel.' He laughed and shook his head, the way he did when Quigley talked to him about women, and said, 'Thanks anyway, Tom. But that's fucked now. I've got to go, flight's board-ing. Nice to see you again.'

There you have it. Just manners, that's all, but he has something. I cannot help rooting for him to somehow succeed. He walked out of Cloud Nine and bumped into a young lady as he looked up at the flight information. He knocked her wheeled travel bag over and sent her stumbling, and she cursed him. But before she had the chance to fly into a tizzy, he had apologised, caught her gently by the elbow, allowing her to regain her footing, and picked her bag up. Then she smiled up at him and apologised too. They laughed a little. He said something and they shook hands. She pointed towards the departure gates and they walked off together into the crowd.

It is all too easy for him, you see. That's why he will never learn. Although, I suspect, as he gets older, he will wake in the middle of the night with increasing regularity, in cold sweats, trembling and queasy, unable to explain the tears and anxiety and with no means to fight them. But until then, while he is still young enough to be worshipped by the world for his beauty, and insipid enough to pass little offence, his short-sighted passage through life, his litany of easy ways out, will continue.

So long as the world values the aesthetically fortunate above the endeavourers, the passionate, and the compassionate, and hands life to them on a plate, people like Stuart will never find out that the road is long, and magnificent youth is only a short part of it, until it's much too late. He will tell us he has no choice, that he cannot face his quandary with courage and dignity, and then he'll smile at us, in that pleasant, courteous way of his, and walk away scot-free; the world has never made the beautiful do anything they didn't want.

JOHN TOOMEY was born in 1975 in Dublin, where he now teaches English at Clonkeen College. *Sleepwalker* is his first novel. Further information, including an extract from his forthcoming novel and some of his short stories, can be read on his website www.johntoomeybooks.com.

THE JOHN F. BYRNE IRISH LITERATURE SERIES is made possible through a generous contribution by an anonymous individual. This contribution will allow Dalkey Archive Press to publish one book per year in this series.

Born and raised in Chicago, John F. Byrne was an educator and critic who helped to found the *Review of Contemporary Fiction* and was also an editor for Dalkey Archive Press. Although his primary interest was Victorian literature, he spent much of his career teaching modern literature, especially such Irish writers as James Joyce, Samuel Beckett, and Flann O'Brien. He died in 1998, but his influence on both the *Review* and Dalkey Archive Press will be lasting.

PETROS ABATZOGLOU, *What Does Mrs. Freeman Want?*
MICHAL AJVAZ, *The Golden Age.*
The Other City.
PIERRE ALBERT-BIROT, *Grabinoulor.*
YUZ ALESHKOVSKY, *Kangaroo.*
FELIPE ALFAU, *Chromos.*
Locos.
IVAN ÂNGELO, *The Celebration.*
The Tower of Glass.
DAVID ANTIN, *Talking.*
ANTÓNIO LOBO ANTUNES, *Knowledge of Hell.*
ALAIN ARIAS-MISSON, *Theatre of Incest.*
IFTIKHAR ARIF AND WAQAS KHWAJA, EDS., *Modern Poetry of Pakistan.*
JOHN ASHBERY AND JAMES SCHUYLER, *A Nest of Ninnies.*
HEIMRAD BÄCKER, *transcript.*
DJUNA BARNES, *Ladies Almanack.*
Ryder.
JOHN BARTH, *LETTERS.*
Sabbatical.
DONALD BARTHELME, *The King.*
Paradise.
SVETISLAV BASARA, *Chinese Letter.*
RENÉ BELLETTO, *Dying.*
MARK BINELLI, *Sacco and Vanzetti Must Die!*
ANDREI BITOV, *Pushkin House.*
ANDREJ BLATNIK, *You Do Understand.*
LOUIS PAUL BOON, *Chapel Road.*
My Little War.
Summer in Termuren.
ROGER BOYLAN, *Killoyle.*
IGNÁCIO DE LOYOLA BRANDÃO, *Anonymous Celebrity.*
The Good-Bye Angel.
Teeth under the Sun.
Zero.
BONNIE BREMSER, *Troia: Mexican Memoirs.*
CHRISTINE BROOKE-ROSE, *Amalgamemnon.*
BRIGID BROPHY, *In Transit.*
MEREDITH BROSNAN, *Mr. Dynamite.*
GERALD L. BRUNS, *Modern Poetry and the Idea of Language.*
EVGENY BUNIMOVICH AND J. KATES, EDS., *Contemporary Russian Poetry: An Anthology.*
GABRIELLE BURTON, *Heartbreak Hotel.*
MICHEL BUTOR, *Degrees.*
Mobile.
Portrait of the Artist as a Young Ape.
G. CABRERA INFANTE, *Infante's Inferno.*
Three Trapped Tigers.
JULIETA CAMPOS, *The Fear of Losing Eurydice.*
ANNE CARSON, *Eros the Bittersweet.*
ORLY CASTEL-BLOOM, *Dolly City.*
CAMILO JOSÉ CELA, *Christ versus Arizona.*
The Family of Pascual Duarte.
The Hive.
LOUIS-FERDINAND CÉLINE, *Castle to Castle.*
Conversations with Professor Y.
London Bridge.
Normance.
North.
Rigadoon.
HUGO CHARTERIS, *The Tide Is Right.*
JEROME CHARYN, *The Tar Baby.*
MARC CHOLODENKO, *Mordechai Schamz.*
JOSHUA COHEN, *Witz.*
EMILY HOLMES COLEMAN, *The Shutter of Snow.*
ROBERT COOVER, *A Night at the Movies.*
STANLEY CRAWFORD, *Log of the S.S. The Mrs Unguentine.*
Some Instructions to My Wife.
ROBERT CREELEY, *Collected Prose.*
RENÉ CREVEL, *Putting My Foot in It.*
RALPH CUSACK, *Cadenza.*
SUSAN DAITCH, *L.C.*
Storytown.
NICHOLAS DELBANCO, *The Count of Concord.*
NIGEL DENNIS, *Cards of Identity.*
PETER DIMOCK, *A Short Rhetoric for Leaving the Family.*
ARIEL DORFMAN, *Konfidenz.*
COLEMAN DOWELL, *The Houses of Children.*
Island People.
Too Much Flesh and Jabez.
ARKADII DRAGOMOSHCHENKO, *Dust.*
RIKKI DUCORNET, *The Complete Butcher's Tales.*
The Fountains of Neptune.
The Jade Cabinet.
The One Marvelous Thing.
Phosphor in Dreamland.
The Stain.
The Word "Desire."
WILLIAM EASTLAKE, *The Bamboo Bed.*
Castle Keep.
Lyric of the Circle Heart.
JEAN ECHENOZ, *Chopin's Move.*
STANLEY ELKIN, *A Bad Man.*
Boswell: A Modern Comedy.
Criers and Kibitzers, Kibitzers and Criers.
The Dick Gibson Show.
The Franchiser.
George Mills.
The Living End.
The MacGuffin.
The Magic Kingdom.
Mrs. Ted Bliss.
The Rabbi of Lud.
Van Gogh's Room at Arles.
ANNIE ERNAUX, *Cleaned Out.*
LAUREN FAIRBANKS, *Muzzle Thyself.*
Sister Carrie.
LESLIE A. FIEDLER, *Love and Death in the American Novel.*
JUAN FILLOY, *Op Oloop.*
GUSTAVE FLAUBERT, *Bouvard and Pécuchet.*
KASS FLEISHER, *Talking out of School.*
FORD MADOX FORD, *The March of Literature.*
JON FOSSE, *Aliss at the Fire.*
Melancholy.

FOR A FULL LIST OF PUBLICATIONS, VISIT:
www.dalkeyarchive.com

My Life in CIA.
Singular Pleasures.
The Sinking of the Odradek
  Stadium.
Tlooth.
20 Lines a Day.
JOSEPH McELROY,
  Night Soul and Other Stories.
ROBERT L. McLAUGHLIN, ED.,
  Innovations: An Anthology of
  Modern & Contemporary Fiction.
HERMAN MELVILLE, *The Confidence-Man.*
AMANDA MICHALOPOULOU, *I'd Like.*
STEVEN MILLHAUSER,
  The Barnum Museum.
  In the Penny Arcade.
RALPH J. MILLS, JR.,
  Essays on Poetry.
MOMUS, *The Book of Jokes.*
CHRISTINE MONTALBETTI, *Western.*
OLIVE MOORE, *Spleen.*
NICHOLAS MOSLEY, *Accident.*
  Assassins.
  Catastrophe Practice.
  Children of Darkness and Light.
  Experience and Religion.
  God's Hazard.
  The Hesperides Tree.
  Hopeful Monsters.
  Imago Bird.
  Impossible Object.
  Inventing God.
  Judith.
  Look at the Dark.
  Natalie Natalia.
  Paradoxes of Peace.
  Serpent.
  Time at War.
  The Uses of Slime Mould:
    Essays of Four Decades.
WARREN MOTTE,
  Fables of the Novel: French Fiction
    since 1990.
  Fiction Now: The French Novel in
    the 21st Century.
  Oulipo: A Primer of Potential
    Literature.
YVES NAVARRE, *Our Share of Time.*
  Sweet Tooth.
DOROTHY NELSON, *In Night's City.*
  Tar and Feathers.
ESHKOL NEVO, *Homesick.*
WILFRIDO D. NOLLEDO,
  But for the Lovers.
FLANN O'BRIEN,
  At Swim-Two-Birds.
  At War.
  The Best of Myles.
  The Dalkey Archive.
  Further Cuttings.
  The Hard Life.
  The Poor Mouth.
  The Third Policeman.
CLAUDE OLLIER, *The Mise-en-Scène.*
PATRIK OUŘEDNÍK, *Europeana.*
BORIS PAHOR, *Necropolis.*

FERNANDO DEL PASO,
  News from the Empire.
  Palinuro of Mexico.
ROBERT PINGET, *The Inquisitory.*
  Mahu or The Material.
  Trio.
MANUEL PUIG,
  Betrayed by Rita Hayworth.
  The Buenos Aires Affair.
  Heartbreak Tango.
RAYMOND QUENEAU, *The Last Days.*
  Odile.
  Pierrot Mon Ami.
  Saint Glinglin.
ANN QUIN, *Berg.*
  Passages.
  Three.
  Tripticks.
ISHMAEL REED,
  The Free-Lance Pallbearers.
  The Last Days of Louisiana Red.
  Ishmael Reed: The Plays.
  Reckless Eyeballing.
  The Terrible Threes.
  The Terrible Twos.
  Yellow Back Radio Broke-Down.
JEAN RICARDOU, *Place Names.*
RAINER MARIA RILKE, *The Notebooks of*
  Malte Laurids Brigge.
JULIÁN RÍOS, *The House of Ulysses.*
  Larva: A Midsummer Night's Babel.
  Poundemonium.
AUGUSTO ROA BASTOS, *I the Supreme.*
DANIËL ROBBERECHTS,
  Arriving in Avignon.
OLIVIER ROLIN, *Hotel Crystal.*
ALIX CLEO ROUBAUD, *Alix's Journal.*
JACQUES ROUBAUD, *The Form of a*
  City Changes Faster, Alas, Than
  the Human Heart.
  The Great Fire of London.
  Hortense in Exile.
  Hortense Is Abducted.
  The Loop.
  The Plurality of Worlds of Lewis.
  The Princess Hoppy.
  Some Thing Black.
LEON S. ROUDIEZ,
  French Fiction Revisited.
VEDRANA RUDAN, *Night.*
STIG SÆTERBAKKEN, *Siamese.*
LYDIE SALVAYRE, *The Company of Ghosts.*
  Everyday Life.
  The Lecture.
  Portrait of the Writer as a
    Domesticated Animal.
  The Power of Flies.
LUIS RAFAEL SÁNCHEZ,
  Macho Camacho's Beat.
SEVERO SARDUY, *Cobra & Maitreya.*
NATHALIE SARRAUTE,
  Do You Hear Them?
  Martereau.
  The Planetarium.
ARNO SCHMIDT, *Collected Stories.*
  Nobodaddy's Children.

CHRISTINE SCHUTT, *Nightwork*.
GAIL SCOTT, *My Paris*.
DAMION SEARLS, *What We Were Doing and Where We Were Going*.
JUNE AKERS SEESE,
  Is This What Other Women Feel Too?
  What Waiting Really Means.
BERNARD SHARE, *Inish*.
  Transit.
AURELIE SHEEHAN,
  Jack Kerouac Is Pregnant.
VIKTOR SHKLOVSKY, *Knight's Move*.
  A Sentimental Journey:
    Memoirs 1917–1922.
  Energy of Delusion: A Book on Plot.
  Literature and Cinematography.
  Theory of Prose.
  Third Factory.
  Zoo, or Letters Not about Love.
CLAUDE SIMON, *The Invitation*.
PIERRE SINIAC, *The Collaborators*.
JOSEF ŠKVORECKÝ, *The Engineer of Human Souls*.
GILBERT SORRENTINO,
  Aberration of Starlight.
  Blue Pastoral.
  Crystal Vision.
  Imaginative Qualities of Actual Things.
  Mulligan Stew.
  Pack of Lies.
  Red the Fiend.
  The Sky Changes.
  Something Said.
  Splendide-Hôtel.
  Steelwork.
  Under the Shadow.
W. M. SPACKMAN,
  The Complete Fiction.
ANDRZEJ STASIUK, *Fado*.
GERTRUDE STEIN,
  Lucy Church Amiably.
  The Making of Americans.
  A Novel of Thank You.
LARS SVENDSEN, *A Philosophy of Evil*.
PIOTR SZEWC, *Annihilation*.
GONÇALO M. TAVARES, *Jerusalem*.
LUCIAN DAN TEODOROVICI,
  Our Circus Presents . . .
STEFAN THEMERSON, *Hobson's Island*.
  The Mystery of the Sardine.
  Tom Harris.
JOHN TOOMEY, *Sleepwalker*.
JEAN-PHILIPPE TOUSSAINT,
  The Bathroom.
  Camera.
  Monsieur.
  Running Away.
  Self-Portrait Abroad.
  Television.
DUMITRU TSEPENEAG,
  Hotel Europa.
  The Necessary Marriage.
  Pigeon Post.
  Vain Art of the Fugue.
ESTHER TUSQUETS, *Stranded*.

DUBRAVKA UGRESIC,
  Lend Me Your Character.
  Thank You for Not Reading.
MATI UNT, *Brecht at Night*.
  Diary of a Blood Donor.
  Things in the Night.
ÁLVARO URIBE AND OLIVIA SEARS, EDS.,
  Best of Contemporary Mexican Fiction.
ELOY URROZ, *Friction*.
  The Obstacles.
LUISA VALENZUELA, *He Who Searches*.
MARJA-LIISA VARTIO,
  The Parson's Widow.
PAUL VERHAEGHEN, *Omega Minor*.
BORIS VIAN, *Heartsnatcher*.
LLORENÇ VILLALONGA, *The Dolls' Room*.
ORNELA VORPSI, *The Country Where No One Ever Dies*.
AUSTRYN WAINHOUSE, *Hedyphagetica*.
PAUL WEST,
  Words for a Deaf Daughter & Gala.
CURTIS WHITE,
  America's Magic Mountain.
  The Idea of Home.
  Memories of My Father Watching TV.
  Monstrous Possibility: An Invitation to Literary Politics.
  Requiem.
DIANE WILLIAMS, *Excitability: Selected Stories*.
  Romancer Erector.
DOUGLAS WOOLF, *Wall to Wall*.
  Ya! & John-Juan.
JAY WRIGHT, *Polynomials and Pollen*.
  The Presentable Art of Reading Absence.
PHILIP WYLIE, *Generation of Vipers*.
MARGUERITE YOUNG,
  Angel in the Forest.
  Miss MacIntosh, My Darling.
REYOUNG, *Unbabbling*.
VLADO ŽABOT, *The Succubus*.
ZORAN ŽIVKOVIĆ, *Hidden Camera*.
LOUIS ZUKOFSKY, *Collected Fiction*.
SCOTT ZWIREN, *God Head*.